THE MEDICINE MAN

THE MEN
OF WHITE SANDY

SARAH M. ANDERSON

Dedication

To Becca.

I'd like to thank Newton Love and Annette Love Hatton, as well as the Lakota Language Consortium, for all their help with the Lakota translations in the book. Many thanks to Laurel Levy for being an awesome critique partner and one heck of a pediatric nurse. Also, thanks to Mary Dieterich and Mom and Dad for always being behind me—even when I was driving in reverse! I couldn't have done it without you! And finally, thanks to Jill Marsal for believing in this story even when everyone else had given up on it, and thanks to Heidi Moore for appreciating a good skinny-dipping scene.

Prologue

He let his mind go blank as he stared at the fire. Years of practice kept his feet and hands still until he was little more than the stump he was leaning against. The calm that overtook him left little else. In the distance, a coyote set off a round of cries into the night. The crickets called over the breeze like young braves singing to their lovers while the grasses shushed the river like a mother comforting her baby.

The sounds of his world surrounded him and told him he was right with it. He was where he belonged, doing what he should.

If he was patient, he would see his next idea in a vision. Recently, he'd been getting real good at being patient. Patience was getting his work into art galleries from South Dakota to New Mexico, and that one pipe bag he'd made last year was in the Museum of the American Indian in D.C. Patience was making him a major player in the world of Indian art.

He sat for a long time, but time itself wasn't important. What was important was patience, the vision. And the next bag. The longer he sat, the better the idea would be.

At some point between the hoot of a hungry owl and another breath of wind, things changed and the vision took him. The temperature dropped from sixty to six in a heartbeat. The snow seemed not to fall from the sky, but spring straight out of the ground. The fire disappeared into the steam of breath coming from his mouth. He could just make out the low ceiling of smoke that pointed to a village over the next hill.

Peace filled him. Nothing else mattered but this connection to the past, the past that held the key to his future. Nothing else mattered but a winter's day on the plains. He could see it now. The white background. His next pipe bag would be a winter scene.

The thud of hooves drew his attention. A horse, the red paint on his face looking like blood in the snow, ran toward him from the east. White flakes were kicked up with each stride, shrouding the horse in a cloud of ice.

A horse. A red-and-white paint horse running through the snow. The image assembled itself in his mind's eye. Tanned leather, long fringe, beaded tie done in the same white. It would be a beautiful bag.

The horse ran right past him, so close that he was lost in the ice cloud. He waited. This was the end of the vision. As soon as his eyes cleared, he'd be back in front of his fire, next to the river on an early May evening. And then he could get started on his leather.

But it didn't happen. Instead of the past leaving him behind, it pulled him deeper into the vision. When his eyes cleared, he saw the horse was gone, and he was colder than he'd ever been in his life. Feeling suddenly a little lost in time, he looked around the place he was in. And what he saw only added to his confusion. Instead of four prints in the snow, he saw only two headed toward the village.

He stared at the tracks. Not hooves—not a horse. Human. Small human prints. It looked like the heels were dragging a little, fanning the snow out in a long tail behind each step. He didn't know what to make of them, but he tucked the shape and size away in his mind. Maybe he would do a pair of moccasins too. He hadn't done mocs for a good long while.

Just a pair of mocs couldn't be why he was still here freezing his ass off in the snow. The village. Something in the village was pulling on him. He began to follow the tracks, tripping through the snow banks. He didn't remember walking being this hard. Usually, if he moved at all in his visions, he seemed to float above. But not now. The cold air tried to rip the breath from his chest as the snow clawed at his feet. He fought on, trying to remember that this snow wasn't really here, and that he wasn't about to get frostbite chasing down a horse that left delicate human footprints. This was all just a vision. Nothing more.

He lost his footing and slid the last few feet down the hill and into the safe circle of tipis. It was a little warmer in the circle, sheltered from the wind behind the hill. He stood, dusted the snow from his braid and looked for the tracks.

And saw nothing but bodies.

Panic stuck in his throat as he began to count the dead. Five here, seven there—the numbers climbed quickly. Dressed in the traditional buckskins, the people—his people—lay on the ground where they'd fallen, their pocked skin almost as white as the snow that held them in its grasp. There was no blood, so it wasn't a war party or the blue-coat soldiers come back again.

He looked at each member of his family, held

forever in death's grasp. There was no one left to perform the death rites, no one to keep their souls until they were ready to be judged by Owl Woman.

The sickness had come.

Through the haze of horror that blinded his eyes almost as much as the wind-whipped snow, he tried to focus on what he knew. He knew what—and when—this was. This was the smallpox epidemic, and it had wiped out whole branches of his tribe, the Lakota tribe, back in 1831. A hundred and seventy years ago—a past long dead.

Or was it? Why was this particular past coming back to him now? Why had the horse—the footprints—led him here?

He looked for any sign of life. Some had lived: the tribe had survived this sickness. Someone had to have lived.

There were the footprints again, but this time they were different. The tracks stopped next to each body, and what looked like knee prints were pressed into the snow. Someone else had been here. Someone else knew of the sickness.

He studied the tracks. For the life of him, he couldn't tell if the horse—the person—who'd left them had brought the sickness or had tried to stop it. Tried and failed. Everyone here was dead, except for him.

The horse appeared again, agitated and wild. Foam dripped out of its mouth. The horse was sick too. And it was charging. He couldn't move. He couldn't get out of the way of this death bearing down on him.

"What do you want?" he shouted, hoping the horse could hear him, praying it would listen.

"I came here looking for you," a voice said. It didn't come from the horse, but from the wind around him. He couldn't tell if it was a threat or a promise. The horse—death—blew blood out of its nose as it ran faster and faster at him.

He closed his eyes, bracing for the impact. Instead, the cold, the snow, the horse, the voice all disappeared, and he found himself once again sitting in front of his fire on a cool May night. His blood was pounding, and he was so dizzy he was sure he was going to throw up. After a moment, the feeling passed. It always passed.

But what he'd seen didn't pass.

The sickness was coming again. And someone was coming with it.

Chapter One

Thank goodness, Dr. Madeline Mitchell thought as she hurried into the sterile gown and snapped the shield over her face. Anything to get her away from all those half-hearted well-wishers at her farewell party.

"Drugs!" the woman—girl really, probably no more than seventeen—who was sprawled on the stretcher screamed. They hadn't even made it to a room in the E.R. yet.

At least it's not a boring night, Madeline thought as she bent to check. The baby was already crowning. The girl screamed again, and another inch of the head emerged. They would barely have time to get to the room. Drugs were out of the question. She was just going to have to tough it out.

Madeline let her training take over. She loved the E.R., loved the unexpected. In fact, right now she was loving the unexpected more than she normally did. It was her last night working before she bailed on Columbus, Ohio, and to bring a new baby into this world as her final act at the hospital seemed fitting. She was doing a last little bit of good.

Madeline followed the stretcher as they raced down the hall, keeping her hand on that little head. *You can do it, baby*, she thought, almost as much to the girl as to the infant. "I want you to push," she said, keeping her voice low and steady as the door shut behind them. Then she looked at the nurse for some explanation as to why this girl was in the E.R. and not the maternity ward.

The nurse shrugged. "Her mother said she'd been in pain all afternoon. Thought it was an appendix. When we told her the daughter was in labor, the mother passed out in the waiting room."

"Where's the on-call O.B.?"

The nurse rolled her eyes. "Your guess is as good as mine."

"*Drugs!*" The girl's voice careened off the walls. The head gained another inch.

"She's a screamer," the nurse said under her breath.

The girl was probably in six degrees of shit with her parents right now and was about to have a natural childbirth, whether she wanted one or not. Madeline could see from the terrified look in her eyes that she felt alone. The last thing she needed was a snippy nurse making her feel even smaller.

"I'm right here, honey. You're not alone," Madeline said in her most soothing tone as she shot the nurse the look that everyone referred to as the Mitchell sneer. It came in very handy at times like this. The nurse backpedaled and shut the hell up. "You can scream if it helps, okay? But I need you to push."

The girl nodded and sucked in a huge breath. Madeline barely had the chance to wish for earplugs before she was cradling the newborn baby boy.

Perfect, she thought as she did the quick check. Of course, they'd run tests on him—it sounded like he'd gotten no prenatal care—but he was perfect. The girl, who was now sobbing, had needed Madeline right then more than anyone else in the world, and she'd been there for her.

This is what she lived for.

In the middle of the adrenaline rush, a tinge of sadness snuck up on her. She'd never see either of them again, never know if they turned out all right and lived happily ever after. She was leaving. The weight of her decision hit her in the sternum.

"I can't believe you'd rather go to some Indian reservation than stay here and do *this*, Dr. Mitchell," the nurse said, her voice dripping with cynicism as they waited for the afterbirth.

"I'll still be doing *this*," Madeline shot back, keeping her voice low. The mother of the girl had been wheeled in on a matching stretcher, and they were both crying. It's not that Madeline didn't feel for their situation, but she didn't allow herself to get too attached to patients in the E.R. Caring about patients was a recipe for insanity. "I'll be the only doctor within a hundred miles." Pregnant teenagers, gunshot wounds, car accidents—she expected to see more of the same on the reservation. "But don't forget, I'm double certified. I'll be doing general practice. A lot of preventative stuff. Those people just need a good doctor."

The nurse scoffed, an attitude that was shared by more than a few people at the hospital. "Yeah. Good luck with that."

Madeline had heard the gossip whispered down silent hallways. Darrin, her recent ex, had spread more than his share it. They all thought she was nuts, and in her weaker moments, Madeline was afraid they might be right. Her sister, Melonie, was the only one who thought Madeline was doing the right thing.

Maybe she was nuts, maybe she wasn't. That didn't change a thing.

The Lakota Sioux on the White Sandy reservation in South Dakota needed a good doctor. Madeline needed—well, she wasn't sure what she needed anymore.

She looked at the baby, mother and grandmother, all bawling their heads off in nearly perfect three-part harmony. She needed this, this rush from doing her job and doing it well. But it wasn't enough anymore.

She needed something else.

She hoped to hell it was out West.

Chapter Two

This couldn't be the West. The thought popped into Madeline's head as she crested a small hill and saw what she could only pray wasn't the White Sandy Clinic and Hospital. But there wasn't another building in sight, and she'd followed the directions. The squat building looked like someone had chucked cinder blocks at each other, and the depressing gray color did little to detract from the peeling metal roof or the front door that was patched with half a sheet of plywood. Above the plywood were the scratched, faded letters that spelled out Clinic. This was it, her home away from home for the next two years. It was as if the place had been pillaged years ago and no one had bothered to fix it up since then.

Her stomach fell. She'd expected rustic, sure. Her little cabin was rustic. This? This was squalid. Maybe Darrin had been right. This was idiotic—the dumbest thing she could do. Career suicide.

Ugh. Darrin. Her nervous stomach tried to revolt on her, but she kept things firmly under control and talked some damn sense into herself. Darrin had nothing to do with this. Darrin wasn't here, and that's the way she liked it. Besides, she shouldn't jump to conclusions at 7:37 in the morning. At least things couldn't get much worse.

And then they did.

She barely got her new Jeep parked when a rusted-out truck careened into the lot behind her. The first—the only—thing she saw in the rear-view mirror was the shotgun in the gun rack. *Shit*, she thought, but that was as far as she got before the truck's door opened and a guy the size of Maine hopped out of the driver's seat. Madeline's jaw dropped. Jesus, he was huge, with one of those biker-style do-rags on his head and tattoos visible at twenty paces. And he was armed.

All she could do was lock her car door, although the guy could probably remove it with one hand tied behind his back. He cricked his neck, looked around and headed straight for her.

She should have gotten a gun. Or some mace. Or a baseball bat. Anything that might level the playing field with the tank that was... smiling?

"Sorry I'm late, Doc," the tank yelled, loud enough to be heard through the glass.

"Excuse me?"

"You're Dr. Mitchell, right?" Madeline noticed that he was wearing blue scrubs with a medical-style badge hanging off the pocket of his shirt.

Moving slowly, she rolled down her window. "Yes, I am. And you are... ?"

"Clarence Thunder." He waved again. Up close now, she could see the anchors tattooed on his arms. He noticed she was looking. "Navy Medical Corps, retired," he said with a tired salute. "Chief—well, only—nurse here on the White Sandy."

"You're the nurse?" Excellent. Shock and surprise were exactly the first sorts of impressions she wanted to make. At least she wasn't being overbearing, right?

He shrugged, seemingly amused with her confusion. "Fresh out of lady nurses around here. I'm all you got. Come on in."

A tattooed tank named Thunder was all she had? What had she gotten herself into?

The clinic was better on the inside than it was on the outside. The floors were swept, the lights all flickered on, and there was no mistaking the comforting smell of chemical clean. "Like I said, sorry I'm late. Indian time, you know."

No, she didn't, but she wasn't going to own up to that level of ignorance in the first three minutes. "It's fine," Madeline replied with what she hoped was a friendly, easy-going tone as she scoped out the joint. Style-wise, the waiting room was what one might term original, as in everything in it looked like it was original to the building, circa late 1960s. The Naugahyde chairs were held together with duct tape, and she saw a grand total of four tattered magazines. She could barely see the huge desk underneath the rotary phone, an old computer and about two thousand files. No filing cabinets?

Clarence sidestepped the desk with a level of grace she wouldn't have attributed to a man his size. "After Tara gets the patients all checked in, I bring them back here." He waved to four exam tables, one of which had stirrups for gynecological exams at the ready. On the other side were two hospital beds.

The room was wide open. Each bed was backed against the far wall with a small tray separating them. No monitors, no blood-pressure machines—no walls. "No walls?"

"We got them curtains a few years ago." Clarence shrugged, gesturing to the tracks on the ceiling. Each one ringed the four exam tables. And tied against the wall were the curtains in question. The pleats on three of them were still crisp. Only the one around the gyne table looked like it ever got pulled. "Someone thought we needed them. Can't seem to recall why."

For the first time, she noticed his accent. He clipped the ends of his vowels, which gave his voice a lilting quality. It seemed an odd fit on a man who looked like he did, but not unpleasant. "Doesn't that violate HIPAA? Patient rights?"

"Don't really matter. Everyone here's family." Clarence fixed her with a stare that walked a fine line between amused and irritated, and she resolved to be more agreeable before she pissed off her one and only nurse.

Before she could even process that thought, the door whooshed open. "Clarence? Dr. Mitchell? It's me, Tara."

Tara, it turned out, was a plump young woman with big hair and bigger earrings. She was wearing a skin-tight red T-shirt and low-cut jeans that left little of her muffin top to the imagination. "Hi. I'm Tara Tall Trees. I'm the receptionist—and I do the transcribing," she added, propping the door open with a fan.

Okay, the names were crazy, but she was the one who'd come to the Indian reservation, right? She was the one who loved a challenge, right? She smiled as warmly as she could manage with her head swimming. "I'm Dr. Madeline Mitchell. Nice to meet you."

She didn't get the chance to make any more chitchat. Suddenly the waiting room was mobbed by people who looked like seven levels of hell. The time for pleasantries was over. She had a job to do.

It didn't take her long to realize that the job was going to be a hell of a lot harder without actual supplies. The normal conversation went along the lines of, "Where's the iodine?" Or saline or cotton swabs or vaccines or any number of things a clinic needed to function on a daily basis.

"Don't have any."

"When are we getting some?"

"When someone pays us."

Over and over and over. The clinic didn't have any supplies beyond four bottles of Tylenol that were about three days from expiring, two boxes of bandages and half a box of hypodermic syringes. She'd brought supplies, sure, but a few boxes of bandages and needles weren't enough to hold her through the morning. By eleven, the supply closet was empty of everything but alcohol swabs.

She didn't have time to get frustrated. The patients came in droves. Diabetics who were in danger of losing feet, what seemed like dozens of people with the stomach flu, and people who were going blind from chronic alcohol poisoning. Few people actually looked at her, unless she caught them staring out of the corner of her eye. Half of them didn't even talk to her, just to Tara and Clarence.

The worst was a guy who came in looking like he'd wandered right out of a cage match. He was compact and muscled with his head shaved on the sides and his hair was pulled into a tight, tribal-looking braid. Which was intimidating enough, but with the flesh wound he was sporting on his shoulder? Mercenary, was all she could think. That, and what did the other guy look like? Clarence wouldn't tell her what his name was. "That's nobody," was all she got out of anyone. No one looked at him, and he looked at no one.

And then she was alone with him, behind the curtain. If he wasn't so damn intimidating, he'd be a good-looking man—definitely one of the healthier ones she'd seen today. However, the blood-soaked shirt she cut from him looked anything but good, and the old scars on his chest were even worse. A trickle of fear cut through her stomach as she snapped on a new pair of gloves. What had happened to this man? *Nobody*, she repeated to herself as she began to dig for the bullet. Just nobody. "How did this happen?"

Nothing. Not even a grunt of pain as she packed the wound with the last of the gauze. It was like performing surgery on a statue. She found her hands shaking as she wondered just who the hell nobody was, and what, exactly, he'd done to get shot. The list was long.

Okay. So this guy was terrifying. She still had a moral obligation to make sure her patients received the best care, as long as they weren't ax murderers, right? "You'll need to come back in within a week for me to check the wound," she said as she opened the curtain and made notes in a blank file. She thought about writing Nobody on the top. "And I'm required by law to inform the authorities, Mister… " she said, hoping to get something out of him.

She felt a breeze rustle her hair. That's weird, she thought as she turned around. The fan doesn't normally…

Nobody was gone.

The trickle became a waterfall of panic. What kind of person just blew out with the breeze—after a bullet wound? Someone who didn't want to be found, that's who. Someone who was wanted. Someone who was dangerous. More than just her hands shook as she tried to walk casually over to Tara. "We've got to call the police," she said, hoping her voice wasn't giving her away—at least not within earshot of patients.

Tara gently shook her head as she answered the phone again. "It was nobody. Tim—he's the sheriff—he'll call us if he needs us," she replied as she handed Madeline another file, like gunshot wounds in unnamed patients were just another day.

And that was all before lunch.

Madeline tried to keep upbeat. Clarence was a hell of a good nurse, and the patients clearly trusted him—far more than they trusted her. Tara was a multitasking genius. She could answer the phone, greet new patients and take histories all at the same time. Madeline had a good team to work with. Now if she only had some supplies to go with it.

"Tara, start a list," she called across the room upon discovering the only bottle of penicillin was expired.

"We don't have any money," Clarence repeated with a grunt as he lifted an old woman without her feet out of a rusty wheel chair.

She'd been here for three hours and had already heard that seventeen times. *They* might not have any money, but *she* did. "I'll get it. Just write it down."

By the time they stopped for a twenty-minute lunch, the list was up to number forty-seven, and she'd already seen forty-four patients and two emergencies. Tara slipped out with a promise to be back soon, whenever that was.

She was exhausted. She'd sweat through both her shirt and coat, rubbed blisters on top of blisters in her new cowboy boots, and the smoothness she'd flat-ironed into her hair this morning was all but shot. Even though she was sitting on the floor in front of the fan, she was still hot. She'd done more in four and a half hours than she normally did in a twelve-hour shift in the E.R. "Is it always this busy?" she asked between bites of peanut butter and jelly. She needed to get something closer to real food if she was going to sustain this energy level for long, but she didn't have any idea where she'd put groceries in her minuscule kitchen. At least she'd guessed right about there being no microwave in the clinic.

"Nah," Clarence replied from Tara's chair. He had his feet up on an exam table and his head leaned all the way back with his eyes closed. She was afraid he was going to fall asleep on her, but a nap actually sounded like a great idea right now. Add coffee maker to the list. "We just haven't had a doctor for a few months. Kind of a backlog."

"You did this by yourself for a few *months*?"

"It's a paycheck. Sometimes," he added.

Things picked up again at one thirty. Tara made it back in at two. Madeline was beginning to figure out that Indian time did not necessarily coincide with numbers on a clock, but no one else was exactly rushing around either. *Indian time. Just a time zone not found on any map*, she mused as she looked down another throat.

A lot of these people had the same symptoms—stomach cramps, low-grade fevers and occasionally diarrhea. *Seems like everyone always has the same*

17

stomach bug, she thought as she took a few blood samples from the people who seemed the worst. A few samples were all she could take—those were all the vials she had. *Add them to the list.* How huge of a chunk she was going to have to take out of the trust-fund money she'd transferred into her checking account for all this stuff? And how long it would last before she had to do it again?

Her wheels were already turning. After all, she knew people whose hobbies included expensive dinners and charity auctions. The Mitchells had been one of the leading philanthropic families in Columbus. It wouldn't take much to convince people with bleeding hearts and open wallets to have a dinner and charity auction for this clinic. And the hospital back home—maybe she could get Todd in Supplies to ship her at least the bandages that were just past their freshness date? It wasn't like gauze went bad. The drugs were going to be harder. She couldn't weasel extra freebies out of pharmaceutical reps if no reps got within a hundred miles of the place.

Things began to slow down around four, which meant there was only one person left in the waiting room, an old man with gray hair that just hit his flannel shirt collar. He didn't look sick as he sat and thumbed through an ancient magazine. *The end is in sight.* She sighed. *Maybe he just needs a prescription re-authorized.* It would be nice to end on something easy. At least today hadn't been boring.

And suddenly, it got a whole lot less boring. Tara gasped in shock as the fan was kicked out of the door. *Now what?* Madeline spun around in her pitiful supply closet.

Two men stood in front of Tara. Well, one man stood. He was tall and straight, all the more so compared to the broken people she'd looked at all day. His jet-black hair hung long and loose under a straw cowboy hat, all the way down to his denim-clad butt. Even though he was supporting the other man, he was moving from one black cowboy boot to the other, his hips shifting in a subtle-but-sexy motion. He was wearing a T-shirt with the sleeves torn off, revealing a set of honest biceps that looked like carved caramel—the best kind of delicious.

"*Find a nice cowboy.*" Melonie's voice floated back up her from their last conversation. "*Ride him a little. Have fun!*"

Now, Madeline wasn't exactly a thrill-seeking adrenaline junkie. On more than one occasion, she'd been accused of being the party pooper, the stick in the mud, a real-bring-me-downer in the room. Several times, it had been pointed out that she wouldn't know fun if it walked up and bit her in the ass. And that was just what Melonie said to her face. God only knew what everyone else said behind her back.

But there he was, standing in her waiting room. Fun in cowboy boots. No biting in the ass required, because she knew him immediately, and all she wanted to do was find a horse and ride. With him. The heat started at her neck and flashed southward. She could feel her curls trying to break free into a full-fledged frizz with the sudden temperature change, which only made things that much worse.

"Jesse!" Tara said in a voice that was just one small step below shouting. "What did you do now?"

"Give me a hand, will you?" Fun in Cowboy

19

Boots called back to Clarence. He pivoted just a little, revealing the other man who was leaning all of his weight on Fun's right side.

Not good. The second guy's leg was being held together with what looked like broomsticks and duct tape. His right arm hung limp, and his scratched face was contorted in pain.

"Damn, Rebel, what happened?" Clarence was already hefting the broken man—Jesse?—onto the nearest free table, leading to a volley of clenched grunts from the injured man. "I thought we might get through this month without you trying to kill yourself, you know."

Did Clarence really just call this guy *Rebel*? Well, it was official. She'd heard it all today.

Rebel—if that was his real name—was shaking his head when he caught her staring. He had beautiful black eyes, the kind of black that didn't so much show you the window to his soul, but reflected yours back to you. Those eyes widened in surprise. "You know how it goes, Clarence," he said, his gaze bearing down on her with enough heat that the rest of the clinic felt suddenly cool by comparison. "Life with Jesse is always an adventure."

Tara was next to the exam table now, holding Jesse's hand as she felt his head. "Do I even want to know?"

"Not really," Rebel replied, taking his time as he looked her over. His thumbs were hanging from his belt loops, which only made the shifting thing he was doing look more intentional. Aside from the long hair, he looked like every cowboy fantasy she'd ever had. Did he have a horse, or was her imagination way out of control? "You must be the new doctor, ma'am." He took off his hat and nodded. All that black hair, so straight it made her jealous, flowed around him like a cape.

Oooh, her first *ma'am*. From an honest-to-God cowboy, no less. She felt the sudden urge to curtsey, but then realized what he'd said right before the ma'am. She was the doctor, and she had a job to do. Wrenching her eyes from the long-haired cowboy to the patient, Madeline tried to regain her professional composure. "Dr. Mitchell, please. And this is Jesse?"

"Yes, ma'am."

That wasn't helpful. "I need to know how this happened, Mister... "

"Rebel," he said, those hips still moving.

She was *not* staring like a schoolgirl at this man. "Excuse me?"

"Just Rebel, ma'am."

A shiver ran down her spine. One more ma'am and she might swoon. "Dr. Mitchell," she said with more force as she turned to her patient. Clarence had finished cutting the duct tape off. "And how did this happen?"

"Dirt bike," Rebel said with a shrug. "Thinks he's going to make the X-Games circuit."

"Jesus, Jesse." Tara edged ever closer to hysteria. "That's your *fresh new start*? You're going to get yourself killed!"

There was something else going on here, something that went a little deeper than the friendly compassion Tara had shown everyone else.

"Nobody's dead yet." Madeline kept her voice low, hoping to regain some semblance of control. "What exactly happened on the bike?"

21

Rebel finally stopped looking at her. She could tell, even though she had her back to him, because her neck stopped sweating. Then he was standing by her side, pointing to the splint. "He rolled it. Heard his leg sort of snap." Tara's face turned white as Jesse groaned, but everyone else just nodded.

"And the arm?"

"Hit the ground funny. Obviously."

Madeline considered the situation. They only had four films left for the X-ray machine. In good conscience, she could only take two films—one for the leg, one for the shoulder. "Only two," she said to Clarence, and he nodded. Hopefully, she'd get the shots she needed on the first try. The phone rang. "Tara." But the young woman didn't move. "Tara, the phone."

"I got it," Rebel said, moving so fast that he picked up the phone before the third ring. "Clinic."

"Um, Clarence?" She wanted to tread carefully—first impressions and all—but she'd never worked anywhere where a patient just jumped into the fray. But Rebel wasn't a patient, her brain noted. And was an entirely different matter. "He can't answer the phone—can he?"

"Sorry, Doc." Clarence wheeled the X-ray machine over to Jesse and loaded the precious film. Mentally, Madeline added film to the list, which made it the most expensive item out of all of the must-haves. "Rebel helps out some. He knows how to answer the phone, but he hasn't learned the machine yet."

He helped out? This was bordering on insane, but she tried to ignore that fact. Frankly, at the moment, she could use a little help. Really, was this any different from a normal day at the E.R.? The only difference was that she didn't know everyone. She didn't know Rebel.

Yet. She glanced back at him. She didn't know him *yet.*

"Hiya, Irma," Rebel was saying as he sat in Tara's chair. "Yup—new doctor." Despite her confusion, Madeline's ears perked up. What would Fun in Cowboy Boots say about her? "Yeah, she's a little busy right now. Jesse crashed his bike. No, really." His eyes settled on her again, sending her temperature up a notch. God, was she imagining things, or was he interested? "She looks like a good one."

Not imagining *that.* Her cheeks warmed at the compliment. If things got much hotter, she was going to officially melt.

Now Tara was crying. "What about Nelly, huh?" She was never going to take her phone away from Fun named Rebel. "You promised you'd help out with Nelly more now that you're home, Jesse," Tara sniveled. "How are you going to do that if you're all busted up?"

Days of Our Lives. Madeline cut the rest of Jesse's shirt off. That certainly isn't any different than Ohio, she thought with a smirk. Jesse had *Army* tattooed on his biceps. Ah. He must be home from the Middle East.

"How about Thursday?" Rebel was saying. "Earlier would be better. I think you'll like her."

Okay. Yes. This was insane. Beyond certifiable. But she still had a broken bone to set. She forcibly directed all her attention to her patient. "Get him some of that Tylenol. Sorry, Jesse, but it's all we've got."

Jesse nodded, his eyes watering. "Do we have enough fiberglass?" she asked Clarence. Because all signs up to this moment pointed to no.

"We don't have fiberglass. We got a little plaster of Paris," he said as he shifted Jesse around on the bed. "Rebel can mix it while we do this, if it's okay with you."

Plaster of Paris? No one used that stuff anymore. And Rebel could mix it? What the hell? She turned to look at the man in question. He whipped his hat off his head again. "I help out," he explained, somehow managing to look both sheepish and sexy. "But only if it's okay with you."

She looked from the ancient X-ray machine rattling to life to Jesse's broken bone and back to Rebel. "Do you know how to mix plaster?"

Anything sheepish about him disappeared, and her temperature shot up another few degrees. "Yes, ma'am."

"Rebel's okay," Tara said between sniffs. "Better than Jesse is."

"I'll do better," Jesse muttered as Madeline tried to position his leg for the best shot. "Promise—*Ow!*" He tried to sit, but didn't manage much more than some unproductive shouting.

Lord, she had her hands full, and nothing about Rebel said he was a problem. Well, not the bad kind, anyway. She nodded, and Rebel spun on his heel and made straight for the supply closet in one smooth motion. Madeline knew she shouldn't just stand there and watch him walk away from her, but she couldn't help it. She'd never seen jeans sit on a man like that. But then, she'd never seen a man like Rebel.

"Uh, Doc?" The humor in Clarence's voice snapped her out of her little cowboy fantasy. "The X-ray?"

Excellent. Everyone was noticing. She hadn't been staring, she reasoned. She'd been keeping an eye on a strange man in her supply closet. That's all. "Of course," she said, trying to play it cool as she bent over Jesse's leg. It didn't look swollen—hopefully it was a minor fracture so she could cast it now. To be sure, she'd have to get the angle just right... "Tara, does Jesse have a file?"

Tara nodded, but she made no move to leave Jesse's side. "You were supposed to watch Nelly tomorrow so Mom could have a break. Now what?"

The old man from the waiting room appeared at her shoulder. He said a bunch of stuff, but the only thing Madeline understood was "Jesse," and even that was iffy.

So that's Lakota, she thought as Jesse nodded. Didn't sound anything like it looked in the textbook she'd tried to study from.

"What?" Tara demanded. "Albert, you know I don't understand."

"He said bring her over. Jesse can read her stories," Rebel informed them, arm-deep in a bucket of plaster of Paris.

Okay. So Tara had a daughter—Nelly—and Jesse was the most likely father figure. She still had nothing on Rebel, and who the hell was Albert? But none of that mattered. She didn't have to understand any of the drama to do her job. "Okay, everyone who's not broken, please go to the waiting room. I've got to shoot this film." Although she wasn't sure the walls of the clinic were

25

enough to protect them from the X-ray's radiation, she shooed them around the corner anyway.

Everyone crowded near the front door, and Madeline found herself standing side-by-side with Rebel. He was still moving, mixing the plaster with his bare hand. Each muscle in his arm twitched in turn, leaving no question in her mind. This was a man who was good with his hands.

"You got a first name?" he asked, so low that she wasn't sure she'd heard him at all. But he was staring expectantly at her.

She opened her mouth, but then caught herself. She knew nothing about this man, including whether or not he was the sort of person who should know her first name. And as far as she was concerned, an attractive set of musculature and a couple of well-placed *ma'ams* gave him no right to expect anything from her. "You got a real one?"

His eyebrow moved up as the corner of his mouth curved into something that might have been a smile if it hadn't been so focused. "Rebel is my real name."

She knew she was staring at him, but she couldn't help herself. If she could, she'd stare all day long, but that would undoubtedly be an even bigger problem than it already was. She had to stand with her whole arm hanging out in the room because the cord didn't stretch. The X-ray machine rattled and hummed and finally clicked. She didn't even want to think how old it was, but it was all she had, and there wasn't enough money in the world for a new one. Some things would have to wait.

Twenty minutes later, Madeline had set Jesse's femur with absolutely no plaster to spare and was reviewing his hefty medical chart. Clarence dug up a used sling for Jesse's separated shoulder. Tara finally roused herself from his bedside to add fiberglass to the list while Rebel was talking in quiet tones to Jesse. Albert had disappeared, only to reappear with a mop and a bucket. He began to mop the floor and wipe down each exam table with the kind of efficiency that said he'd been doing it for years.

Madeline had regained her bearings now that everyone had stopped talking all at once, and she was pretty sure she'd come off as cold and overbearing to the man who emptied her trashcan. "I'm sorry—Albert, is it? I didn't realize you worked here. It's nice to meet you."

Albert smiled and nodded his head. He said nothing.

Madeline tried again. "Thank you for cleaning up. I appreciate it."

"He doesn't speak much English," Clarence said as he carried the sheets they'd used as table covers back to the world's loudest washer. Apparently, it had been invented before ball bearings.

"Oh." That was a problem. She was unable to talk to a full one-third of her staff? Big problem. She made sure to slow down this time. Keep it simple. "Well. Thank you."

"He can hear, you know." Rebel was at her side again, shifting his weight from one foot to another. "You don't have to yell."

It should sound like a criticism, but the way it came out of his mouth was something much closer to a sweet nothing he was whispering in her ear. The heat spread from her stomach up to her face. She hated blushing, that betrayal of a physical reaction. And this

Rebel was making her blush with every single word he said. She took a deep breath and ignored the heat. "I wasn't yelling."

He moved his hand, like he was about to reach out and touch someone—her—but he caught himself. "You got louder, *Doctor*."

"I apologize if I offended your delicate tympanic membranes... " She couldn't bring herself to say *Rebel*. Just couldn't. The man had to have a real name. Even something like Tall Trees.

"If?" A lazy grin snuck across his face, and for some reason, Madeline was reminded of one of the movies she'd watched in preparation for the big move—*Dances with Wolves*. The way he moved, the way he looked at her—he was like the wolf moving through the grass. He didn't miss a trick. If she wasn't careful, he'd have her outflanked before she knew what was happening.

Not like that would be a bad thing. Not all bad, anyway.

She remembered he'd translated for Tara earlier. "Do you speak Lakota?"

He shifted, and his hips stilled. *Thank goodness*, Madeline thought. She had no idea how much more of that she could take.

"More than most people." And with that, he began to tap a heel onto the aged linoleum.

The perfect ending to this day was a sound like a ball-peen hammer beating itself into her brain. Which was nice, actually, in that it reminded her that no matter how hot—literally and physically—this man was, flirting did not belong in her clinic. "Please tell him I appreciate the job he's doing."

28

Rebel nodded his head and said words she didn't have a hope or a prayer of ever understanding, much less pronouncing. She must have been out of her mind thinking she was going to get *that* from a book. But Albert smiled again. "Thanks," he said, his accent so thick it was almost unintelligible.

Okay, she thought with a genuine smile. *We can start at thanks and go from there.* She turned her attention back to Jesse, who had at least stopped moaning. "When was the last time you had your vaccines updated?"

A hush fell over the clinic as they all turned to stare at her like she'd farted in the elevator. "Uh, there's a new adult booster shot for the chicken pox," she went on and wondered what she'd done this time. "Reduces the chances of getting shingles."

"Not interested," Rebel said, dismissing the very idea in the same tone he might use to shoot down a suggestion that they all picnic on the moon today.

Not interested? Madeline didn't care if he was interested or not. As far as she was concerned, the flu shot was not optional. "But I don't see where he's even had his hepatitis vaccinations. And everyone should get the flu shot—do you know how many people I saw today that had the stomach flu? This whole population is susceptible to H1N1 and other seasonal flu viruses."

"Not interested." Rebel dropped his head as his shoulders hunched forward.

He looked like he was going to spring at any second, and all that nervous energy was going to uncoil on her in the worst way possible. *Oh, shit.* Outflanked. And he was going to rip her to shreds.

Clarence came to her rescue, God bless the man. He cleared his throat and stepped between the two of them—ostensibly to carry the scissors back to the autoclave be sterilized. "Even when Rebel pays us for the X-rays, we won't be able to get that stuff. We've got too many other things we need."

Payment? All she'd heard all day was that no one paid. She looked at Rebel. "You pay?"

Rebel narrowed his eyes, but he started shifting his weight again. "I need an invoice first. But I pay my bills."

Amen and halleluiah, someone who did. If someone else was going to help cover the cost of supplies, she'd do her damnedest to make nice. "I'm sure Tara will have one for you in a few days, after she runs it through insurance."

The laugh came out of nowhere. One second, Rebel looked like a dangerous, wild animal. The next, he was doubled over, slapping his knee like she was Milton Berle and someone had hit her with a powder puff. And it was contagious too. Tara tittered, and she heard Clarence snort from the back room. Even Jesse managed a weak smile. Great. She'd gone from being insulting to insulted in one swift move.

"Insurance? Doc," Rebel said as he wiped his eyes, "you're on the rez."

"So?" That didn't come out right, but man, she hated being the butt of jokes. And right now, she felt like one huge ass.

"So, no jobs equals no money and no insurance."

Nothing. She'd spent all her time studying, only to get to the final exam and discover she'd been preparing for the wrong subject. Instead of that foolish language textbook, she should have been looking at census reports or something. Anything. Her ignorance of the situation was embarrassing, but there was no way in hell she was going to let him see that. It didn't matter if she was outflanked. "Well, someone's got to pay for something. Otherwise, no clinic, no doctor, no medicine."

And they were right back to that lazy smile as he shifted from one foot to the other, like he wanted to mesmerize her with his hips. "The last doctor made it five months."

He said it like he'd asked what her name was, but the challenge was unmistakable. She fought back the smile, knowing full well it was far too early to break out the Mitchell sneer. He had no idea who he was dealing with. Madeline Mitchell didn't back down. Period. She squared her feet, ignoring the blisters. "I signed a contract for two years. I keep my promises."

He held her gaze, the noble Indian and proud cowboy all wrapped up into one irritatingly handsome package. Then his gaze slid from her to where Tara was mopping Jesse's brow. She thought she saw a look of resignation pass over his face, but it was gone so quickly, she was sure she was imagining things. "Then I guess we have one thing in common."

One thing.

That was it.

Chapter Three

F"aster, Webel! Faster!"

Rebel pivoted to look back at his niece. Nelly Tall Trees was perched on her saddle, her rag doll carefully mimicking her position. She was rocking back and forth, as if she could convince Tanka to go faster with all forty-two of her pounds.

"I didn't hear the magic words," he teased, facing forward again.

The silence was drawn out. *Kids*, he thought with a smile. He'd spent how long reminding her what the magic words were? And still it took her a minute.

"Please, Webel?" He bit back the laugh at her mispronunciation. It was like Elmer Fudd was asking, not a little girl. "Please can we go faster?"

"You didn't ask in Lakota."

She growled at him, his little wolf-in-training. He didn't bother to reply. He knew that if she thought about it hard enough, she'd use their language. "Why do I hafta?"

"Because you are Lakota."

"Daddy doesn't speak it."

Maybe Nelly would grow up to be a lawyer. At five tender years, she could argue with the best of them. "He understands it."

"Mommy doesn't even understand it." Oh, she would be a great lawyer. She'd led him right into that. How much was law school these days? More importantly, how much would it be in twenty years? He would have to sell a lot of bags, that much he was sure of.

Nelly made her closing arguments. "Why do I hafta learn it?"

She was good, but there was no way in hell a five-year-old could out-argue him. He could throw a million things at her, things like the fact that their native language would die if kids didn't learn it, or that it was a part of them, just like the sky. Instead he went for the obvious. "Because if you can speak Lakota and your mom can't, how would she know if you say something bad?"

This important fact brought more contemplative silence. There's just no arguing with facts, Rebel decided. Not even for little kids.

He snuck a look back at Nelly. She sat tall in her saddle, and he could see the proud lineage of her tribe in her baby face. She loved her saddle—which was good, considering the bag he'd traded for it was worth almost ten times what the saddle was. But that's what uncles did for little girls whose daddies were fighting other people's wars. It was worth it every time he finally let her go faster and saw that toothless grin again.

"You might tattle on me. Teacher says tattling is not allowed."

"Nell-Bell. Would I do that?"

"No... " She didn't sound completely convinced.

Rebel waited. He could be patient when he

wanted to be. Still, it took a few minutes. Nelly had trouble with the vowel sounds. "Webel, *oh'ánkoya*."

"Good! That was good, Nell-Bell." He touched Blue Eye's sides, and the mare picked up the pace to a slow canter.

Tanka followed suit, leading to the "*Whee!*" that the wind picked up and wrapped around both of them.

Rebel wanted to go faster too. He loved nothing more than to give Blue Eye all of her lead and let her run as wild and free as a horse got these days. In her third summer, Blue Eye was, hands down, the best horse he'd ever owned. And he'd owned a lot of them.

Too bad no one but Nelly would ride with him. The language wasn't the only part of the tribe that would die if the kids didn't learn it. And with Jesse out of commission for the next few months—a year, maybe—it was up to Rebel. Like normal.

Blue Eye was pulling hard, just itching to leave old Tanka in the dust, but the clinic was just over the next hill. Rebel brought her back to a walk, and she snorted in disgust.

"Aww, Webel!" At least Blue Eye wasn't the only one disgusted right now.

"Sorry, kiddo. We're almost here."

"Mommy says the new doctor is mad."

"Oh?" Crazy or angry? He wasn't sure Nelly knew the crazy definition. He'd go with angry, but as far as he was concerned, crazy was not off the table. Because, if she wasn't a little nuts, what the hell was a doctor with stunning blue eyes and a smart mouth to match doing in the middle of the White Sandy?

Dr. Mitchell. She had a thin face that, on a less attractive woman would look horsy, but on her it just looked regal. Everything about her was long and lean, and despite the tied-back hair and sexless lab coat, she still managed to look delicate. Feminine. Beautiful.

"What else did your mom say?" A question that had nothing to do with those blue eyes. Or those legs. Nothing at all.

"Just that Daddy better not whine."

He chuckled as they wove their way to the hitching post through the cars haphazardly parked around the clinic. "Sounded a lot like whining to me when I got there." He reached up and pulled Nelly off her horse. "You won't tattle on your daddy, will you?"

Her little pug nose wrinkled with the weight of the decision. "I guess not—not if he's gonna keep reading me stories."

Yeah, Nelly is her mother's daughter. Rebel grinned at the little girl. *"Thunkášila* Albert made him promise. He'll keep his promise."

"That means grandfather, right? I thought Albert wasn't my grandfather. He's yours." Yup. Nelly was going to be a great lawyer.

"Thunkášila Albert is everyone's grandfather," he scolded her as he tied the horses.

Everybody's grandfather—even Nobody's. After Rebel dropped off Nelly, he had to go check on Nobody's wound. "Nelly," he said as he lifted her down, "you promise me that if you or your mom or grandma start to feel sick, you'll tell *Thunkášila* Albert or me right away, okay?" The sickness was coming. That's what the vision meant. But he couldn't bear the thought of Nelly getting sick. Not before he figured out what it was. Not before he figured out if there was a way to stop it.

35

"Yes, Webel," she said with a dutiful tone as he lifted her over the fan that was propping the door to the clinic open. And then she was gone, wriggling out of his hands and sprinting through the crowded waiting room to Tara's arms. "Mommy! Mommy, Webel let me go faster!"

"Hi, sugar." Tara glared at Rebel over the top of Nelly's head. "How fast?"

"Not fast enough," Nelly said with full lip-pout action.

Tara was not a big fan of anything faster, not when every time Jesse went faster, he broke something new. Time to cover. "Jesse was getting pretty tired, and Albert had some stuff to do," he explained, fully aware that the whole waiting room was listening. "So I brought her."

"Tara!" Dr. Mitchell yelled, pretty much eliminating all doubt about what kind of mad she was. "This speculum is broken! Where are the others?"

"Check the top drawer!" Tara rolled her eyes. "All day long, she yells," she said in a voice just loud enough that the only person who wouldn't hear it was Dr. Mitchell. "All day long."

"Those are all broken too! Where are the ones that *work?*"

"We don't have any others!" Tara shouted back. "Rebel, do me a big favor and pay your bill." She dug out a hand-written bill with the adding-machine paper stapled to it. "The sooner she can go buy her damn supplies, the sooner she'll stop being a—"

"We don't have a single speculum that works?" Dr. Mitchell appeared before them.

Rebel was immediately reminded of a mad scientist. Her cornsilk hair was working its way loose from the same bun thing she'd had it tied up in yesterday and looked like it was standing straight out from her head, which made the elegant length of her face look deranged. Her cheeks were flaming red, but her eyes flashed with nothing but ice. Ice notwithstanding, she looked like a woman who had just gotten everything she wanted from a man. Images of her naked, twisted in sheets in a bed or bare to the air under the night sky, flashed in his mind. Against his will, his pulse picked up a notch. It had been a long time since he'd tried to give a woman what she wanted, but he was starting to think he might like to give it another go.

At least she wasn't looking at him. That reduced the chances of her noticing his sudden state of discomfort. Instead, she slammed the broken whatever-it-was down on the desk. Her voice came out exasperated—and tired. Two days, and this place was already wearing on her. "Add plastic speculums to the dam—"

"A-hem," he said, cutting her off mid-curse word. Nelly didn't need to be hearing that—not more than Jesse already said it, anyway. "Dr. Mitchell."

Her mouth still hung open with the unspoken word as she shot straight up. Her hands flew to her hair, the same thing she'd done yesterday, practically the first reaction she'd had to him. "Oh. Uh… "

Damn, Dr. Mitchell flustered was only making him more flustered. To cover for what was becoming an embarrassing situation, he got behind the computer monitor. "Dr. Mitchell, this is Nelly Tall Trees."

"Oh. Hello there." Dr. Mitchell did a half wave from a safe distance, as if she was afraid of a little girl. She looked like she was under arrest, what with her hands behind her head like that. She wore no jewelry, he noticed. No bracelets dangled off either slim wrist, no necklace hid behind the collar of her shirt. She didn't even have stud earrings. She was unadorned. Naked.

Nelly buried her face in her mom's shoulder. "This is just a one-time thing." Tara looked like she'd been busted mid-cookie snatch. "My mom had something to do, and Jesse was supposed to watch her..."

"Well." Rebel could see Dr. Mitchell forcibly getting herself back under control. Her mouth snapped shut, her hands dropped away from her hair and she picked up that broken thing and jammed it into her pocket. "Yes, Jesse. How is he today?"

"He'll have to stay off of dirt bikes from here on out," Rebel said, shifting his weight so his zipper stopped intruding. "But he'll live."

"Well." She looked down at Nelly, who had graduated to cautious peering at the new white woman on the rez. "Hello. I'm Dr. Mitchell. I'm the new doctor."

The last three doctors who'd thought they could save the world had all told the kids to call them Dr. Jerry, Dr. Blaine, and Dr. Nate, but not the new doctor. She seemed almost as afraid of Nelly as Nelly was of her.

What was her name? He was dying to find out. He wanted to wrap his tongue around it, and then maybe wrap his tongue around a few other things.

Ow. His zipper was intruding again. *Damn white women.*

Dr. Mitchell waited, but she got no response from Nelly. Unexpectedly, a warm smile broke out on her face. "Tara, this shouldn't be a problem. And please add... speculums... to the list." She turned fire-red again.

His zipper was going to kill him.

"Rebel came in to get his bill," Tara said. She turned demanding eyes to him. "*Didn't* you, Rebel?"

"Sure." He took the bill and looked it over. And looked again, because he was sure his eyes were playing tricks on him. "One *thousand* dollars?"

"I understood that you paid your—*horse!*"

"What?"

But then he heard the rest of the waiting room gasp as Nelly squealed, "Blue Eye! Get out!"

Rebel spun to see that Blue Eye was straddling the fan, no doubt enjoying the breeze as she checked out what all the hubbub was about.

"Horse!" Dr. Mitchell screamed again. "Horse in the clinic!"

"Get, shoo, Blue Eye." Finally, the chance to get his pants adjusted. He grabbed the mare's lead and backed her out of the clinic. "Stay out here, or you'll have the mad doctor after you."

Blue Eye knocked his hat off his head and sniffed his hair, which was her way of saying, "Can we go now?"

Rebel knew she'd become an increasingly large pain in the ass until they got the hell out of town and back to the wide-open spaces again. "Give me a second," he muttered as he cinched the lead down tight and went back in. If he was lucky, he had five minutes before the horse figured her way out of the tie again. But he wasn't ready to leave, not just yet.

Dr. Mitchell was waiting for him, her eyes all ice and her cheeks all fire again. Her crossed arms were suddenly making that lab coat a whole lot less sexless as she huffed at him. "Horses do not belong in this clinic," she said, like that wasn't some obvious statement.

He grinned and saw the way her eyes got... deeper, somehow. It had been a long time, but not so long that he'd forgotten what that look meant on a woman's face. That was attraction, pure and simple. "She was just curious," he said, trying to stretch time just a little. The longer he stalled, the more he could look at her. "Not a big deal."

She was a sea of emotions. He thought he caught a glimpse of amusement under the attraction, but then both were gone, and she wore the meanest look he'd ever seen on a woman. He wasn't sure he'd ever seen eyes that damn blue, and he was positive that no one had ever tried to kill him by glaring alone. "Pay your bill, sir. And control your animal. Clarence! Bring me the next patient." And she stomped off.

He watched her go. What he wouldn't give to see her without that doctor's coat on. He strongly suspected that underneath she had a long, elegant body. The kind of body that gave a man just enough to hold onto, but no more. The kind of body that someone should be properly appreciating.

The kind of body he couldn't see right now. But what he could see was the way she sort of wobbled in her boots, like she was hurting.

Moccasins. A woman like that—a woman who was on her feet all day, yelling at people about medical supplies—a woman like that could probably use a nice pair of moccasins.

He kept his voice low. "Tara, what's her name?"

Tara rolled her eyes with expert precision. "Madeline, Madison—something Mad." She snorted as she answered the phone. "Suits her too."

Something Mad.

That just about described how she was driving him.

"Hello, I'm Dr. Mitchell." Madeline drew the curtain behind her. This entire clinic was in violation of HIPAA practices. Like the divider curtains kept anything private from anyone else. If this were Columbus, she'd already have been sued seven times over. Not that anyone here seemed to notice.

She glanced down at the chart. Another strange name. Although, to be fair, her name was probably weird to them. "And you're Mr. White Mouse?" She looked up from the chart to the old man slumping against the exam table. His hair was a dingy gray, and when he smiled, he revealed a mouth minus most of its teeth. At least he didn't have bloodshot eyes. She was damned tired of cirrhosis of the liver. Damned tired.

He nodded, his head bobbing forward just enough to stir his hair. White hair, White Mouse. *At least he isn't Mr. Mighty Mouse.* She frowned to keep the giggle back. Knowing her luck, Mr. Mighty Mouse would be in next week. "What seems to be the problem?"

Mr. White Mouse smiled and nodded again. And said nothing.

Madeline took a deep breath. Clarence was stitching a kid's chin back together, and Tara was no help in these situations. So she tried again. Slowly. "What's wrong?"

Mr. White Mouse's brow wrinkled, like he was concentrating extra hard. "Sick," he finally got out, his accent so thick that she could barely make out the word. The one word.

41

This was going to be a long day. *Better bedside manner. Better bedside manner.* She forced her best caring look. "Where?"

Progress. He nodded in understanding and then pointed at his crotch.

Well. That had gone south fast. She poked her head out the curtain. Clarence was still trying to get that kid closed up, and Tara was checking in what looked like a tour bus full of patients. She was on her own here.

Ten minutes later, she peeled her glove off while Mr. White Mouse hitched up his trousers. She looked at the old man, his face understandably twisted with confusion and maybe just a little pain. But he still managed a kind smile, full of trust and hope.

His prostate was the size of a grapefruit. He needed to get to the hospital. The surgery would have to be immediate—who knew what kind of strings she'd have to pull to this man on the docket? Given his age, he'd probably have to go to an assisted nursing facility, and maybe stay through the chemo and radiation.

And she had no idea how to explain this to a man who barely spoke English. She needed Clarence, damn it. If he hadn't gotten that kid stitched up yet, then they'd just have to wait. She flung back the curtain and found herself face to face with Rebel.

"What the... ?" she squawked as she stumbled backwards. He caught her arm and pulled her up—and right into his chest.

"Hiya, Rebel," Mr. White Mouse said behind her.

"Hiya, *Thunkášila*," Rebel replied, still holding onto her arm. Still holding her.

She could feel a chest that matched those arms. Could feel it right through her coat and ugly blouse. Could feel it right down to her very core. Her mouth began to move. "Speak English," was the first thing that sputtered out. Excellent. She sounded like a bigot.

"Learn Lakota," he shot back with a grin. A distracting grin. "This is our land." Again, part of her brain knew he should be angry with her—she was kind of being a jerk—but he just seemed amused. Suddenly, she was aware that his thumb was rubbing the underside of her arm.

Was this a joke to him? She would not let this man distract her with something as petty as a gentle touch. Not any more than he was already distracting her, that was. "This is my clinic."

She wasn't mistaken. His whole hand was moving over her upper arm, like he was checking to see if she had the muscles to deck him or something. His head dipped down and he locked his eyes onto hers. Her breath caught in her throat. "You're just renting it for a few years. Some of us will still be here long after you're gone."

Damn it all, he was intentionally distracting her, what with the caresses and the intent gazes and all. Trying to use her weakness against her. Trying to get rid of her. "You aren't even giving me a chance. You expect me to fail."

Something about him changed. Some shadow crossed his face, and he let go of her. "No," he said as he stepped around her, his mouth passing inches from her ear, "I don't." The tension was gone from his voice, and he sounded almost mournful. "But you have other promises to keep."

Was he quoting Robert Frost? To her? Maddening, that's what the man named Rebel was. Soft touches, happy voice, strange words she didn't know—what the heck was *Thunkášila*, anyway?

"*Thunkášila*," he said again, shaking Mr. White Mouse's hand. He turned to look at her. "It means grandfather."

Okay. Yes. The pain in her ass was hijacking a medical consultation. But they looked like they knew each other. Rebel could translate for her, and no one else besides her gave a rat's ass for privacy.

"I need your help."

"Oh?" And the playful wolf was back in the room, shifting back and forth again, grinning like a man who held all the cards.

"I need you to tell Mr. White Mouse that I think he might have prostate cancer." Rebel's eyebrows shot up, so she pressed on. "Now, I don't know when I can get him into the hospital in Rapid City for a surgical appointment with the specialist, and the chemo will take some time after that, but—"

Rebel held up his hand and cut her off. "Stop."

"Excuse me?"

"You think he has cancer?" The way he said it made her feel like the time her old Camry had died on her, and the first guy to come to the assistance of a damsel in distress had asked if she'd tried turning the key. Rebel was making it perfectly clear that not only did he expect her to fail, he thought she was an idiot.

Well, he could take his expectations and shove them. And if he needed help, she had at least four pairs of gloves left. She'd be happy to lend a helping hand. "Yes. That is my professional medical opinion. He needs surgery, chemo, possibly radiation, and I would try my damnedest to get him enrolled in a clinical trial."

"I see." He turned to Mr. White Mouse, who looked like he was bored at a tennis match. "And, Dr. Mitchell, can you tell me what his life expectancy will be if he agrees to such an aggressive handling of his possible cancer?"

What the hell was that, Perry Mason? She took a deep breath to keep from losing the last of her cool in the closed space of a fabric room. "Average survival rates depend on a variety of factors, including reoccurrence and—"

"Given. Average life expectancy?"

"Three to five years." She managed to keep the *you asshole* to herself.

"I see." He looked at Mr. White Mouse again. "And if we do nothing?"

"Doing nothing means certain death."

"We all die, Doctor. Or did you miss that day in class?"

He was trying to piss her off, trying to get her off her guard so he could finish outflanking her and drag her down to his level. "You paid your bill yet?"

Boy, she'd love to be able to appreciate that smile—warm as the summer sun that was baking the clinic, but sultry in all the good ways. Every time she thought she had him cornered, he flashed that smile at her, which suddenly made her feel as if she wasn't even playing the right game.

"In cash. For the supplies. And you're out of plaster of Paris."

Her one and only paying client. The relief washed over her, but she fought to keep from looking grateful.

One eyebrow snuck up, giving him that playful look again. "How long with no treatment?"

"One to three years."

"Yup."

Yup? Yup *what*? Nothing this man said made a lick of sense, except for the parts that pissed her off. She understood those just fine.

Finally, he started translating. Mr. White Mouse nodded as Rebel went on. Occasionally, the two of them would look over to her, like she was a candy striper instead of the head honcho around here, but that was it.

After what seemed like an eternity in the waiting room for Hell, Mr. White Mouse shook Rebel's hand, nodded at her and walked out.

She looked at Mr. White Mouse, at Rebel and back to Mr. White Mouse. "What the hell did you tell him?

"To go to a sweat lodge."

"Excuse me?" That did it. She was going to lose it, right here, right now. In the three days she'd been here, she'd had a nameless man with an unreported bullet wound, a horse in the clinic, and now this—a strange man with a stranger name sending her patients away against medical advice. No wonder the last guy only made it five months. This place was insane. She yanked the curtain shut so she could at least pretend she was losing it in private. "What the hell is a sweat lodge?"

"Calm down, ma'am." His voice dropped a notch and he turned to face her.

Oh, he was going to do the old speak-in-quiet-tones thing, the very thing she did when she needed to calm a patient? Screw him. "I'm not your ma'am. I'm Dr. Mitchell to you."

He leaned in, so close she could feel his breath on her flushed face. "You're really Madeline, aren't you?"

The air crushed out of her chest and her heart, which had been moving along at a nice, super-pissed clip, threatened to stop entirely. All at once, she realized they were obscured from everyone else in the clinic by the curtain. They were almost alone. And he was almost going to kiss her.

"Yeah, that's what I thought," he said, dipping his head down to hers. He waved his hand—not touching her face, not touching her hair, but she felt the coolness of the air move over her. "Madeline."

He was outflanking her, plain and simple. Mesmerizing her with his deep voice that said her name like it was something sacred, something worth protecting. Holding her with his soft eyes. Hypnotizing her with his easy movements. Waiting until she was completely defenseless. And then he'd go for the kill.

So what if she wouldn't mind being taken down right now? Dr. Madeline Mitchell didn't go down without a fight. "You tell me what a sweat lodge is. You tell me why you sent my patient away against medical advice. You tell me what your real name is, or I'll have you arrested for trespassing." She wanted to wince at that last part. She had no idea if she could have him arrested or not. But it was too late. It was out there.

If he only had a longer nose, he'd look exactly like a wolf grinning at his prey. Her.

"I didn't send him away against medical advice. You said so yourself—he's got about three years, one way or the other." He leaned back, his heel tapping again. Always moving—but not moving in on her now. She let go of the breath she hadn't realized she'd been holding. "*Even if* he had the money to pay for tests and surgery and chemo and radiation, *even if* he had a car that could get him to Rapid City and back, *even if* he let you poison his body in hopes of saving it, he's got about three years. He's sixty-eight. He's already lived longer than most of us will on this rez."

"So you won't even try? You won't even let *me* try to cure him?"

He scrunched up his face with disdain. "With surgery and controlled poisoning? You might *cure* his body—that's a big might—but you will not *heal* him. We'll go into a sweat lodge, and the elders and I will heal him. That's what he needs in his twilight."

Sweat lodges? He was speaking her language, and she still had nothing. "I could still have you arrested."

He called her bluff without blinking an eye. Damn, those eyes—those eyes would do her in. Here she was, trying to kick him out, and he was looking at her like... like... like she didn't know what. Those eyes didn't give away much. "Rebel is my real name." He tipped his hat, old-school. "Madeline."

And then he was gone.

And all she could do was watch him walk away.

Chapter Four

A t 8:15 on Thursday morning, Rebel was in the waiting room, sitting next to Irma Speaks Loud. He was fully aware that he'd been here every single day this week and that he didn't have to stick around for Irma's appointment—her English was just fine. He was also aware that he could not get his leg to stop jumping and that Tara was staring at him out of the corner of her eye.

He was more than aware that Dr. Madeline Mitchell was wearing a skirt today. A blue-jean skirt that came to just below her knees but hugged everything it touched like an old friend. Her legs were pale, almost milk-white. Those legs said she didn't normally wear skirts. Those legs said she had a good reason for wearing that skirt.

She had on those boots again too. They were right pretty boots, he figured, chestnut with blue stitching. Matched her eyes. But they pinched her feet. He could tell by the way she splayed her feet out to the side when she walked. Probably blisters on the heels. He thought about making her a pair of mocs, then realized he was thinking of the pair he'd seen in the vision. They'd look good on her.

However, even if he made her a nice pair of

mocs, she might very well throw them back in his face. After all, she'd seriously considered calling Tim on him yesterday—as if Tim would actually arrest him. But she didn't know that.

She spun around and caught him watching her. Her hands flew to her hair again—this time, it was tied in a low tail. It swung down to just between her shoulder blades. He liked it down, but something about it seemed off. Not quite right.

A fact that was not helped by the way her face twisted into something ferocious as she walked up to him. "Hello, *Rebel*." She sounded like she'd hit a piece of gristle in the middle of a good steak, but it didn't matter. She'd said his name. It had the potential to be music to his ears. "Back again?"

He willed his leg to be still, and it ignored him. "Brought Irma in."

Her eyes shifted to Irma, and she softened. It was a pretty thing to watch, to see the woman inside try to come out. "And you're here to translate?"

Irma cackled, her good humor filling the room. "I don't need no translator. I figure if I got to have someone drive me in, I might as well get someone easy on the eyes to do it, yeah?"

He chuckled with Irma, which helped keep him from staring at the prairie-fire blush that flamed across Madeline's cheeks. Damn, she just got prettier all the time.

"Well. That's… good." She did a damn fine job of ignoring her physical reactions, Rebel decided. She was relieved that she wouldn't need a translator, but she acted like it was no big deal. The boots were clearly rubbing her wrong, but she wore them anyway.

She blushed like a schoolgirl, but refused to even acknowledge that he was getting to her.

Somewhere, deep inside a pissy doctor who couldn't stand the sight of him, was a woman named Madeline. He thought he'd seen her yesterday, right about the time he'd thought about kissing her in the middle of the afternoon, just to see what she'd do. But the pissy doctor had overruled the woman named Madeline with such ease that she probably didn't even know she'd done it. Second nature, that's what it was.

He wanted to know what her first nature was. He could be patient if he had to be. But he wasn't feeling patient today. Hence the fact that his leg would *not* stop jumping.

She was staring at him. And not in the good way. "Was there something else you needed?"

He'd bet money that particular look didn't exactly win her friends, wherever she came from. She was *that* good at it. "Nope."

Her lips thinned. "I'm sure you've got someplace else to be."

"Not really." She didn't like someone challenging her directly, that much was clear. She was used to being in charge. Probably the oldest child, he decided.

Her hand slicked back, smoothing her ponytail again. As far as personal tics went, it was odd. "Don't you have anything else to do?"

He settled his butt into the chair. "Not today." Not when he could sit here all day and watch her fight herself. Beads would keep.

In a flash, her demeanor changed and she smiled, the smile of a woman who got exactly what she wanted. His blood ran hot. "Good. Then I'm sure you

51

won't mind helping Clarence unload the supplies. Since you're so familiar with my stock closet."

Oh, he'd like to be familiar with a whole lot more than that. But if she wanted him to prove himself by carrying boxes, then so be it. At least then he'd have a good reason for still being here. "Yes, ma'am."

"The white Jeep," she said, dismissing him with a wave. "Irma? Come on back."

He had to look around, but he finally found the white Jeep parked in back. He should have guessed that a vehicle that nice and new was hers. Not many cars like that around here. And who would buy a white car? Back when he'd gone off the rez, white cars were all driven by drivers paid good money just to take wealthy old ladies from point A to point B. She didn't look that old.

Clarence had a stack of boxes on a hand truck. "Hiya, Rebel," he said with a grunt as he lifted another box.

"Hiya, Clarence. That's a lot of boxes."

He looked from the hand truck to the Jeep. "I think she managed to get forty boxes in here. And so far, they all weigh a ton."

Rebel peeked in. Boxes were crammed in, floor to ceiling, window to window—passenger seat included. "What on earth did she get?" He'd only given her a grand. A grand went a long way for him, but he didn't think it would cover this much. He picked up a box marked *FRAGILE. X-RAY FILM."* A *ton* didn't begin to describe it.

"Everything, I think. There's got to be five thousand bucks' worth of stuff in there."

Wow. That's why she bought a white Jeep. She

was a wealthy lady. Just not old. "I brought Irma in. I can help until she's done."

Even with the two of them, it still took over an hour to get all the supplies in. As they wheeled the last boxes in, Rebel noticed Tara was smiling. It didn't happen very often, not unless Nelly was behaving herself. "Better day today?"

Sipping a Diet Coke, Tara nodded. "She hasn't yelled once. It's been almost pleasant. I thought she might be even grumpier about spending all that money... "

His curiosity got the better of him. "How much?"

"More than eleven grand." Tara's voice was a true whisper, like she was afraid to name the number out loud. "She gave me the receipts to file. That's a lot of money."

Rebel whistled. That wasn't a lot of money. That was a *hell* of a lot of money.

Who the hell was Dr. Madeline Mitchell?

It took nine hours to unpack eleven grand worth of medical supplies. He even took Irma home and then borrowed her car to come back and keep helping, much to Blue Eye's disappointment. When Albert showed up, Tara left to get Nelly at four thirty, marking the official end of the work day. Clarence held out until five thirty before he bailed. Albert asked if he should help, but she must be picking up on some of the language, because she yelled from the stock room that Albert was sweet for asking, but he should go home and check on Jesse, which Rebel duly translated.

And it was just the two of them.

By seven, they were done. She sprawled out at Tara's desk, her head down as she ran her hand over what was left of her pony tail. There wasn't much there, but damn it all, it was smooth.

Rebel took up residence on the floor in front of the fan, watching her through narrow eyes. She was exhausted. Would she own up to it, or pretend everything was fine?

"Thank you for your help, Rebel." It was muffled by the crook of her arm, but he heard it anyway. It wasn't the first time she'd said his name, but it did mark the first time she said it without sneering.

The fan wasn't cooling much. "Glad to help. That was a hell of a lot of stuff."

"I believe the technical term is a *shitload* of stuff." She pulled her head up and smiled weakly as she rotated her head from side to side. She was funny. He found her unintentionally humorous, but she could even be funny on purpose—when she wasn't trying to run the world.

"You got all that last night?" True, he was dancing around the eleven-thousand-dollar question. But every pass got him closer to some of her truth.

She shot him the *I-got-what-I-wanted* look. With her mussed hair and tired smile, she definitely looked like she belonged in a bed. Or at least a sleeping bag. "That medical supply place didn't want to stay open past eight, but money talks, you know."

Getting closer. He edged away from the fan. "That didn't look like money talking. That looked like money screaming."

Her back stiffened and she spun the chair away from him. He was losing her. "Don't worry about it."

He didn't want to lose her, not yet. "Can I worry about you?"

"Can you? Sure. I can't stop you. But I'm not giving you permission." Damn it all, he'd lost her.

Right before his eyes. "You *may* not worry about me. I'm fine. It's just been a long week."

Did she think he was going to buy that load of shit? "You can't *live* here. The clinic is not a life."

She snorted. "Says the man who's been here every day of the week and isn't the least bit sick."

Busted. But she wasn't the only one who could ignore the obvious. "That's not why I'm here."

"Then why?" She spun around to face him. The exhaustion was gone. Instead, he found himself staring into clear eyes the color of winter ice. No defenses, no second nature. She was just a woman, and he was just a man.

Who wasn't quite ready to own up to the truth. He actually wasn't so sure on the reasons himself. He pulled himself to his feet and shook the stiffness out of his back. Sitting on linoleum was a world of different from sitting on sand. "I doubt you'd understand."

"Sure. I don't understand the language, the customs, why over half my patients have the flu. I don't understand why you tell my patients there's nothing I can do for them when that's not true. I don't understand why my landline won't work. I don't understand a damn thing." She was on her feet, backing away from him. "Least of all you."

He swallowed. He'd pushed when he should have pulled. "I can check into your landline."

She shook her head, like she couldn't believe what he was saying. "Don't you have a job? Someplace to be? Anywhere but here?"

Now they were getting somewhere. She was pulling again. She was the kind of woman who needed to pull. She was *that* good at it.

"Sure. I work."

After she ran her hand over her hair again, she crossed her arms in frustration. Or was it protection? "Where?"

"Wherever I want."

He would be lucky if he got out of here without her strangling him. At least he could tell that was what she was thinking. "Doing what?" She liked to pull. She liked the control. So she could just keep pulling.

He shrugged, like he wasn't sure. "What I want."

"For whom?" For a woman who'd seen patients all day, and unpacked supplies all evening, she was suddenly looking quite feisty. And there were no patients around this time. He could kiss her now, and the worst thing that could happen would be that she stabbed him with a scalpel.

As long as she didn't hit a major blood vessel… he might risk it. "For me, myself and I." She glared at him, and he knew he'd earned it. "This is the rez," he added, trying to shrug it off. "Things are different here."

"Tell me something I don't know." She turned, looking at the whole of the clinic. He knew it had to come up lacking.

Again, he tried to imagine what she'd given up to come, and *why* she'd given it up. Others had come, filled with misguided hope about saving the noble savages from themselves. Those were the ones that lasted weeks, if not days. But she gave no indication that was the reason, and he didn't have a clue. "We're glad you came," he offered, hoping to make peace.

"We?" She pivoted, and suddenly, Rebel found himself looking at Madeline.

"Me. I'm glad you came."

Slowly, the smile developed like an old-fashioned Polaroid. Free from Dr. Mitchell, Madeline was beyond beautiful. It took everything he had not to step up, take that angelic face in his hands and kiss her. "Thank you for your help," she said again, each word coming out precisely measured.

"Anytime," he said. "Glad to do it." *For you*, he silently added.

She held his gaze for a moment longer, and then, in a heartbeat, Madeline was gone. "Will you be gracing the clinic with your presence tomorrow?" Dr. Mitchell said, putting the desk between her and Rebel.

That was it—the sign that he should not kiss her. Not tonight anyway. "Not if you don't want me to."

She bit her lip, and he saw her. Madeline. Madeline wanted to see him tomorrow, no matter how much he irritated Dr. Mitchell. Who would win? "No," she finally said with crushing certainty. "I do not want to see you tomorrow."

Second nature. She probably didn't even know she'd done it.

But he did.

By the time he got the car back to Irma's and rode over to Albert's, Jesse was in full whining mode again. Just like he'd been when Rebel had last seen him.

"Bro! Come on. At least change the channel for me. I'm *dying* over here."

The familiarity was comforting, in that pain-in-the-ass kind of way. "Suffer. You're the damn fool who broke his leg. Not me."

"I don't remember you trying to stop me," Jesse huffed as he tried to shift on Albert's couch.

Rebel couldn't help but compare Jesse's whining to Nobody's stoic silence. Damn, but he could go for a little stoic silence right now. "Jesse, I gave up trying to tell you what to do when you were seven."

"Some medicine man you are. Can't even tell your own brother when he's going to crash and burn," Jesse muttered, giving up on shifting. He threw his arms over his head to block out PBS. "Just change the channel, Rebel."

"Suffer. You might learn something." Like not to be a jerk, but after all these years, the chances were slim. "Seen your daughter today?"

"*Hanyanke'ci*," Albert hollered from the kitchen, where he was frying venison steaks. Tomorrow. At least Albert was keeping track of these things. But he always did.

"I hate it when he talks Lakota," Jesse whimpered, wrapping his arms over his ears. "I hate it here."

Which meant staying with Albert was good for the twerp. "Nelly doesn't whine this much. You sound like a baby," Rebel scoffed, turning up the volume on a program about seed pods. Static rippled across the TV. He headed into the kitchen where Albert already had the tea cooling. The tension eased out of his body. Man, it was good to come home.

Albert looked over his shoulder and nodded with a tired smile. Yeah, Rebel wasn't the only one who had to put up with Jesse's bitching. But then he squared around. "You like her."

Not a good sign, not when Albert spoke English. "Just helping out," he replied, hoping that was enough.

Albert's smile was a whole lot less tired. "Ayup, *wacánto wagnaka*," he said again, repeating himself in

Lakota. The language may change, but the sentiment did not.

His face shot hot. It could be worse. This was Albert. More than anyone else on this rez, Albert would understand. He had understood long before Rebel had.

But that didn't mean he wanted to stand here and have his grandfather break down his school-aged crush for him. He'd rather take his chances with Jesse. Jesse wasn't nearly as perceptive. What could go wrong?

Lots. Jesse came up firing. "Heard you were back at the clinic again today."

Rebel stiffened. Albert was one thing. Jesse was an entirely different beast. But it wasn't like Albert to gossip. Was word getting around *that* fast? Shit. He was in trouble. "Yeah?"

"Yeah." For a man who was supposed to be in agony, Jesse sure as hell looked like he'd just won the lottery. And, like usual, Rebel would have to foot the bill. "Same as yesterday. And the day before."

Damn it. Damn it all. He should have known this was coming. He'd walked right into it, and now he had no choice but to brazen it out. "So?"

He hated that smile of Jesse's. All the more so because people said that was when they most looked like brothers. He hated smiling like Jesse. He hated *being* like Jesse. "So I thought you swore off white women. Women in general, in fact."

It wouldn't be fair to punch that smile in. The man was defenseless. "This has nothing to do with that."

"Right, right. I forgot. I forgot you were the high and mighty Rebel Runs Fast, better than everyone else.

59

You never chased a skirt. You never did anything for a woman. You certainly never married a white woman. I just forgot." Jesse glared at him from the couch, the TV throwing the blue light of PBS onto his face until he looked like a *sica*, a spirit. And not a good one. "Or maybe it was you who forgot, Rebel. Maybe it was you who forgot who you really are."

Still. Be still. Because moving would mean punching Jesse's lights out. "I hope your leg gets infected."

"What, so you can take me back to the clinic and hit on the pretty doctor again? Go right ahead. I can't hurt any worse."

"Wanna bet?"

"Hey!" Albert appeared in the doorway, wielding the kitchen knife Rebel had gotten him three hunting seasons ago. "Knock it off."

Rebel didn't doubt the old man still had enough in him to at least do some collateral damage with the blade. Well, Jesse would get what was coming to him, that much was sure. "Yes, *Tȟuŋkášila*."

"Not my grandfather," Jesse said with more pout than Nelly ever got away with. That's what you got when dealing with a grown man who didn't know who his father was. Pouting.

It was time to leave before someone in this house lost it, and he was at the top of the list. "*Tȟuŋkášila*," he said, mindful of keeping the respect proper. And he walked away. He walked away, no matter how good the dinner he'd hunted and given to his grandfather smelled. Blue Eye trotted after him, but he wasn't in the mood to ride right now. He needed to just walk away. He, walked away from his little brother, his mother's only remembrance of a one-night stand with a white man she met at a truck stop. He loved Jesse, but he could not be around him when he was irrational. Not when he reminded Rebel of everything he'd almost been once.

Not when Jesse reminded him of everything he could still be.

He was done with white women.

It was better this way.

Chapter Five

A month. One month. Madeline had made it one long, overworked, underpaid month.

Only four to go until she broke the last guy's record.

She sat outside the High Plains Art Gallery in Rapid City, finishing her latte and enjoying the urban wilderness again. Sidewalks. Dogs on leashes. Self-absorbed hipsters. Bright awnings on freshly painted buildings. Man, she was loving the city today. Not that the clinic wasn't on her mind. She had a Jeep full of medical supplies and canned goods, and had only one more errand on her to-do list. Melonie's birthday was in less than a month, and she had demanded something nice. "Something Native," her one and only little sister had said just over a month ago.

Had it really been a month since she'd had a latte? The days had flown by in a blur of clinic, cabin, clinic, cabin. *Challenging* didn't begin to describe it. Despite her rather childish insistence that she didn't want to see him in the clinic again, Rebel had come in on a regular basis—he seemed to know when the older patients needed a translator. Not that he ever told them what Madeline wanted him to tell them, though.

She'd gotten a shipment of flu vaccine—money

talked, after all. And when it arrived on Thursday, Rebel had shown up and said a whole bunch of things to a whole bunch of people in that language that was so lovely she almost wasn't irritated listening to it. Except that no one would let her vaccinate them. Something about the government—but what the hell did that have to do with the flu? And how had he known that was the day the vaccine would get there? It bothered her, like a micro-cut on her hands she didn't know she had until she spilled orange juice on them.

That man. She wanted to hate him—desperately wanted to hate him—for making her job harder than it already was. But every time she wanted to strangle him, he'd turn around and do something that made her life easier. Her landline had miraculously developed a dial tone one day. He brought in some blocks and a ball, and would sit on the floor with Nelly, playing with fussy babies and talking to them all in soothing Lakota tones until they stopped squalling. And—damn it all—some of the people he talked out of medical advice had the nerve to get better anyway. Mr. White Mouse had come in—Rebel had already been there, waiting—and explained that after the sweat lodge, he was feeling much better. As much as she thought they were all nuts, people who felt better were still people feeling better. She didn't know how an unknown quantity like Rebel made things better, but he did.

Aside from Rebel—certainly not because of him—things were, on the whole, improving. Things had slowed down after the first few weeks. Clarence had been right—they just had a backlog to work through. It had taken some serious wheeling and dealing, but she'd gotten the hospital in Columbus to ship out some stuff.

The gauze supply was safe. Rebel paid a couple of people's bills, and part of a couple of others. Where he got that kind of money, she didn't know, and she'd decided not to think about it too much. A few other people gave her some money, and one woman gave her a quilt for bringing down a child's fever. A quilt in July. At least it was a thoughtful thing. Patients were starting to look at her. Progress.

More and more people were coming in with that stomach bug, though, and that was beginning to be a problem. Some were repeat visits—and she was beginning to worry about the old and the young. Clarence said someone's grandmother had died last week, but she'd never made it into the clinic. And just yesterday, a four-year-old girl had to be carried in by her mother because she was too dehydrated to walk.

As Madeline drank her latte, she worried about that little girl. Not much younger than Nelly was, and so drained she couldn't even cry. It had to be some strain of the flu, but she hadn't heard anything about a new one making the rounds. Madeline kept taking samples, but the lab wasn't exactly in a hurry to get the results back to the White Sandy Clinic. Not even the Center for Disease Control was returning her calls. No one in the outside world was in a hurry to do anything for the clinic.

Well, she was going to do something—Rebel be damned. The battle lines had been drawn. She had a fresh supply of IV drips and two new poles in the back. She had the sinking feeling this flu would get worse before it got better. She could only hope to get her patients vaccinated before people's immune systems got too weak to fight off any other infections. Which lead her thoughts straight back to Rebel again.

She caught herself. That had been last week. Today was Saturday. She was not going to think about sick little girls and dying grandmothers. She was not going to think about Rebel today at all. She was going to finish her to-do list, get her sister a lovely present, and then she was going to do something fun. She deserved a little fun today. After she got Melonie's present, she was going to watch a movie in a dark, air-conditioned theater while eating overpriced, over-salted popcorn, and that was that. Didn't matter what was playing. Trans fats and sodium be damned.

She threw her empty cup under the seat and checked her reflection. Thanks to blasting the a/c, her hair was good. The necklace Melonie had given her as a going-away present—a huge, sea-green disk of turquoise on a brown leather strap—hung just above the deep V of her favorite girly shirt—a pink, short-sleeved sweater that was thick enough she didn't have to wear a bra with it if she didn't want to. She'd even applied some lip gloss in hopes of getting better service today. Plus, her bag was a Hermes—a twenty-year-old Hermes that she'd inherited after her mother died—but still. Nothing got service in an art gallery like the announcement that money had entered the building. It had felt good to dress up a little. Melonie would be proud. She felt less like a doctor in the trenches and more like a normal woman.

It took less than twenty seconds. "May I help you?" The saleslady was the kind of delicate redhead that probably earned money on the side doing *tasteful* modeling sessions for *serious* artists. Like Melonie had done for a while.

"Yes. I need a gift for my sister." She bit back Melonie's *something Native*. "Something nice."

65

The saleslady's eyes hit the turquoise, the bag and the boots in one fell swoop. Then she smiled warmly. "Of course. I'm sure we have something you'll both love."

Yeah. Madeline mentally snorted. Something expensive.

The tour began with sculpture and moved on to paintings. They paused so that Karen, as the young saleslady insisted Madeline call her, could get them some coffee. Then they continued on to jewelry.

Nothing was quite right. There were some beautiful things, things Melonie would like, but nothing sang to Madeline. Not at those prices, anyway. She kept thinking how many antibiotics she could get for a two-thousand-dollar, signed Fritz Scholder print.

"We also have some lovely Native beadwork. Original pieces," Karen offered as she led the way up a sweeping set of stairs behind a velvet rope. Madeline kept her smirk to herself. That's what a Hermes bag got a girl. Behind the velvet rope.

"Original is good." After all, Melonie was one of a kind. She'd like something no one else had.

This was more like it. Shirts dripping in color, moccasins with every square inch covered in tiny beads, hair ornaments, chokers—all definitely beautiful. Her eye was immediately drawn to a long, green—well, bag, she guessed, with an old-style pipe next to it, all under a glass case at the end of the aisle. "That's beautiful."

"Isn't it?" Karen perked up with hope as she unlocked the case. "It's a ceremonial pipe bag. Brain-tanned buffalo hide, hand-carved soapstone pipe on a locally harvested cottonwood stem. Not a reproduction, but an original. One of a kind." She took out the bag. There was something oddly sensual about the way her fingers stroked the fringe. "It's by a local artist. Jonathan Runs Fast. He's one of our top sellers, and is perhaps the most important artist in this medium in the world. His work is in museums. Mr. Steinman—the gallery owner—got one of his pipe bags in the Museum of the American Indian in Washington." She held it out to Madeline. "Go on. You can hold it."

Madeline moved carefully. She wasn't likely to drop something like this bag, but still... The leather was as soft as any baby's bottom. "Wow." She didn't know leather could be better than silk. This was brain-tanned? She'd overlook the gross factor. She didn't have sheets this soft, for crying out loud. She studied the complicated pattern on the body of the bag. "What's it supposed to be?"

"The buffalo on the prairie after the spring rains, I think."

Madeline squinted, but she could see the brown things were supposed to be the buffalo, and the green would be the grass. Abstract, but also representational. Melonie would totally groove on this. "He carved the pipe himself?"

Karen's eyes were glowing with something between desire and awe. "He does everything by hand—even hunts the animal and tans the hide."

A man who both hunted and wielded a needle and thread? She would believe that when she saw it. "A local artist?" She didn't know any local artists, but she knew semi-local Indians. She might be able to get non-gallery verification about this sales pitch. Clarence had to know someone who knew something. Clarence knew everyone.

Karen pointed to a framed sheet of paper next to the pipe. "He lives somewhere out on the White Sandy Reservation, not too far from here."

Madeline froze the moment the word *White* was out there. That was local. Too local. Moving at what felt like a glacial pace, her eyes found the paper. There, under the title "Jonathan Runs Fast: Traditional Master of Fine Art" was a picture. Sure, the guy in the picture was minus the straw cowboy hat, and his white, button-up shirt was underneath a dark sports coat. But the man in the picture looked exactly like her professional pain in the ass—the vaccine-hating, non-translating Rebel himself.

"Sure," his voice came back to her. *"I work. For me, myself and I."*

"Do you know anything about him?" she got out, hoping she didn't sound like she was having a coronary event. One of the most important artists in the country was spending his free time telling her patients not to get the flu vaccine? What the hell? The shock that twisted through her gut was beyond physically uncomfortable. It was downright painful.

"Oh, my," Karen said, her eyes going dreamy. "He's such an... unusual man. He goes by the name Rebel. Mr. Steinman—the gallery owner—says he lives in a tent in the middle of nowhere. Mr. Steinman said he doesn't have a phone, doesn't own a car." Karen's tone of voice made it clear she thought the whole thing sounded like something out of a romance novel. No wonder the saleslady looked like she was in love with the bag. She was in love with Rebel. "He's... amazing."

The shock twisted again, like a scalpel cutting without anesthesia. "Oh?" What kind of amazing were they talking about here? And why did that matter? Madeline choked down the confusion that swirled in her throat as she scanned the rest of the sheet. Master of Fine Arts from the University of New Mexico. Gallery shows in Rapid City; Taos, New Mexico; New York City; and Washington, D.C. Best in Show awards. Notable Recognitions. Outstanding New Artist.

The pain in her ass was an Outstanding New Artist. He had an MFA.

His name was Jonathan. Jonathan Runs Fast.

"How do you get a hold of him if he doesn't have a phone?" How did anyone get a hold of him? If Jonathan *Rebel* Runs Fast didn't have a phone, how did he know when to show up at the clinic? The confusion was swirling right on up to cyclone territory. Fast.

"We don't." Karen leaned in and dropped her voice from saleslady to co-conspirator. "Mr. Steinman went looking for him once, got lost and was almost eaten by a coyote. Mr. Steinman said that Rebel rode up out of nowhere and rescued him. He said Rebel took him back to his camp, and it was nothing but a tent in the middle of nowhere. He said Rebel was some sort of medicine man, said he kept souls in his tent. Mr. Steinman said he'd never been so afraid of dying in his life." She looked over her shoulder in fear. "Mr. Steinman doesn't like the clients to know that, of course... "

"Of course." She could just see it too. Rebel appearing on that one-blue-eye, one-brown-eye horse of his, chasing off wild animals and rescuing clueless white men. But that was all she could see right now. Because a medicine man? He thought he was a *medicine man*? Some quack with a Fine Arts degree was telling her patients what to do? Her cyclone of confusion had her heart pounding so hard she thought she was going to start popping blood vessels in her ocular cavities. Maybe she already had, because she was seeing red.

"But we don't have to get a hold of him. He usually shows up right after we sell one of his bags." Karen looked like she wanted to pet the bag again. "He usually makes ten or twelve a year, and they go quickly. One of a kind."

Madeline was barely aware of clutching the bag to her chest like she was afraid to let go of it. "How much?"

The smile was barely contained victory. "Mr. Steinman has been shopping that particular work around. The pipe and the bag were designed as a set—"

Rebel had designed them as a set. "How much?"

Karen was openly beaming now. "A private collector in Okinawa expressed interest—"

Screw Japan. "How much?"

"$3,700."

She had known he had a real name—she'd always known. A real name that was well known. A real name that meant something.

She thrust the bag out to Karen, whose face was aglow with commission expectations. Madeline would have spent that money on supplies anyway. And since Robin Hood Rebel seemed to take it upon himself to overcharge the rich and pay the medical bills of the poor, she might as well get something besides irritation out of the deal. "I'll take it. And you don't know how to get a hold of him?"

"No. He's unreachable."

We'll just see about that.

By the time she was in the car, she was beyond pissed. He'd tricked her—no, tricking would be a good joke. He'd flat-out lied to her. He'd lied about his name, about where he got the money to pay all those medical bills, about what he did with his life. He'd jerked her around for fun, and God only knew what his sick motives were for jerking around innocent, sick people.

He was about to find out that no one jerked Madeline Mitchell around.

She opened her phone and gave thanks that she'd both bothered to put her staff's numbers in it and that she was in a city where she got service. She dialed Clarence first. Clarence knew everyone. Clarence knew Rebel.

It was only when he picked up that Madeline realized that she was about to make a fool of herself. She couldn't just tell Clarence she was going to kill Rebel, and could she have directions to his secret hiding place, please? "Uh, hey, Clarence," she backpedaled quickly, trying desperately to figure out how not to sound like a raving lunatic. "Uh, listen, I was looking for something arty for my sister, and—"

"You should ask Rebel," the big man said with a yawn.

Excellent. She'd woken him up. But asking Rebel was *exactly* what she had in mind. Try to sound casual. Casual. "Oh, yeah. I'll do that. Do you know where I can find him?"

"He ain't easy to find."

So I heard. She took a cleansing breath. "Would

Albert know? I was going to call him next." Like Albert would even understand her. She was pretty sure Albert and Rebel were related, but she hadn't even gotten close to cracking the family code on the rez. She waited. She'd call Albert if she had to, but she didn't think she'd have to.

Finally, Clarence sighed so heavily she swore she could hear him roll his eyes. "You don't have to bother Albert. It's summer. Rebel's got a spot down on the White Sandy. Go west by the burnt-out bar until the road ends. Should be a short walk after that."

The burnt-out bar. She'd driven past that on her way off the rez today. "Thanks, Clarence. And sorry to bother you on the weekend."

"Yeah, yeah. And, Doc? Don't get lost." He hung up.

She wasn't worried about getting lost. Rebel had rescued Mr. Steinman, after all.

By the time she got done, someone was going to need to rescue Rebel.

The road ended with no warning. One second, she was driving way too fast on a gravel road; the next, a gate overgrown with wild trees appeared out of nowhere. Madeline slammed on the brakes and careened to a stop with inches to go. Her heart, which had already been pounding in a simmering rage, kicked back up another notch. Damn that man. He was out to foil her at every turn.

A short walk, Clarence had said. But she didn't see a river, or a creek, or anything that passed as water. Didn't matter. Nothing—not even a gate—was going to keep her from putting that man in his place.

She fished out a half-full water bottle and headed west as fast as she could in her boots.

After ten minutes, she began to wonder about the *short* walk she was on. After twenty minutes, she began praying for a hat to block the hot sun. By the time she'd been wandering around in what seemed like circles for half an hour, her feet were killing her and her water was gone. Suddenly, she crested a small hill and saw water. Stumbling through gnarly underbrush, she ran.

Only to discover that it had been a mirage. Nothing but more flatness.

Bad sign, she thought as she tried to re-orient herself west. Confusion and disorientation were bad signs. She was starting to think she'd be lucky if a coyote tried to eat her, because otherwise she was going to get heat stroke in the middle of nowhere. And there was nothing good in that.

Her legs got heavier and heavier, but she forced them to keep going as she kept her eyes off the horizon so they wouldn't trick her again. Finally, she saw the smoke off in the distance. He was out here, she thought as she prayed she wasn't hallucinating that thin, white wisp. She was closer than Mr. Steinman had been, so that was something.

Damn, but her feet hurt. The longer she walked, the more she wondered what the hell she was doing. This was one of her more poorly planned ideas, that much was certain. Tracking his ass down had seemed like a good—no, great—idea at the time. She'd been so furious on the drive back from the gallery that she'd decided to have it out with her professional pain in the ass once and for all.

But that was currently the least of her worries. She needed something to drink and a cold shower, and she needed them STAT. She'd been stumbling her way through scrub brush and tall grass for what felt like days in boots that were not designed for anything more taxing than plush carpeting. And she was paying the price. Big time. Grass was stuck up under the legs of her jeans, scratching her skin more with every step. Sweat was running down her scalp, and her underwear was sticking in places it was never meant to. By the time she found Jonathan Rebel Runs Fast's camp, she'd be lucky if she didn't look—and smell—like Bigfoot in need of a flea dip.

The sound of water reached her ears, the promise of cool relief almost enough to bring tears to her eyes. Water. Rebel would have to wait. She needed to bring her core temperature down before her symptoms began to cascade. It was the least she could do for her poor feet.

But she'd have to find him soon. Of course he'd be near water. But he wasn't stupid enough to drink it, was he? Well, if he was, that wasn't her problem. Not until he got dysentery. Then maybe she'd care.

She broke through some scrawny trees and discovered herself on the bank of a decently wide river. *I'll be damned.* She blinked several times, just to be sure she was really seeing it. *The sand is white.*

Just ahead was a long, sloping hill, so low that it was maybe only seven feet tall. The front of the hill had been shorn off by hundreds of years of water running over this very spot. The top of the hill was covered by more of the scrawny trees, but they looked less anemic up there than they did down here. And there, right in middle, was a tent.

He really did live in a tent. It wasn't just a load of bull. He was for real.

Real like the small fire crackling in a pit at the bottom of the hill, less than five feet from the river. Real like the pot hanging over it, bubbling with what smelled like stew. Blankets were spread out on either side of the fire. Looked like he was expecting company.

Excellent. She was intruding. If she had parked close, she'd bail. This was not a good idea, much less a great one. What had she thought she'd accomplish by barging in on him? He had plans, and God only knew what a man like Rebel considered *plans*.

But the water was gurgling on its merry way past the campsite, just begging her to kick off her shoes and come on in. She turned to look at the river. She'd come so far... maybe for only a minute. Then she'd see if she could find something to drink that didn't look like it was crawling with microbes, and it would be time to go. She spun around, looking for a place where she could sit down and wrench her boots off.

And found herself face to chest with a dripping wet, *shirtless* Rebel. Well, almost face to chest. He was still a good six feet away from her, just finishing knotting a towel around his waist.

His bare waist. She could see the oblique muscles, cut from solid rock, just above his hips. And it wasn't a hell of a big towel. There was no way he had on anything else but one dinky little towel and a whole lot of muscles.

She was staring when it hit her. *Holy hell, what am I doing here?* Not a good idea. She should not be here, not with him looking like some sort of water god, not with her on the brink of a medical emergency. She should not be here *at all*.

His smile seemed a little less lazy this time as his eyes took in everything—the sore feet, the sweaty shirt, the hair that was about ten seconds from full-fledged frizz. Everything. The smile left lazy behind and headed straight for intent. "Hmm. Not who I was expecting."

"You were expecting someone?" Great. Add besotted teenager voice to the long list of things that were wrong with her at this exact moment in time. But that was the best she had because, faced with that chest, she felt exactly like a besotted teenager she'd once been, watching Patrick Swayze teach that lucky Jennifer Grey how to dance in the water for the first time. The moment puberty had officially begun.

And damn it all, she was about five feet from living that delicious dream in real life. If she didn't pass out from her plummeting blood pressure first.

At this exact moment in time, he was everything—everything—she wasn't. He was cool, calm, collected, mostly undressed and in no apparent danger of swooning. "Someone. Didn't know who. Thought it might be… Nobody. If I'd known it was you," he looked over to the pot, "I wouldn't have made the stew. I hope it'll be okay."

See, now, that was exactly what he normally did—spoke words she understood individually, but all together? He wasn't making a single ounce of sense. "You made me dinner?"

"It's got a little while to go." His eyes moved again—and she realized that was the only part of him that was moving. No ball-peen-hammer heels, no tapping fingers, no swiveling hips. He was completely, utterly still. The only movement was the trickle of water down bronzed skin and off the ends of his hair.

This was officially getting weird. Hell, it was already weird. It was getting a whole lot weirder.

"So, you wanna go?"

The question caught her off-guard, but not quite as much as the *yes* that almost popped out of her mouth. She didn't know for sure what she would have been saying yes to—Leaving? Swimming? Go at *it?*—but with the way he was just *looking* at her, she didn't think she was going anywhere anytime soon.

And she was starting to think that maybe she was okay with that.

She managed to get a, "Where?" out, but she couldn't fool him, not one bit.

He tilted his head to one side, setting all that loose hair tipping off to the right. "You look hot. I don't have anything air conditioned, but the river would help those blisters you're working on."

Well. At this particular point in time, perhaps *hot* was the best she could do. "I don't have a suit."

He had the nerve to chuckle. "So? Neither do I."

Now would be a good time to start breathing again. Right now. "Uh… "

"You came from the east, which means it's about a mile and a half back to your Jeep. I don't want you to get heatstroke or anything." Rational—at the same time he was completely, totally irrational.

Get naked? In a river? With him? *Oh, let me count the ways this is a bad idea.* "Uh… "

Great. Just great.

And then he moved. One careful step at a time, he

closed the distance between them until there was less than a foot. One measly little foot between hot, sweaty and panicked and cool, wet and calm.

She swore she could hear "The Time of My Life" echoing from somewhere. "I don't think this is such a good idea."

"You're hot. You're blistering. You need to cool off."

"I'm fine." And that sweat trailing down her face? That had nothing to do with anything, thank you very much. At least she was still sweating, right?

Twisting his mouth into that canine grin, he shook his head at her lousy lie. And then, moving slow enough that it hurt her deep inside, he reached up and felt her forehead with the back of his hand. His hand was cool, damp. Her temperature dropped a whole degree—at least on her head. "Why do you do that?" he asked.

She tried to pull away from his touch, gentle and yet exquisitely dangerous, but he suddenly had her face in his bare palm. That alone was enough to hold her. "Do what?" Excellent. Her voice was starting to quiver. All she wanted to do was run into the river, water god be damned. She was going to crack.

"Ignore what you really want." His thumb moved over her cheek, leaving a cool trail in its wake. "What you really need."

"I don't need anything." She was sure that wasn't true—she'd come here needing something—but at this exact moment in time, she was having a lot of trouble remembering what that was. She didn't need anything. Other people needed *her*. That was how it worked.

"Everyone needs something, at least some of the

time." He should sound like he was scolding her for not knowing that simple fact, but nothing about him said scolding. "And right now, you need to cool off."

He stepped in, close enough she could see herself reflected in those black eyes. Close enough she could smell the river water. Close enough she could taste him, if she wanted.

He slid his hand down from her face, across her collarbone, over her shoulder and down each and every one of her vertebrae with enough pressure to weaken her knees. Then he grabbed her top shirt and began to pull.

"What are you doing?" she spluttered, finally finding her hands. She grabbed at his forearms—rock solid—and halted his movement.

He let her stop him. "You don't want to ride home in wet clothes, do you?"

There it was again, that rational irrationality. "I don't want you to look." And she was right back to childish.

He shook his head, his smile not moving a bit. He knew *exactly* how childish she was being. "You're a doctor. You see people naked all the time."

She swallowed. His hands were still on her waist, but he was tracing her ribs through her tank top now. Her shirt was half up. For the love of God, it *couldn't* go up any farther. "That's different. I'm a doctor."

His eyes narrowed and his hands stilled. "Are you saying no one has ever seen you naked before?"

Excellent. Just freaking wonderful. She was so horrid at this… this… this whatever they were doing that she was coming off as a virgin. A bad virgin. "I didn't say that."

Did he look relieved, or was she imagining things? Either way, his hands started to move again, edging up ever so slightly and taking her shirt with them. "Let me guess. The first boyfriend, your parents hated. The other, they loved."

How did he do that? How did he just know about Bryce, her one attempt at teenaged rebellion? How did he just guess that Dad had referred to Darrin as son from the second date onward? How did he know anything?

There was that grin again, the one she wanted to push into his head when he shot it at her in the clinic. But they weren't in the clinic. They weren't even in a building. They were standing on a sand bar, next to a river, under a hill.

She was pretty sure. If she was suffering from heat stroke, she might be imagining this whole thing.

He leaned in and pressed his cheek against hers. She was *not* imagining that, that much she was certain. "So which one did you leave to come here?"

He hadn't kissed her. And she was disappointed about that—why? "The one Dad loved."

"That's kind of what I thought." And her top shirt was over her head, leaving her feeling naked in a tank top.

"Madeline," he said, his voice pushing its way past her heated daze and pouring cool, clear water on her soul. His hands found her shoulders again, tracing the straps of her tank top. "No bra?"

If possible, she got hotter. "Don't need one when I'm not in the office." She'd long ago given up on being jealous of Melonie's fabu set of girls, but in an instant, she wished she had something more to bring to this particular little party.

"Hmm. A necklace." His fingers undid the leather strap of her necklace without hesitation, which didn't leave a doubt in her mind that a bra wouldn't have slowed him down a bit. He let the ends of the necklace trail off her skin. "Madeline," he whispered again, his accent taking each syllable and making it something different, something new. "I won't look." His eyes locked on hers with laser-like intensity. "I promise."

And then he went for the tank top.

By now, Madeline was powerless to stop him. His voice had her mesmerized. The heat wasn't helping. The promise of cool release was all she could think about.

That, and she didn't know what to do with her arms. The tank top was a lot tighter than her top shirt had been. Her elbows had to go somewhere, and she was desperately afraid she was going to clock him in the nose. Of all the problems with this moment, that was the one that unexpectedly had her frantic.

He solved the problem for her. His hands guided her arms up as he stripped her of her shirt, and then he dropped the shirt behind him so that her arms were around his neck. Which brought their bare chests within a breath of touching.

Her eyes were not focusing like they should. She knew she needed to cool off before the heat stroke got serious, but all she could think was that with one stiff breeze her nipples would be introducing themselves to his bare skin.

On the bright side, at this distance, he couldn't see said nipples. She had that going for her.

"Mad-e-line," he repeated, each syllable a prayer said by a man hell-bent on sinning. He slid his hands down her exposed back, each fingertip finding something new to explore. Then he was undoing her button, then her zipper, then his palms were flat against her skin, sliding under the jeans and pushing them down. "Madeline."

Name. Names. His name. Despite her befuddled state, a dim, flickering light went off. "Jonathan," she whispered, suddenly aware of how dry her mouth was.

He froze. Absolutely froze against her, and damn it all, her nipples went rock hard. She ignored her stupid nipples and focused on the victorious fact that she had outflanked him. For once, she had outflanked him. "Jonathan Runs Fast."

"Who told you that?" His voice was off-balance, scared even.

"Karen. From the High Plains Gallery. I bought a green bag. With pipe."

He swallowed—her eyes were level with his Adam's apple. "You overpaid in commission."

She was going to enjoy this. She thought. Already, her perceived victory was leaving a funny taste in her mouth. "It was worth it, *Jonathan*."

His hands went hard against her. "Don't. Don't call me that." He swallowed again. "Please."

"Why not?"

He leaned away from her, catching her eyes and holding them tight with his again. "Because." His fingers found her face again, and he cupped her cheeks. His eyes weren't looking at anything but hers. "That's what my ex-wife called me."

Chapter Six

If possible, her cheeks shot even redder than a summer tomato as everything soft about her in his arms turned to steel. "Excuse me? Your *ex-wife*?"

He didn't want to talk about Anna. He wanted to get Madeline into the water, get her cooled off so he could heat her up again. But, as usual, Anna had popped up out of nowhere, leaving him to deal with the wreckage. "Not a big deal. One of those starter marriages. Over before it got going, really."

Which was kind of how his afternoon was beginning to feel. Over before it got properly started.

"Why?" she demanded, managing to look a little ferocious even as she sounded like she'd been swallowing sand.

"She took one look at the rez and ran screaming." Against his will, his hands began to slide down, grabbing more of what he couldn't see. Her skin had a give to it that just begged a man to grab another handful.

"Don't," she snapped, lurching away from him.

He caught her around the waist. Too much more distance, and he might accidentally look. Which would only make her madder—and that wasn't what anyone needed right now. "You need to cool off."

Her eyes darted to the river behind him, and she bit her lip. She wanted to go—she *needed* to go. But would that second nature of hers override what was just a simple, basic need?

"I won't look," he said, trying hard to sound like it didn't matter to him one way or the other. "I promise."

He felt the sigh start low in her chest before it moved up to her eyes. Which just about turned his brain to jelly. Her, right *here*. No sexless coats. No patients. No Jesse. Just her. She tried to glare at him, but all she could manage was some pitiful version of her normal sneer.

"Fine." She sounded like she was doing him a favor, but he'd take it. "But I'll do this myself, thank you very much."

He stared into those icy blues for a second longer before he scrunched his eyes shut. "You tell me when I can open them again, okay? Just go slow getting into the water. Watch your footing. There's a little bit of an undertow."

She nodded. Reluctantly, he let go of her waist and pivoted in the direction of his water cooler. "You need some water," he called over his shoulder as he fumbled around for a cup.

"I am *not* going to drink river water. Do you have any idea what kind of microbes or contaminants could be in that stuff?"

He wanted to laugh at her, but he didn't want to spill the cup he was filling. "Madeline, do you really think I'm dumb enough to drink this straight? I have a purifier system. My water is cleaner than what comes out of your tap, I bet." Besides, he didn't think she needed to be worried about the water.

The trickle of water told him the cup was full, while the sound of grunting behind him said she was struggling with those boots. Again. "I'm going to set this on the stump. You come in the water when you're ready, okay? You need to cool off."

"What about you?

"I'll be in the river." Flinging his towel onto a bush to dry again, he waded in.

She gasped, a quick, involuntary sound. The sound tickled over his nerves like the sweetest breeze. Oh, yeah. She'd looked.

The water welcomed him back, the current swirling around his legs as he went deeper. He sidestepped a sinkhole as the cold water hit his groin like a slow-swung sledgehammer, which was just as well. She wasn't the only one who needed to cool off.

He needed to get his head together right now. He could not even think about thinking with his dick. She'd been in Rapid City. She'd bought that green bag—God only knew how much she'd paid for that.

But more importantly, she'd talked to Karen. Karen, who treated him like a god descending from Olympus. Half the white world treated him like that—some mystic Indian god at whose feet they desperately wanted to worship. Just like Anna. Which was good for his brand image, but bad for his soul.

And now Madeline knew about Anna, about his art—about everything. He knew why she was here. She was pissed. She had merely underestimated the prairie in summer, that was all. As soon as she unwilted a little, she'd probably let him have it.

He could hope, anyway.

His ears looked for him. Over the gentle lap of

the river, he could hear her sniff the cup, then take a drink. He heard her swallow the rest in huge gulps. "There's more in the cooler, but don't drink it too fast. You'll upset your belly."

"I know that," she snapped. A little less wilted with every second. "If I get dysentery, I'm holding you personally responsible."

Like this was all his fault. Well, maybe just a little. "I'm not the one who walked a mile and a half during the hottest part of the day, you know."

She snorted, but he still heard the water give way to her foot. "Don't change the subject."

"Which was what again?" The way her bare legs were slicing through his river? The way she'd shiver when the coldness hit the hidden spot between her legs? How hard her nipples would get when they got wet? He cleared his throat and moved deeper into the water, in case she was still looking. She'd made no such promises, after all. "Is that your lack of preparedness for a summer hike?"

"We were discussing why you have a real name that you hid from me. You lied."

"Rebel *is* my real name. Albert gave it to me."

"I don't understand a damn thing you say." She waded up next to him, and, despite sounding pissier than hell, let out a deep, satisfied sigh. She was crouched way down in the water, so that it covered everything important but her shoulders. Out of the corner of his eye, he could see their round, shimmering softness. "I didn't say you could look," she snapped, taking another step into deeper water. "I don't understand why you didn't just tell me you're this big, important artist. I don't understand how you know things if you don't have a phone out here, things like when Mr. White Mouse has an appointment or when the vaccine was coming in. I don't know a damn thing about you."

"Sure you do. You know I went to college, I make bags and that some people pay way too much money for them. You even know I was married. What else is there to know?"

"And when were you going to tell me about that, huh? For all I know, you're secretly a serial killer, Jonathan. Go to hell." In slow motion, she walked away from him.

And right toward a sinkhole. "Madeline—stop!" But he was too late. In a heartbeat, she disappeared under the water, leaving nothing more than an errant ripple in the water. It was like she'd never even been there.

Couldn't she swim? Maybe not. Maybe the current had her. Oh, shit. Without thinking, he ducked under the murky water and grabbed for her. And came up empty. She was slipping through his fingers just as surely as the water was.

Panic struck at him. Where was she? The river would keep her, if it wanted. But that wasn't what he wanted, not by a long shot. *No*. Not her. Not now.

He kept grabbing, kept coming up empty. Finally, after what was probably no more than ten seconds, but ten seconds that took five years off his life, he got hold of her arm and hauled her to the surface.

Sputtering, she spit water in his face before she choked down a tortured breath. "Madeline! Are you okay?" *Please, please be okay*, he prayed. Just be okay.

She threw her arms around his neck. Her whole body was shaking. "Don't let go, Rebel," she pleaded as she coughed up more of the river. "Don't let go of me."

She was okay. Scared, and probably about a minute from worrying about dysentery again, but otherwise okay. Relief surged through him. No matter what, she was okay, and he'd keep her that way. He hugged her to his chest as he silently thanked the river for giving her back. "I won't. I promise."

Nodding into his neck, she coughed a few more times. But then she relaxed in his arms a little.

And he remembered they were both naked. And holding each other. And there were no zippers to intrude on anything this time around. Each part of hers was pressing into each matching part of his.

Holding tight, he shifted her so both of her legs trailed off to one side, so he was holding her like he held Nelly when she wanted him to spin her around. One arm under her shoulders, the other around her waist. Safer this way. She didn't let go of his neck, though, didn't demand he unhand her this instant. She just let his arms hold her against his chest, let her hand rest on his shoulders.

He found himself spinning in slow circles, letting the river get to know her, letting her get to know the river. Dancing, in a way, to the music of his land. The water burbled by in apology for scaring her, while the wind shushed through the grasses with a murmuring calm. Peace filled him.

It was working on her too. He could tell that, despite the dunking, she was doing better. Her skin was much cooler to the touch and she'd calmed down.

In fact, she was letting her toes peek out of the water as they went around and around. After a while—he didn't know how long, and he didn't care—he felt all the steel leave her body as she let him and the water carry her.

Suddenly, this position didn't feel any safer. His left hand was on her ribs, just below her breast. His other hand was in the small of her back, itching to get back to where it had been headed earlier. He willed his hands to be still on her skin. He was just helping her cool down. He was just making sure she was comfortable in the water. He was just helping a friend. That's all. He was not going to find out what secrets her body was ready to give up. He was not going to push her. He was not going to do anything with Dr. Madeline Mitchell.

Nothing she didn't want, anyway.

Soon enough, her calm passed. "Tell me about it." Instead of anger or frustration, instead of the superior pissiness that was her second nature, she sounded contemplative. She wasn't pulling. She was just asking.

"Which part?"

One hand left his shoulder and trailed down his chest until it reached the water, where it joined her toes in having a nice time. The slow suction of her breast pulling free from his chest almost sent him to his knees. Without even trying, she was going to bring him to his knees. "All of it."

Goose bumps danced up and down his skin—an involuntary reaction, and one he hadn't had in a long time. What he wouldn't give to see if she had any, but he'd promised. Damn it. To keep temptation at bay, he rested his chin on the top of her head. "Albert had a vision when I was born."

She jumped in shock, but said, "Really?" like it was no big deal.

White people. They never believed in the spirit world, except when it was convenient for them. He chuckled into her hair. "Really. He is a powerful man. Who just happens to have a job mopping floors."

Her fingers cut small waves in the never-ending river. "Are you a powerful man too? A medicine man?"

"Yes. I'm not trying to steal your patients, you know. We just believe in trying the traditional ways first—although I'm not about to set any bones. If it came down to a life-and-death situation that only antibiotics could fix, then bring on the drugs."

He could actually feel her weighing that statement. "Do you keep souls?"

He chuckled again. "Karen is… reliable in her gossip. But yes, I do. I hold onto a person's soul for a year after they die, and then I release it so it can make the final journey to be judged by Owl Woman. Like Saint Peter at the Gate," he added. Everyone knew about Saint Peter.

She thought on that for a moment, which was a change of pace. She was trying to understand, really trying. His respect for her grew. "And this is connected to your name? Albert gave you your name, you said."

"He did. When I was born, he saw that I had one foot in a moccasin, and one in what he called 'those shoes people wear when they want to walk on their money'."

"Penny loafers?" She giggled, and he felt her head move up. She was looking at him. "He had a vision of you in penny loafers?"

He waited for the water to carry her disbelief away. "Crazy, I know. He said people tried to get me to wear the moccasins, but I was not happy. Then people tried to get me to wear the loafers, but I wasn't any happier. I was unhappy until I chose for myself. And then I was happy. And that was the vision. He said I would rebel in both worlds until I found my place. Hence Rebel."

"And?" She wasn't sure she was going to believe it, but at least she wasn't dismissing him outright. Which was a pleasant thing—that and the way her fingers were lying flat against his neck, digging in with just enough pressure to make sure he wouldn't forget she was there.

As if that were a risk. "And that's what happened. People recognized my talent early on. Walter White Mouse taught me to tan leather. Irma taught me how to string the beads on sinew. Burt taught me to carve. Everyone taught me something."

"What did Albert teach you?"

"Everything." Everything he was, everything he would ever be was because Albert had raised him right. "He taught me how to be Lakota."

"What about your parents?"

Old memories, memories he'd long ago tried to make peace with, ran free again. "My father left to find work and never came back. Mom—well, after she had Jesse, she got more and more gone. She died of alcohol poisoning." But after all these years, the memories didn't run far. He managed to get himself back under control again.

She made a pained little noise. "I... I didn't realize... "

Desperate to avoid pity, he forged ahead. "That's just how it is on the rez. That's why I wanted out." Out of the crushing poverty, out of the way of life that wasn't living at all. He hadn't wanted to be an Indian, not if that was what being an Indian was. He remembered opening the acceptance letter to the university, and knowing for sure that it was the best day of his life, because he could leave and never come back.

"So you put on penny loafers?"

He found himself hugging her, making sure she stayed close. Making sure he could feel all of her against his chest. And she didn't protest. Not even a thread of steel tightened her body. "Not literally. Someone knew someone, who pulled a few strings, and I got to New Mexico. And it didn't take long to figure out that no one wanted anything by a dirt-poor red man. When people buy Indian art, they want a little piece of the Indian. And the Indian they want a part of is this… this… this *thing* that only exists in the imaginations of Hollywood directors and romance writers." It still got his hackles up. No one—not a single damn person—had ever seen just him. They'd only seen what they wanted to see. "So if you want to be a *serious* Indian artist, you have to be this Indian that you never were and never will be."

She was silent, but then she looped her arms back around his neck and held him even tighter than he'd been holding her. "That was surprisingly cynical."

"*That* is life in the art circuit. I just had to figure out which pieces of myself I could give away with each painting, with each sculpture, with every single thing I made—and which pieces I could keep."

"And you got married." There wasn't a single note of pity in her voice, not a single tone of poor-little-you. Neither was there any recriminations, no accusations of betraying his people, his family.

That, more than anything, was why he was dancing in the water with a white woman in the middle of a summer day. He wasn't an object, a thing to be bought and sold, but he wasn't a thing to be pitied or ashamed of either. He was just a man. Holding a woman.

"Anna." This memory was harder to contain. He told himself it was because it was newer. He barely remembered his father, after all. "She was not that different from Karen at the gallery."

"Are you sleeping with Karen?"

Now *that* was a distinctive note of jealousy. "No. I gave up women a long time ago."

She leaned back, way back, in his arms, until her head was half dipped in the water again. Then she pulled his face down until he had no choice but to look at her. "That comes as somewhat surprising news to me."

Hell, she was beautiful. Just beautiful. The water had her yellow hair slicked back, and she had a teasing, flirting grin on her face. Her eyes, always so ice cold, held nothing but unresolved challenge for him. Like he was only halfway up the glacial wall he was climbing.

"Recently, I've thought about reconsidering that stance." Careful not to lose his grip on her, he shifted to free a hand and stroke her face. Then he noticed her hair.

Trailing behind her in the water, it was wavy. All of it. He lifted her head out of the water a little and the wave didn't stay in the water. It only got wavier as the water dripped free. "You have curly hair?"

She jumped in his arms, her hands flying to her head. The exact same motion she did every time she saw him. "Oh! Uh, well, uh… damn. The water."

The light bulb was bright when it went off. She had curls. That she hated. At least now he knew why he thought she always looked a little off. She was just hiding her true self.

"No, I like them." He pulled her hand away from her hair and held it to his chest. She splayed her fingers out against his skin on contact. "I bet it only makes you prettier." But probably not as pretty as the pink-rose blush that started on her cheeks and went south. Suddenly, he was feeling a lot warmer in the water. "I'd like to see it all curly."

"You're doing it again," she murmured, her eyes dropping back to watch her toes. "Changing the subject. You got married… "

When he was done with this subject, he'd show her changing. "Yeah. Anna. My ex-wife." He forced himself to look away from the woman in his arms and think about the woman who would never be in his arms again. "She was the daughter of this wealthy collector. She worked at an influential gallery for a major player in the art world. She was, well, beautiful. Pale skin, black hair—like Snow White, but without the silly dress."

He felt the shock pass through her body. "You were married to a white woman?"

Again, there wasn't any pity, and absolutely no accusations. She was just surprised.

"Yeah. For about eight months."

She nestled her head back into the crook of his neck and was silent. Maybe eight months wasn't too

94

long of a time. He wondered how long she'd been with the one her father had loved—the one she'd left to come here.

"And then it ended?"

"Yeah. Badly."

"What happened?"

"It... I... " The guilt reared its ugly head. If he hadn't been so convinced that she was his ticket to the big time, if she hadn't been so convinced that he was her ticket out of Taos... "She wanted to own a piece of this Indian I was supposed to be, this brand image I'd built."

"Is that who you are in that picture? The one in the gallery?"

"Oh, that." Now it was his turn for his face to get hot. He never felt less like his brand image than at this exact moment. "Yeah. That's me as a commodity. Jonathan Runs Fast. Serious Artist."

She stilled, but just for a second before her chest was rubbing against his. She was laughing. "Which piece of you did I overpay in commissions for?"

Yeah, she owned a piece of him. No doubt, she considered it leverage of some sort. "The piece that waits for the first day of summer sun to come set the world free from the spring rains." He'd thought of that bag from his spring spot, up higher in the hills, where he could look down on the prairie and watch the world wake up. "But don't worry. I'll get that piece back next spring."

"*Jonathan*. I think I like Rebel better," she murmured as she touched his reddening cheek.

God, he wanted to kiss her, but that would be pushing it right now. She'd get mad and flustered and accuse him of changing the subject again. "By the time I married her, I'd given away so many pieces that I didn't have much left." The emptiness had clawed away at him until his dreams were filled with nothing but grass and river, wind and sky. "I needed to come home, come back to this land and remember what it meant to be a Lakota again. What it meant to be a real Indian again."

"Did she come with you?"

"For about three days. Then she left. And I never did." For eight months, Anna had treated him like he was the Indian, the noble savage she was personally educating. And then she'd see Albert's shack, seen the wasteland that was his home, and in a heartbeat, everything had changed. The noble devotion had sunk under the weight of disgust. Horror. Sheer shock that he would even consider coming home to a bunch of Indians too drunk to do anything but drink some more.

Which is how the other half of the white world treated him. A thing to be feared. A thing to be contained.

A thing.

The divorce had been quick and uncontested. He'd signed the papers by mail.

Her hand was back on his chest, like she was checking his heartbeat. "Did she ever see this place?"

"No." This place stayed pure, unfouled. And now Madeline was here. "The only people who come here are people looking for a medicine man."

"Really?" Suddenly, she was leaning up against him, her mouth as close to his ear as she could get and stay covered by the water. "I came here looking for you."

Her voice trickled down his neck, down his chest, until its warmth overpowered the cold water. "You found me."

While he looked down at her, hoping to kiss those lips, to finally taste that mouth, she was grinning at him. She was toying with him. Maybe he had a little of that coming his way.

"But you wear cowboy boots now, not moccasins or loafers."

Don't push it. But he didn't know how much longer he could *not* push it, because she was pushing him. He laughed. It felt good. "True. Visions are always open to interpretation, you know."

She stretched out, her skin moving under his until he was afraid he would have to let her go, just to keep from touching her in all the wrong, right ways. "You have visions, too?"

Her body—her body was begging him to come on in, the water was fine. But her brain was still tap-dancing around things, like it was some sort of test he had to pass. She was going to drive him mad.

"I had to learn how to see them. It took a lot of practice. I have to be patient and completely still."

Now she laughed, throwing her arms wide into the water. If he looked down... Mad. He was absolutely mad. For her.

"How much practice?"

He wasn't looking, but he couldn't help touching. He moved his hands over her ribs, half-stroking, half-tickling. And she responded by splashing him.

"Years," he said, finding a belly button that was a surprising outie. His fingers moved over it with something that was far less tickling and far more something else. "Years of practice."

Her breath caught in her throat as he rubbed her belly. A nice belly, gently rounded out under smooth skin. Firm, but soft. His fingers itched to find out if the rest of her was just as soft, just as firm. He'd touched so much, but it wasn't enough. Not enough to make up for the last six years of no one to touch.

And then she was gone, twisted right out of his arms and moving toward his side where he couldn't see her. She moved slowly, testing her footing. She was in no mood to be rescued again. Damn. He stood there, surprised by how cold her sudden absence left him.

"I think I've cooled off enough now. I'd better get out of this river before I catch something. I'd like another drink of water."

She sounded like she was trying to convince herself.

Rebel sighed and closed his eyes. He'd pushed instead of letting her pull, and Madeline had slipped right through his hands.

She'd come here looking for him, but what would she take with her when she left?

Chapter Seven

What was she doing? "I'd like another drink of water." Really? That was really what she'd *like*? She wanted a damn drink of water more than she wanted him to keep touching her, his hands moving over her body with something that was close to reverence? She'd come pitifully close to marrying a doctor—a man who'd performed delicate surgeries on delicate areas—and she'd never, ever been touched by a man who was as good with his hands as Rebel was.

The confusion on his face just made it worse. Damn it all, his arms were still stretched out in her direction, which made him look like he was nigh onto begging to get her back.

This should be a victory. Once again, she'd completely, totally outflanked him. She'd won this round, fair and square.

Funny how winning felt like losing.

Slowly, his arms drifted back to his sides at the same speed his eyes closed and his face went blank. "The stew should be done," he said, his voice as blank as his face. "I've got a clean towel in the tent. I'll bring it down for you." He turned to go, but then paused. "Will you be okay in the water?"

God, what was she doing? He'd given her

everything she'd asked for today—and more. He'd kept his promise, told her what she wanted—needed—to hear, and she was still going to be a bitch?

No, she almost said. No, she would not be okay, not until he got that ass she was afraid she'd hallucinated over here and picked her up and went right back to a kind of freedom she'd never even dreamed existed before she fell into the river and right into his arms. "I'll, uh, try not to drown." Which was not the same as being okay in the water.

He looked over his shoulder at her, even though his eyes were still closed. The surprised blankness was gone again, and she caught the edge of his lazy smile again. "Do that. I'll be right back."

And then he walked out of the water.

Despite the heat that surged through her, she shivered. Not some sort of deranged hallucination. That was, hands down, the finest ass she'd ever seen. Rebel's back came to a narrow V before his rounded cheeks dovetailed into legs that rippled—though she couldn't tell if it was the water sheeting off them or the muscles twitching, but everything about that man said not only was he good with his hands, he was good with his legs.

Suddenly, she found herself wondering what he looked like on that horse with the bi-colored eyes. He might not be some Indian from an imagined past, but that didn't mean she couldn't imagine what he'd look like now. Legs twitching, hair flying, heart pounding as the horse raced through virgin grass.

Why, oh, why hadn't she ever snuck a look at him riding away from the clinic?

Too soon, he was wrapped up in the towel again. "I'll be right back," he said, bounding up the hill with all the grace of a deer. Clearly, that was something he did a lot. All those muscles were earned the hard way.

Treading water, she waited as she tried to screw her head back on straight. It wasn't that she'd freaked out when it had suddenly became a very real option that he was about to begin exploring her topography. No, it had nothing to do with the unexpected shock of something that sunk to her very center. Nothing to do with the certain realization that there would be nothing pitiful about sex with Rebel.

If he even had a bed.

No, she reasoned, her reaction had merely been the safest thing. If he'd actually gotten... anywhere, well, he'd have broken the natural-fluid seal her body had erected for the express purpose of keeping dirty river water on the outside, where it belonged. Yes, that was it. She was just concerned about microbes and stuff.

Sure.

The sun was getting lower in the sky. She was going to have to get home somehow. And she didn't think she could walk back to her Jeep in those boots again. Just the thought of putting those instruments of torture back on her feet made her almost forget about everything.

Right until Rebel popped out of the tent. Then she forgot about her feet altogether. "You still down there?"

"I don't know where else you'd think I'd go," she shouted back. "You live in the middle of nowhere."

"You should see the middle of nowhere I live in during the spring." He was dressed now, sort of. A pair of cut-off jeans, the fringe billowing out behind him with each stride. "Makes this place look populated. Here's your towel. Tell me when I can look, okay?" He draped it over the bush and turned to the fire and the pot that held dinner.

Making sure mud squished under her feet before she committed, Madeline left the water behind. She felt almost like a whole new woman. Almost. God only knew what her hair was going to look like after that.

"You don't live here year round?"

"Nope. The river floods in the spring, so I go up into the hills." He stirred the stew and began ladling it into bowls, his undivided attention on the meal—and not on her. He kept his promises. "In the fall, I go south a little farther. The river drops, and the water gets real shallow here."

She wasn't in the water anymore. She could drop this towel and parade around to his front, where he'd have to look at her, right?

And then what? He'd leap over the fire to have his way with her?

No. Knowing him, he'd probably just close his eyes.

He sat on his heels, messing around with the fire. His back—she could really stare at it, now that his backside was covered again—was a symphony of muscles moving together. Had she ever just admired? Had she ever looked at a man and not seen the sum total of parts that did and did not need to be fixed? Maybe this is what artists did—admired the form— because his form was *amazing*.

"Uh," she said, trying to slip her panties back on without getting too much sand in them, "what about the winter? Don't you get cold?" Yeah, that's it. Just a couple of half-dressed friends discussing the weather. Nothing abnormal about any of this.

"Well, no." He chuckled, and all those muscles chuckled with him. Hell, she felt like laughing a little, now that she thought about it. "Not when it gets real cold. I find a place to crash—always a floor for me at Albert's—or I head into the city. I do most of my gallery stuff in the dead of winter. Spent almost a month in New York last February."

The photograph popped up again. She still had trouble seeing that urbane, sophisticated man as the same one in cut-offs, ladling stew into bowls. But that didn't mean he couldn't pull it off.

She got her tank back on and her jeans safely zipped. There. She felt mostly better now. "You can look."

His head jumped up, but then he slowly looked over his shoulder. "You look... good."

Now, how was she supposed to take that? Good that she no longer looked like she was going to faint? That her hair was throwing all caution to the wind? That she only had on one shirt?

He turned back to the stew. "Water's behind you."

Yes, that's right. She was thirsty. And, now that she thought about it, hungry. And whatever was in it, the stew smelled better than anything she'd dumped out of a can in the last month.

Cup full of water, she sat down on one of the two blankets and hugged her knees to her chest. The sun was hitting the hills in the distance at a sharp angle, bathing the trees in gold while the grass was in shadows. Somehow, she knew the sunsets here were even better than the ones she saw from her little cabin.

Rebel handed her a bowl and just sort of folded cross-legged onto the blanket. Her blanket. He wasn't touching her, but he was more than close enough to do it if he wanted to.

She was not going to think about that right now. Right now, she wanted dinner. She pulled her knees up and tried to balance her dinner bowl on them, all the while wondering if he'd hunted the meat himself.

"So, what about you?" he said between spoonfuls of the most mouth-watering stuff she'd ever eaten.

Maybe this was deer meat? She wasn't sure she'd ever tasted it before. "What about me?"

"Correct me if I'm wrong, but you just dropped a couple of grand on something I would've happily given you. You single-handedly supplied the whole clinic. You don't seem to mind not getting a big doctor paycheck." He fixed her with the kind of look that didn't so much expect an answer as demand it. "Tell me about it."

"Oh. That." Suddenly, she didn't know how to approach this situation. Not that she'd ever thought him dumb, but in less than twelve hours, he'd gone from being the enemy to something closer to an equal. Much closer. "My father was the first person to successfully implant an artificial heart in Ohio."

Rebel stared at her with that pleased smile on his face. "A good doctor?"

"He was one of the best."

"I should have known that." The tone of his voice said he heard the *was* loud and clear. "And your mother?"

"Partner in her law firm. She was the top divorce lawyer in Columbus before she died. But she handled cases pro bono for a women's shelter too. A lot of times, we'd serve Thanksgiving dinner there."

"How old were you?"

"What, when she died?"

He nodded. The dusk was settling over them. In the light from the fire, his face took on an otherworldly look. He really did look like a medicine man. She swallowed. If she didn't think about Mom, it didn't hurt. Not much, anyway. She braced for the rush of emotion. "Nineteen. I was a sophomore."

Mom had hidden her breast cancer diagnosis from Madeline until after she'd finished her finals so it wouldn't impact her grades. Mom had died a month later. For a long time, the if-onlys had ruled Madeline. If only Dad had been an oncologist instead of a cardiologist. If only Mom's regular doctor had ordered the mammogram sooner. If only Madeline had been older, farther along in her studies.

If only Mom had lived.

But instead of the wave of emotions she always tried to block out with more work, something strange happened. The predictable sorrow mixed with the guilt didn't come. Instead, she just felt a sense of peace. It was unsettling.

Silently, Rebel set his bowl aside and stoked the fire until the glow surrounded them. Staring into the flame was like being hypnotized. That sorrow-and-guilt slush was there, but she could see it was old, tired. It needed to rest. It was ready for her to let go of it.

"Did you get to say goodbye?"

"Yes—to her." Mom had come home one last time. Melonie had been scared, terrified by nightmares, but Madeline had been the strong one.

105

Mom had needed her to be there and hold her hand. And Madeline had needed to be there. But the moment her chest had stopped rising, stopped falling, the if-onlys had started.

The flame danced and flickered, turning wood to ashes, and ashes to dust. *Goodbye, Mom*, she thought. *I love you.*

And, just like that, the if-onlys were gone.

She looked up, feeling like she did when she delivered a baby. The heady rush of freedom had her smiling. Hell, she almost felt like laughing.

Rebel wasn't looking at her. He was staring at the fire. "But not your father?"

Dad—well, Dad hurt, but in a different way. "He died of a heart attack in his sleep last year." The leading cardiologist in Columbus dead at sixty-seven from a massive coronary event. And if Melonie had been upset when Mom died, she'd been inconsolable about Dad. Melonie had started on the if-onlys. If only Madeline had gone into cardiology like she was supposed to. If only Madeline had read the signs a little better. If only they both hadn't gone out to dinner without Dad that night. It hadn't been more than three hours after the funeral before Melonie had burst back into Madeline's guilty silence, sobbing so hard that Madeline had barely been able to understand her apology. Which had almost made it better, but not quite. "It was just one of those things." That's what she told herself, anyway. That was what she had to tell herself.

He nodded. So he hadn't guessed everything. She was willing to bet he didn't have to guess about much more now. "That's not how your—younger sister, right? That's not how she saw it."

Her jaw dropped, but she tried to snap it shut. Unsuccessfully. It was like he was reading her mind, and if that was the case, she was screwed. Big time. "You're doing it again."

The firelight caught the faint smile. Could he get any better looking? "I didn't change the subject."

She tried to glare at him, but something in her wouldn't let her. She couldn't find a part of her that was irritated, not even a little. Just wonderment. "If you tell me you had a vision that I had a younger sister, I'll throw a boot at you."

Oh, there was that blush again. Or maybe it was just the sunset that made his face glow like that. "You are, I beg your pardon, a bossy know-it-all who has to be right all the time. Pretty standard for an oldest child."

The sudden—well, not quite an insult, because it was probably all true—took her back. "Excuse me?"

"If I had to guess, I'd say your sister is some free spirit who always got away with everything. Like Jesse."

This was becoming a disturbing trend. Was there anything he hadn't guessed right on today? "Well, maybe not just like Jesse." Sure, Melonie had the unique capacity to drive her bonkers, but Madeline didn't take on personal responsibilities for her, not like Rebel seemed to do for Jesse. Still, there might be enough similarities to rub him wrong. "Free spirit doesn't begin to describe her."

And she didn't get away with everything, just more than Madeline did. "She's artistic, but unfocused. One year she's in England, studying the masters. The next, she's learning how to weld so she can understand outsider art better. Some of her stuff is okay… " And God only knew what Melonie would do in front of

107

someone like Rebel—a verifiable hunk who was a verifiable artist? Madeline put her money on swooning.

"So what does she do with her art if she's not any good?"

"Actually, she spends a lot of time doing after-school stuff with city kids. She's a big believer in the healing power of art and all that." It occurred to Madeline that Melonie would love Nelly. She could just see the two of them drawing huge murals on the side of the clinic, or making sculptures out of found objects, or whatever it was Melonie did that made kids love her. Melonie and Nelly would really tear up this town.

"And you spent *how much* on that bag for her?"

He was doing it again. Maybe she should focus all of her efforts on not thinking about his body. Maybe she should be thinking about the Stay-Puft marshmallow man. Safer than thinking about verifiable hunks. She tried to shrug off her amazement. "It was your work, you know." Yeah, that's right. No big deal, not several grand on ceremonial pipes, not skinny dipping and certainly not the way he was looking at her, like he really was reading her mind. "I figured I would have spent the money on supplies anyway, and you'd probably use most of it to pay someone's bill. She's a nice sister. She should get something out of it."

"Hmm," he hummed, and she swore she felt the vibrations from a foot away. Then he turned to look at the fire again. "I'm sorry about Walter."

The flying lead change whipped her head up. "Excuse me?"

"Walter White Mouse. I wasn't trying to piss you off. I didn't know about your mother when I sent him away."

She looked at him. All the playfulness gone from his face, all the movement gone from his body. Was this what he did when he saw those visions? "It's okay. He got better." It was a hard thing to admit, but she hadn't been about to do anything for Mr. White Mouse. It was harder still to say what came next. But she wanted him to hear it. "And you were right. He couldn't have afforded any of that anyway." She cleared her throat. "Why don't you like vaccines?"

He began to move again—not much, but she could see his fingers tapping on his leg. "Did you know that the government once gave my people blankets contaminated with smallpox?"

She blinked at him. If she only knew what he was going to say next. If she only had a clue. An inkling. The barest of hints. And yet... She answered carefully. "I read about that in school."

"But you didn't really believe it." When she didn't contradict him, he added, "And sick cattle. Institutionalized eradication."

What was he implying? "You don't think I'd give people tainted vaccinations, do you?"

"Not you—not on purpose." The cynicism was back. She didn't like it on him, not one bit. "I said the government did it. We're just being... careful. Have you considered the possibility that it's not the flu that's making people sick?"

"I'm pretty sure it's not smallpox," she snapped. "All the flu symptoms are there. You should be telling people to let me vaccinate them. Nobody wants the swine flu on top of the stomach flu." On the bright side, at least he wasn't spouting some nonsense about autism as his justification. So there was that.

He laughed. He laughed? What the hell? Still smiling, he turned to look at her. Less cynical. More like he knew something she didn't know. "Gotten any of those samples back? Got any proof it's the flu?"

She felt like she was back in that exam room with him telling Mr. White Mouse to go to the sweat lodge again. He was holding out on her, but what the hell would a Traditional Master of Fine Arts know about viruses? "I'm going to call the lab on Monday."

He looked at her and smiled. "Let me know. I'm not trying to make your life harder. Besides, they make some of those vaccines with mercury. Not good for anyone."

The silence settled over them with the twilight. She didn't believe anyone was out to get him—them— but she wouldn't disagree on the larger principle. He had his reasons for doing what he did. It wasn't just to drive her crazy. It was because he was trying to protect people. And he wanted proof.

He got some more wood for the fire and refilled her cup. Watching him move around the campfire was enough to make her wish she had a camera, or some paper and pencils, or something to help her remember this moment. She wasn't a sentimental kind of woman, but she'd give anything to keep the sight of his brown skin glowing in the flickering light in her memory. She didn't have dreams this good. The tension from the vaccine debate faded in the warm glow of a summer evening. She'd never been camping before, but she was starting to think she might like it.

However, even this living dream had to bow to the pressures of reality. Her blisters began to throb. Sooner or later, she was going to have to get home.

Later wouldn't be so bad, would it?

He knelt in front of her, backlit by the fire. She could just see his eyes as they moved over her and kept going until they reached the blisters. "How bad are they?"

"They're fine." The moment the words left her mouth, she shuddered. The reaction had been involuntary—but she knew he wasn't buying it. If he ever had. She thought she saw his eyebrow arch. "Actually, they're not so good."

"There, that wasn't so hard, was it? I'll be right back."

Damn, but he moved fast when he wanted to. Within seconds, he was invisible in the dark, only the sound of his bare feet crunching on grass to tell her he was still there—somewhere. "Where are you going?"

"I've got a rack wagon. Keep all my supplies in it," he called back from the dark.

She had no idea where he was—except she could tell he wasn't up in the tent. In what she hoped was the far-away distance, a coyote howled. Mr. Steinman popped back into her head. She didn't want to be eaten by any wildlife today, please and thank you. And she didn't want Rebel to be eaten either.

And just as easily as he'd disappeared, he was back in the circle of light. "Let me see." Sitting on his heels like it was the easiest thing in the world, he slid one hand down her calf and picked up her foot. She leaned back on her elbows, only a little nervous about this contact. They were dressed now. She wasn't overheating. They weren't in the water. And he was still touching her.

Nail polish. She needed a pedicure in the worst sort of way.

He whistled. "These are hard core." His finger

lightly stroked the sorest spot on her heel. Madeline winced. "Quarter-sized. Very impressive." Then he was smearing something on each and every blister she had with a light enough touch that it only hurt a little.

So very good with his hands.

Have a little fun, Melonie's voice whispered in her ear. *I order you to have a good time.*

She didn't know how much more fun she could handle. Didn't skinny dipping count as enough fun for one day? Besides, there was the small issue of protection. As in, she didn't have any. And that was sort of a deal-breaker. Unintentional pregnancy was low on her list of things to do today. She cleared her throat. "What is that? Bear fat or something?"

"Traditional healing medicine," he intoned as he set the finished foot on his thigh and started on the other one. His accent was suddenly twice as strong. "Its powers are mystical."

And if she wasn't mistaken, he sounded like he was trying not to laugh. "What do you call it?"

A single finger traced up her sole. "Neosporin."

The giggle was as involuntary as the shivers had been earlier. He caught her foot as she tried to kick him. "You drive me crazy." And that was fun, in and of itself.

Suddenly, he wasn't fixing her blisters. He wasn't touching her feet at all. His hands were up and down her calves, the palms rubbing front to back with that same slow, steady pressure that had been all over her back. When he'd undressed her. When she'd let him undress her.

"Is that such a bad thing?" he asked

No. No, it wasn't. Nothing about this was bad, not even the blisters. *That* was two consenting adults, alone, in front of a romantic fire. True, it was mid-July and hotter than hell, but still. This was textbook stuff.

This was seduction. It had to be. And as he moved over her muscles like he'd spent a lifetime practicing for this very moment, she wasn't sure she could remember her perfectly valid reasons for *not* succumbing. "Are you trying to seduce me?"

Really? Did she really just say that? Out loud? Oops.

He didn't move. Not even to breathe. She was pretty sure. "No. I'm not trying."

Embarrassment flooded her system. *He* drove her crazy? She drove herself insane sometimes. Leave it to her analytical little brain to ruin a perfectly fun time by trying to quantify things.

Sure seemed like it was time to go home.

But then he was moving again. He spread her legs wide apart and, just like a wolf getting ready to pounce, he *crawled* up between them. She watched him, powerless to do anything but hold the whimper in. *Crawled.* He was coming. For her.

His mouth grazed her breast at the same moment his groin touched hers. The sudden flash of heat that spiked between the two spots had nothing on the fire. His hips—oh, God—those hips that she'd seen rock countless times from across the clinic were suddenly rocking into hers, back and forth, over and over. Each time he moved against her was something new, something different.

Something *good.*

Didn't matter that she was dressed. Didn't matter if all this contact was through layers of fabric. Didn't matter that she'd tried her best to ruin the moment.

Her body convulsed as his groin hit a spot she didn't know she had. This time, she couldn't fight back the whimper. Her body was beyond her control.

But not his.

By the time he made his way up to her face, she was helpless. "This," he said, his voice low and serious and six different kinds of sexy, "is trying."

When his lips touched hers, everything that had been soft about her shot stiff with the jolt that hit her. If she'd thought the shock she'd felt in the river was painful enough, this was downright agony—in the best possible way. Her nipples acted on their own, her legs weren't listening to her, and even though she'd been thorough in drying off, she was suddenly damp all over again. And her arms? Her arms were around his neck again, where they'd been all afternoon, pulling him down so that she could kiss the hell out of him.

Third time's the charm, she thought. Bryce had been a bumbling teenager, where the thrill of getting caught had far outlasted the actual thrill of having her lips smashed with braces. Darrin, well, he'd been a fish. Open, close. Open, close. Repeat until bored. Just like their sex life.

But this? Rebel scraped his teeth along her lower lip with just enough pressure to drag her mouth open. Her blood was past pounding when he swept his tongue in. This was seduction. For the first time in her life, she was being seduced. Properly.

When he pulled back, his chest was heaving just as fast as hers was. He wasn't just jerking her around. He *wanted* her. *Her.* Not her family name, not her lucrative profession. Just her.

"Madeline." His voice, husky with need,

strummed her in places she didn't know could be played. But he knew the right tune. "Mad-e-line." With each sound, he moved his hips. Too much more of this, and it wouldn't matter that they were still both wearing jeans.

He would be amazing. Hell, who was she kidding? He *was* amazing. And this was about to get a whole lot more amazing.

The three months since pity sex with Darrin suddenly weren't the longest three months in her life. No, she was suddenly quite sure she'd never really, truly had sex. Sure, she'd gone through the motions, but this wouldn't be just a physical copulation. This wasn't just sex, but something deeper, something more powerful than she'd ever dared to imagine, much less hold in her arms. This wasn't *just* sex—was it?

"Stay with me," he whispered as his fingers found curls. "Stay here with me."

Not just sex. Not with him. "I… " He kissed her again, his whole body surging up to convince her that staying was the only, best option. Her body quaked underneath his.

"Stay," he breathed. "Please."

Chapter Eight

P lease." He didn't beg—he never begged, because he'd never had to—but even to his own ears, he was getting awful close. She felt so right under him, so right against him, that he couldn't imagine her not staying there. Her curls, perfect in their wildness, spread out under her head, crowning her in silken glory as her eyes fluttered. She made that little whimpering noise again, a high, tight noise in the back of her throat. He leaned down and caught the noise with his mouth.

He'd beg if he had to. He'd never tasted anything as exquisite as the sound of her need. She needed him. She wanted him. And he'd do his damnedest to give it to her. All of it.

Her body—damn the jeans—her body moved in perfect counterpoint to his. It gave when it needed to, met his with a show of sheer force when it had to. She dug her fingers into his back and pulled him up when she wanted more, but they were feather-soft against his skin when he pulled back. Her parted lips were begging for another kiss while her cheeks were still flushed from the last one. He propped himself up on one hand and let the fullness of her breast fill his hand. "Please." He was begging. He had no choice.

Her nipples were at full attention as he rolled his

thumb over her breast. Perfect—just enough to hold. Just like her. But then her head popped up and her eyes popped open, and he saw the alarm. The worry. The regret. And she grabbed his hand.

"I don't have anything." The change that came over her was plenty painful to watch, but more painful to feel. Her soft, giving center jerked away from him. She untwined her legs from his. Then she put her hand on his chest and pushed. She pushed him away. "We have to use something."

The anger was a flash in the pan. For a white-hot second, he was furious with her for letting him get this far, and beyond furious with himself. He was going to have blue balls for a week, all because neither of them had a damned condom.

But then he looked down at her. The corners of her lips—that he'd been kissing—were pulled down into a frown. Her eyes had none of the challenge, none of the superiority that marked their earlier battles. Instead, she looked like she was going to cry.

That made two of them.

He let the anger leave his body. It didn't take much of the desire-turned-frustration with it, but just enough that he could think straight. Of course they needed something. He wasn't some stupid, hormonal teenager who thought only with his dick. He was a grown man, who already took care of enough accidents—Jesse, Nelly, and others—to last him a lifetime.

And, more than anything, he couldn't push her. She was right. She was also miserable. Her lip quivered even though she couldn't meet his gaze anymore. He couldn't push her. Not now, not ever.

Which meant it was time for her to leave.

117

Pulling his hand free from hers, he touched her cheek and then kissed the same spot. This wouldn't—couldn't—be the end of it. Just the end of it right now. "Come on," he said, trying to keep the disappointment out of his voice as he pulled back. "I'll take you back to your Jeep."

But before he could get any farther, she lurched up and caught him around the neck. "I'm sorry."

He let himself savor holding her tight to his chest. Sorry was going to be the state of his balls after this, but there was nothing to be done about it. Alternative methods of solving the problem were probably out—she'd been worried enough about dysentery. He kissed the top of her head, then her forehead. The heat was missing. But that was for the best, right? "It's okay." He pulled her to her feet, but he couldn't quite let her go. His arm was around her waist before he could stop it. And she let him hold her. He needed to get her out of here before she drove him completely, utterly mad. "I can't let you put those boots back on."

She nodded into his neck. Every second she stayed was making it that much harder to let her go. "I don't have another pair of shoes. I'm sorry I wasn't better prepared. For any of it."

He willed his hands to let her go. And mercifully, they listened. "Trust me, this isn't as bad as heat stroke. I'll be right back."

Moccasins. A woman like her could use a nice pair of moccasins. He had just finished a pair. Her pair. True, they were simple, just a medicine wheel in black, white, red and yellow on the top. Nothing fancy about them. But somehow, he knew she didn't need fancy. She needed functional.

While he dug the moccasins out of the container, he whistled. Blue Eye was around here somewhere, and she knew to come when he called. Hopefully, though, she wouldn't take her time. The sooner he got Dr. Madeline Mitchell back to her Jeep, the less trouble he'd get both of them in. He could only hope she wouldn't freak out when he tried to get her on the horse. Every time he rode up to the clinic, he could tell she was praying Blue Eye wouldn't barge back in. The saddle—where had he put his saddle? Trying to find that thing in the dark wasn't going to help a damned thing.

"Is everything okay?" she called up the hill. She sounded worried. Nervous even.

That's when he remembered Karen, who unfailingly related the unfortunate tale of Steinman every chance she got. She couldn't know the coyotes never bothered him. "I'm coming right back down," he called back as he slipped on his own mocs. And he whistled again. If that horse didn't show up in two minutes, she wasn't getting any carrots this week. End of story.

He was halfway down the hill when he heard it. That now-familiar sound—light and happy—filled the air. She was giggling. She didn't giggle at the clinic, but today she'd been free and easy with amusement. She'd been so damn close to being free and easy with him.

He slammed the brakes on that train of thought. Blue balls and horseback riding did not mix. Besides, what the hell was she giggling at? Then he saw why. Blue Eye had come when called, and was snuffling Madeline's hair. And Madeline was laughing.

Suddenly, after this whole day, he wasn't sure he really knew her. "I didn't think you liked her," he said, making damn sure he didn't push.

Madeline shot him the kind of look that made him wish he had a cold shower at the ready. "Correction. I don't like her in the clinic. She's really a beautiful paint. And whistle-trained? I'm impressed." She waved her hand in front of Blue Eye's blue eye, and Blue Eye's head jerked. Madeline gasped, and then giggled again as Blue Eye nudged her. "I thought she was blind. I thought a blue eye was a blind eye."

She sounded like a woman who knew which end of the horse was the front. "Not always," he said, watching her feel along the muscles in Blue Eye's neck with an air of knowledge. Hell, he half-expected her to pick up Blue Eye's feet and check her confirmation.

"Do you ride?"

Her sly grin widened into a high-beam smile.

Oh, yeah, she rode. "How long?"

She looked at him through lowered lashes, and he was instantly aware that seduction was a two-way street, and she was currently behind the wheel. "I rode dressage for almost twenty years. Did quite well too." Dressage. If he remembered correctly, that was that fancy English style—Anna had made him watch the Olympics once. The animals had been things of beauty, like ballet in motion. And she'd done that—for two decades? Wow. And then she made everything worse, in the best sort of way. "I'd love to ride with you."

The shock stilled him. He knew he shouldn't just stand there and stare at her, but damn it all, he couldn't do anything but that. Nothing moved, not a single thing. He felt like he was about to fall into a vision.

But it wasn't a vision. It was just a beautiful woman named Madeline, standing in the flickering light of his campfire, stroking the nose of his horse, ready to ride with him.

With him.

She shot him a look out of the corner of her eye, knowing and yet still coy. Shit. He had to get her out of here right now, before he decided he wanted her to stay forever. "I, uh—" he cleared his throat, "—made these. For you." He held out the moccasins.

Her eyes widened in surprise. "For me?"

"Hope they fit," he said as he sat her down on the stump, dusted the sand off her feet and slid them on.

They did. "Oh," she breathed as she wiggled her toes. "I... don't know what to say."

"That may be a first." But the sound of her breathless and pleased was doing a number on him again. She tried to swat at his shoulder, but he caught her and pulled her into another kiss.

His brain was screaming no, no, *no*, but his body wasn't paying a lick of attention. Sure, she didn't speak the language, wanted everyone to get those damned vaccines, and probably still thought he was at least three degrees of nuts.

But she was here. She'd been here for a month. She'd seen the worst of his people up close and deeply personal, and she hadn't run screaming. Instead, she was hell-bent on making the world a little better.

And she was kissing him back. Not just Jonathan Runs Fast, Traditional Master of Fine Arts, not just some fake Indian god she thought she was worshiping. Just him.

Blue Eye nudged him in the back with enough

force that it nearly knocked them both over. "Oh, yeah." Ornery horse. Who was doing exactly what she needed to. "Can you ride bareback?"

She closed her eyes, took two measured breaths and stepped away from him. Right. Control. She had some to spare. "I probably won't fall off. Give me a leg up."

He cupped his hands, and she stepped up and in the blink of an eye, was settling onto Blue Eye's back like she'd never been away from it. "Interesting," she murmured, shifting her legs around. "Different."

He couldn't help but grin at her. She'd be fine by herself, but he wasn't going to let her be by herself. With a running start, he leapt up and onto his horse's back, something he'd been doing since he was six.

"Whoa!" Madeline jumped as he snaked an arm back around that waist. "How the hell did you do that?"

Yeah, she wasn't the only one who still had a few surprises up her sleeve. "Years of practice. Hold on," he added, nudging Blue Eye up to a fast walk.

How many times had he done this? Mounted up on Blue Eye in the summer night and ridden around the rez in the dark, finding coyotes on the prowl, buffalo slumbering and owls keeping an eye on him? Hundreds. Thousands, maybe. But with Madeline in his arms, everything was different.

He couldn't keep his hands out of her hair. It smelled a little of the river, but her own natural musk blended with that to make it something new, something that triggered some primitive part of his brain to want to smell it more. And it felt like raw silk in his hands, soft and smooth with a touch of the texture that made it wrap itself around his fingers like it was alive.

"You like it?" she said, her voice a low whisper.

"Oh, yeah," was all he could get out as he buried his nose in it. The spring rains, that was what she smelled like. The spring rains soaking into the earth, washing away the grit of a winter spent asleep. Every second with her was like waking up all over again. And he hadn't even realized he'd been asleep. "Wear it like this. For me."

And then they were next to her Jeep, and he had her pinned against the door as he tasted that sound she made again, his hands refusing to let go of any single part of her, because every single part of her was right where he wanted it. In his hands. He found her breast again, first one, then the other. As his thumbs traced the outline of hard nipples through the shirt, she shuddered against him. But it wasn't enough. The woman was more than just what she had up top. And he wanted to know the whole woman.

One hand slipped down between them, down between the intruding zippers and unforgiving denim, down until her hips tilted up for him. His fingers found the warmest, wettest, most secret spot and began to rub. She bucked against him, like a young filly just dying to throw off the new saddle and run free.

"Rebel," she whispered, grabbing him by the back pockets and holding on for what felt like dear life. His blood pumped faster than a runaway train through his veins as he tried to get closer to all that warmth. "Please."

Who the hell needed condoms? He was going to lose it right here, right now, and if he was lucky—and he was starting to feel a little bit lucky—she would too. As slow as he could, he put everything he had into rubbing her secret spot.

And then the floodlight hit them.

She let out a muffled scream as he grabbed her and threw her behind his body. The instinct to protect her first was just that—instinct. Save her first. "Who's there?" he demanded, wishing like all hell he'd grabbed his knife before they left. Blue Eye was suddenly in front of them, her head down and her hoof pawing. *Good horse*, the rational part of his brain noted. *Best I've ever owned.*

"Hiya, Rebel," the toneless voice came from behind the floodlight.

"Who is it?" Madeline's voice was shaking, but not in the good way. Her hands were clamped down onto his arm with enough force to leave marks, but he wasn't about to shake her off. Not when she needed him.

"Nobody," he growled, ready to rip his friend's face off for scaring her so badly. He didn't want her to be afraid. Not now, not ever. "What the hell are you doing?"

"You?" Nobody said, turning the question into a demand.

What was *he* doing? Nope. Not a shot in holy hell he was going to stand here and let this man cop that attitude. "Go to hell."

"Who?" Madeline asked weakly.

"Nobody," he repeated. "Show yourself. You're scaring the good doctor."

As he snorted, Nobody lowered the flashlight. After a few seconds, Rebel's eyes adjusted to the light and he pushed Blue Eye out of the way. "Madeline, this is Nobody Bodine. Nobody, you remember Dr. Madeline Mitchell. If I recall, she was kind enough to pull a bullet out of you. Which is more than I'd do for you right now."

"Nobody... Bodine?" Her death-grip on his arm loosened. "You—your name is *Nobody*?"

Rebel glared. If Nobody didn't show some proper respect, he'd have a whole hell of a lot more to worry about than some piddling little flesh wound.

"Yes, ma'am," Nobody finally said. "I'm Nobody."

"I dug a bullet out of you—and you never came back for a checkup." That was better. Rebel shook a little of his fight off. Madeline wasn't terrified—not as terrified, anyway. She was working her way right back over to Dr. Mitchell at a surprising rate. Good recovery, he thought with a smile. A woman who could deal.

"Yes, ma'am. Appreciated that. Rebel checked on it for me." Three sentences in a row—a new Nobody record. At least he was talking to her, Rebel reasoned. He wasn't known for acknowledging white people even existed.

She spun back to him, and even in the scattered flashlight, he knew he was in trouble. She was pissed. All her flight had clearly screamed right on over to fight. Which, while maybe a little dangerous, was a hell of a lot better than terrified. He'd take it.

"*You*? What did you do?"

She was *not* going to like this. "Traditional healing medicine."

Her mouth open and shut. "Neosporin?"

Nobody cleared his throat. "Ma'am, it was a sweat lodge."

125

It was official—this was the worst possible ending to an almost-date he'd ever had. Made *just* having blue balls look like a walk in the park. Her mouth—kissing it seemed like a distant memory—wrenched itself into the ugliest snarl he'd ever seen on her. "You are *not* a doctor, Rebel. Stop practicing medicine before you kill someone. And you!" She turned on Nobody, who had the decency to flinch. "I expect to see you at the clinic for a proper check-up first thing Monday morning, or I *will* call the police. Do I make myself clear?"

"Yes, ma'am," Nobody said, sounding resigned to his fate.

Madeline stomped to her Jeep so hard that Blue Eye skittered out of her way, and Rebel thought it prudent to do the same. Without another word, she fired up the engine and was peeling out in reverse, narrowly missing them all as the gravel went flying.

"This better be fucking good," Rebel snarled. His shoulders squared around and he dropped into a crouch. He might not be able to beat Nobody, but he'd make a hell of a dent trying.

Nobody stared him down, barely even moving an eyebrow. Yeah, there was that damn stoicism again. "They're gonna do it again," he finally said in the tense stillness. "Gun?"

Have you considered the possibility that it's not the flu? Madeline hadn't, but Rebel had. The rancher to the north of the rez was up to something, but no one knew what. Hell, no one else even suspected something wasn't right—except Nobody. He'd been watching, waiting for his chance to get some proof.

"At the camp. Do we have time?"

Nobody nodded as he whistled for his horse. They needed the gun. Nobody had gone unarmed and alone last time, and see where that had gotten him? They mounted up and took off.

They didn't have a moment to lose.

Chapter Nine

*M*ondays suck. That's all there is to it, Madeline thought as she hefted another box out of the Jeep. *Mondays just suck.*

Especially since it wasn't even seven in the morning yet. It wasn't even seven, and yet here she was, frantically unpacking box after box.

No, no, she wasn't frantic. Not at all. She was *not* frantic, panicked, or even nervous. She wasn't agitated in the least about losing her head around a naked Rebel. No, what she was concerned about—yes, that was it, concerned—was his dangerous belief that being a medicine man somehow qualified him to practice actual medicine.

She wasn't perturbed about the fact that she'd let herself get into a vulnerable situation with a man who wouldn't know reality if it smacked him upside the head. She was more concerned that, by blowing that much cash on one of his bags, she was merely supporting his megalomaniac worldview.

She was certainly *not* worried about dysentery. She'd already started an emergency course of antibiotics, just to make sure nothing had taken up residence after her little dunking. No need to panic there.

She wasn't alarmed by the fact that she didn't know where her boots were. Good heavens, she wasn't even the least bit tense about the fact that she was wearing her beat-up sneakers today, because it had been either that or those ridiculously soft moccasins. And she was quite certain that waltzing around the clinic in handmade footwear was akin to just going ahead and announcing that she lusted after *that man* on national television, and she didn't even want to admit to herself that she lusted after that man.

Which did not explain why she was having heart palpitations about the state of her hair. Its curly state. Its unstraightened state. And, what with all the hefting and carrying and unpacking she had been doing since six this morning, her hair was huge. Bigger than Texas.

It was bad enough when Clarence lumbered in and did a double-take, but it didn't get God-awful until Tara arrived.

"Dr. Mitchell!" she gasped, like Madeline had stuck her with a needle. A sharp one. "Your *hair*!"

"Um, yeah." Her hands flew to her mop. Lord, it was worse than a mop. Her hair had nothing on Medusa right now, it was so insane. This whole thing was insane. What the hell was she doing? She was letting her hair take over the planet for what? For that man—Jonathan Runs Fast, for God's sake? He endangered patients' lives on what seemed like a daily basis, completely disregarded her medical authority, and lived in a freaking tent down by the river—and she was wearing her hair down? For *that man*?

He drove her crazy. And the hair was living proof.

"I, um," she sputtered at Tara, whose mouth

hadn't gotten near closing again. Madeline's hair was more than a mistake—it was about to become the blunder of the century. "My flat iron died. This morning. On me." Yeah, that's it. A mechanical failure that had nothing—*nothing*—to do with Rebel. Or any of his muscles. "It, um, does this on its own."

"Oh, my God," she whispered, and Madeline cringed. Here it came. "It's so beautiful! I *love* it."

Now it was Madeline's turn to do a double take. Was she mistaken, or was that admiration? Lots of it?

No one had ever just admired her hair. Back in school, she'd been tormented by all the perfect little princesses who had Barbie's hair and the attitude to match. Happiness had been the day in seventh grade when Mom finally gave in and took her to the salon to get her hair un-permed, as Melonie had described it. Madeline had finally walked through school feeling normal.

But this was different. With what could only be described as jealously, Tara sighed and looked at Madeline longingly as she ran her hands through her own big hair. "I wish mine could do that. The perms never seem to get the curls just right, and it just goes limp on the hot days." The note of disgust was obvious.

"Really? I always wanted it to be so straight... " *Limp* had been a dream, long held and chased at any cost. She'd wasted all that time, all that effort to be something that wasn't real. And just like that, she felt right. All it had taken was the courage to be who she really was.

And damn it all, it was because of Rebel. Again.

Tara's smile was wide. "That grass, it's always greener, yeah?"

Madeline returned the grin. To hell with Rebel. She didn't need him to make her feel special. She was doing just fine on her own, thank you very much. "Yeah. How's Nelly?"

And just like that, the day slid into normal. People—a lot of people—told her they liked her hair, and no one said anything that wasn't complimentary. Tara's mom dropped Nelly off, and the little girl giggled with sheer kid delight when Madeline let her touch it.

It all seemed perfectly normal. Even the part where Nobody slunk in during the late afternoon and attempted to smile politely as she read him the riot act for entrusting his recovery to Rebel seemed normal— by rez standards, anyway. Just another day.

Except for the part where Rebel didn't show up.

As the shadows got longer and longer, the antsiness took hold of her. She'd worn her hair like that for him, whether she wanted to own up to it or not, and he hadn't even bothered to show up and look at it? After all they'd shared—the skinny dipping and the trying to seduce her and the riding bareback in the dark and the hot kisses against a car—and he wasn't even going to come and *see* her?

Damn that man. All of him. Even the good parts.

It was Wednesday before he showed up. Almost five complete days, she thought as he waltzed right into her waiting room at ten 'til five and plopped down in a chair like he'd been waiting on *her*. Five days.

"What are you doing here?" she snapped after the last patient had driven off the lot and Tara was out the door.

131

"Albert's not feeling well." He sounded the same, but his eyes were huge as he stared at her hair. "He wanted me to come in and give you a... hand."

I wish I'd straightened it today, she thought. Just to piss him off. "That's it? That's the only reason you're here?"

"No." His eyes didn't leave her hair and her face grew warm. She ignored it. He could just look. Touching was out of the question. "I have something I need tested." As he stood, he held out a handful of baggies, each containing a swab smeared with something dark and icky looking.

"Drink too much river water?" she snapped, not touching the bags, and certainly not touching him.

"Not mine." He managed to look a little embarrassed. "Something I... found. I want to see if there's anything in it. Anything that could make someone sick. But I don't have access to labs or anything like that. That's why I need you."

"That's why you need *me*?" Maybe she had suffered heat stroke, because she was beginning to think that imagining the whole naked-in-the-river thing would be preferable to the embarrassment she was being swamped by right now. He was acting like he could care less that she'd almost lost her head—and a whole lot more—to a man who she would never, ever figure out. "That's it?"

Everything about him changed. His hips began to sway as his voice dropped. "Madeline," he said. It almost sounded like an apology. It almost sounded like seduction.

He could shove both.

"Hiya, Rebel." Clarence appeared out of

nowhere. Madeline jumped. She'd completely forgotten the big man was still here. "Albert okay?"

"Hiya, Clarence. *Ektawapaya ki hi unkis woglake.*"

Madeline didn't think it was possible to get any madder at the man, but all of a sudden, she was ready to strangle him personally. He knew damn good and well she couldn't understand what he was saying—what the hell was he trying to hide from her?

"Yeah," Clarence said with a nod as his eyes darted between Madeline and Rebel. God only knew what the Mitchell sneer looked like now, but it had to be a good one. Clarence began to retreat toward the door without turning his back to Madeline.

"See you then," Rebel said, not in the least disturbed by the sneer.

"If you make it that long," was Clarence's parting shot, and then only after he was safely outside the clinic.

Rebel just grinned as the sound of Clarence's engine faded. "I like your hair."

"Go to hell."

One eyebrow notched up in surprise. "Are you mad at me?" He asked it like the very concept was foreign to him.

Men. *This* man. "No," she snapped as she turned around and stomped off to one of the exam tables. If Albert wasn't coming in, she might as well get started on getting everything ready for tomorrow. And the day after. And the rest of her pissy life out here. She would not rely on someone named Rebel. "Of course not. I have no reason to be mad. None whatsoever. And I certainly don't care if you go to hell or not. Just go."

Silence met this announcement. She couldn't even tell if he was still in the building, but she sure as hell wasn't going to turn around and look. Instead, she focused on the job. That was why she was here, right? She had a job to do. Sheets in a pile, supplies on the trays restocked. She made a mental note that they needed more iodine the next time she went for supplies.

Her eyes were watering. She blinked, determined not to rub them. Rubbing was a dead giveaway. Of course, telling him to go to hell had been a dead giveaway too. Shit, she was so screwed. She only had four months to go until she beat the last guy's record. She didn't know if she could make it.

"I was busy." Suddenly he was at her side, one hand resting on the small of her back, already moving in small circles.

Her heart wrenched left as her stomach torqued right, and the collision made her more than a little nauseated. She lurched away from his touch, because the mere thought of his hand on her body threatened to take her furious head of steam and throw it right out the window. "I'm sure."

"I'm not used to being certain places at certain times," he went on, taking another step closer.

"I'm not interested in your apologies," she snapped, cutting around an exam table to put something solid between them. "You have nothing to apologize for, as far as I'm concerned."

He was ignoring her. At least that hadn't changed. She kept on walking. The sound of his boots on linoleum drowned out the soft sound of her sneakers. It occurred to her that the clinic wasn't very large. In short order, they'd be doing laps around the damn place.

"I had to go with Nobody. We had to... check on something."

"So?" She cut around another table.

"The something in the bags."

That's it, she thought as she spun around to face him. "And what the hell is in those bags, huh? What's so important that Nobody Bodine had to sneak up on us? What's so important that you disappear for days on end? What's so fucking important?"

He swallowed. "I went to Rapid City after... that. To see if I could get the samples processed myself. I picked up my check from the gallery. I did Albert's grocery shopping for the month. I went to a drugstore. I got some... " This was a first. He looked deeply, horribly embarrassed. "Supplies."

Son-of-a... He wouldn't even answer a direct question. If he thought he had another shot at her, he had another thing coming. "I'm sure you'll find someone who needs *supplies*. I certainly don't."

"And then Albert wasn't feeling good," he hurried on. He took two quick steps, so that there was nothing but the table between them. And she had the feeling that if she tried to bolt, he'd grab her. "He needed me."

"Oh, he needed you? Or he needed a medical professional? Why didn't you bring him in if he was so damn sick? No—" she cut him off with a wave of her hand, "—don't tell me. I couldn't do anything for him. It's not like I know anything about curing people. It's not like I'm a trained professional who's dedicated the last twelve years of my life to helping people. It's not like you respect me a damn bit."

"That's not true," he shot back, and for the first

time in a long time, she saw the wolf in him, ready to attack.

She knew how to outflank him now. She wasn't scared of the wolf. "The hell it isn't. If you respected me even just a little, you'd let me do my job, *Jonathan.* You'd tell me what's in those bags that's so damned important. You'd stop driving me crazy."

He flinched at his name, but it didn't last. Within a second, he had a cold stare fixed on her, and his face was unreadable. "No one else even knows about those bags." His voice was low and serious, but the edge made him sound dangerous. And most certainly not in the good way. "No one else knows that Nobody came looking for me. No one else thinks that maybe it's not the flu. No one else, Madeline. Just you."

"So what is it?" The shout rang out against the cinderblocks until the echo beat her upside the head.

His jaw flexed, and then it was his turn to spin away from her and stomp off. He got to the waiting room before he stopped. His whole body slumped forward, and suddenly he looked tired. She wondered how much sleep he'd gotten in the last almost five days. "I don't know. That's why I need you."

Right back to where they started.

"I need it tested. And no one will give a dirt-poor red man the time of day. I need a medical professional. I need you."

Oh, was he trying to play the pity card? "Clarence is a medical professional."

"Clarence isn't you. I trust you."

There was that heart-stomach collision again. Thank God lunch had been a long time ago. Otherwise she'd be in danger of throwing up in front of Rebel, and she'd rather have her eyeballs gouged out with a dull spoon. "Not enough to bring Albert to see me. Not enough to even tell me what's wrong with Albert."

"He doesn't want you to worry."

"Go to hell." Right back where they started. The clinic wasn't the only thing they were doing laps around.

The nausea built. Sleeping with Rebel was quickly becoming the biggest mistake she'd almost made in her entire life, because it didn't matter. It didn't matter that kissing him had been like being kissed for the very first time after just reading textbook definitions of the act. It didn't matter that he'd reduced her to a quivering mass of jelly with his jeans on. It didn't matter that he thought she was beautiful—more beautiful with her hair all crazy. It didn't matter if he said her name like a prayer, and it didn't matter one little bit that he was a whole lot of wild and just a smidge crazy, and that for one blind afternoon, she'd had fun, real fun. With him.

She wondered what Darrin was doing tonight. Probably watching Charlie Rose or the Military Channel as he drank a martini and ate a microwave dinner. Safe. Peaceful. Well-paid. Comfortable.

Dull, the voice in the back of her head whispered. It was the same voice that forced her eyes to look up and see Rebel staring at her, the pain plain on his face. *Deadly dull*.

"I respect you more than any woman I've ever met."

Oh, hell, she thought as another wave of nausea battered her stomach. His voice was quivering. He was on the verge of tears.

137

"I've never met a woman like you before. You came here willingly, you stay here willingly. This is a hard life, harder when you've given up what you did. But you're still here."

Darrin had never even tried to compliment her. Darrin had never tried to seduce her. And she sincerely doubted that Darrin had ever really trusted her. He respected the family name, but her? She couldn't be sure.

She caught herself. This was not an either/or situation. No way was she going to let something like a sincere compliment break her, not before she broke him first. "I keep my promises. I promised my parents I'd do a little good in this world. I promised my profession to do no harm. I promised the tribal government I'd stay for two years. But I didn't promise you anything, Rebel. Not a damn thing."

He stared at her a while longer. A long while longer. And then she realized he wasn't moving. No hips swaying, no heel tapping, no fingers drumming. Nothing.

"Rebel?"

Nothing.

"*I had to learn how to see them,*" he'd said in the river. "*It took a lot of practice. I have to be patient and completely still.*"

She didn't know patient, but she could see the still. It was like watching a life-sized wax statue of the man. He didn't blink. She wasn't even sure he was breathing.

Breathing was important. Even if she never wanted to see him again, she thought it would be okay if he kept breathing. Independent of her involvement, of course. She edged closer. "Rebel?" And still nothing.

The wisp of panic did little to enhance the nausea as the second hand made a slow round of the clock. Did the man just slip into trances, all willy-nilly? About what? About her? She wasn't even an Indian, for God's sake. He looked more like he was having a petite mal seizure. He was just frozen.

And then, shaking his head, he crumpled back into the seat like so much dead weight.

"Rebel!" And she was practically vaulting over the table to get to him. Kneeling, she pressed one hand to his forehead and the other to his jugular. His pulse was racing and a thin sheen of sweat coated his head. "Stay with me, Rebel," she pleaded. "Please."

That second hand couldn't move much slower, but it was less than a minute before he relaxed under her hands. "It'll pass," he finally muttered, slumping into her arms. "It always does."

She didn't want to hold him, didn't want to comfort him, but she was unpleasantly relieved that he was considerably less freaked out by the whole thing that she was. She should be hoping he'd be miserable, hoping he'd really suffered for making her so crazy, but instead she was just glad to see a weak version of his know-it-all smile.

"Are you okay?"

"Yeah," he said, but she must have scowled at him, because he shot her a sheepish look and added, "I think."

"You *think*? I thought... " Hell, she didn't know what to think right about now. But having a narcoleptic-style vision thing wasn't something she could wrap her mind around.

"Yeah. Me too." He nodded into her neck and

draped his arms around her shoulders. "Just give me a minute."

She gave him two before she broke the silence—and the hold he had on her. "What happened?" She pushed him back a little so she could look at his eyes, which wasn't quite enough to get his hands off her shoulders. *Just steadying him,* she thought as she studied him. His pupils were completely dilated, but his pulse seemed to be settling back into a steady, normal rhythm. *It'll pass, indeed.*

"It's the cattle," he said. No hesitation, no doubt. "I saw the sick cattle."

"What sick cattle?"

"The ones with smallpox."

"What, institutionalized eradication?" He nodded, which made his eyes flutter. *Dizzy?* "What does that have to do with—"

"The samples. They're from a cattle-processing facility owned by a rancher on the edge of the rez." Taking a deep breath, he ran a knuckle down her face. "The rancher that shot Nobody last month."

"What? Rebel, I don't understand."

"Nobody was looking for some of his horses," he explained, like that made any sense.

Sure, she thought, checking his pulse again. Nobody has horses.

"And he thought he saw some ranchers slaughtering some cattle in the open field. That's not normal, not for beef. But when he got closer to try and see what they were doing, he got shot."

"Okay… " His pulse was steady and strong. He was telling the truth. He was finally telling her the truth. Or at least he thought he was—and wasn't that the same thing? "Someone tried to kill him to keep him from finding out what they were doing?"

"That's what we thought. So he went back. And Saturday night, he saw they were getting ready to do it again. So he came and got me."

What was he talking about—industrial espionage? She was finding out what the hell was going on, and she still had no idea. "And this has what, again, to do with your little vision spasm?"

"Understand the past, understand the future."

Her eyes rolled all by themselves. "Enough with the medicine-man crap, Rebel. Just tell me what's going on."

"It's the cattle. That rancher… " He sighed, then leaned forward and kissed her head. "If I tell you, you lose all plausible deniability."

So Albert wasn't the only one who didn't want her to worry. Her heart gave her stomach a firm shove. "I can lie."

That got a smile out of him. "Not to me, you can't."

She ignored the unsettling implication. "Rebel, you can trust me." He'd said so himself, after all.

"That rancher is paid by the government to provide beef to the tribe."

That couldn't be it. Maybe hundreds of years ago, sheer racism led to institutionalized eradication. But businessmen today didn't just kill off paying customers. "And?"

"He owns the land next to the White Sandy. The tribe controls the river, and we won't let him use it for irrigating or anything. He wants our land. For the water rights. If enough people get sick, the tribal council might have to sell the water rights, just to stay afloat."

"Are you sure?" Because that couldn't be *it*. This was the twenty-first century, for God's sake. No one just tried to take out a whole people anymore.

He shook his head in defeat. "No. I don't have any proof beyond what's in those bags. I think he's doing something that contaminates the beef, and the beef is making the people sick. I don't think it's the flu. But I don't know what else it could be. I don't even know if I'm right."

"And you need me to find out."

He kissed her again, this time on the cheek. "I need you, Madeline." His voice was warm and close to her ear. "I've always needed you."

Mush. Her brain went to mush. She knew she was supposed to be mad—furious—with him. She was supposed to kick him out of here, forbid him from darkening her door ever again, and most certainly to stop touching her. But his lips pressed into the sensitive skin just below her earlobe, and she shuddered.

"You're doing it again," she managed to murmur. "Changing the subject."

His lips didn't leave her skin as he spoke. "Have you had dinner?"

"Excuse me?" Talk about changing the subject.

"After we're—" this time, his teeth scraped against her skin, "—done here, I'll take you to see Albert. He's making dinner for us. And you can see for yourself that he's okay. If you don't mind making house calls, that is."

Was there anything softer than mush? Because that was what her brain was right now. Her head was spinning. What else did they have to do? Did he have *supplies* at the ready? Maybe it hadn't been a case of heat stroke. Maybe this was just how he made her feel, because she was light-headed and confused and in real danger of swooning.

Baggies. House calls. Albert. Dinner. He would take her to see Albert.

Damn it all. She had a job to do.

Half an hour later, Rebel let Blue Eye keep an easy lope as Madeline followed in her Jeep. They were cruising at about ten miles an hour on the dirt road that lead back to Albert's house. She was leaning out the window, trying to egg Blue Eye on faster and faster as she beamed that high-watt smile at him, like she couldn't believe her eyes. Dinner was waiting for them—a real dinner, complete with ripe strawberries, the season's first green beans and a fresh-baked chocolate cake. Albert's favorite.

He didn't want to go faster. Faster would mean sooner. The sooner they got there, the sooner she'd see everything. And all he could think was, this was not a good idea.

This is not a good idea, he thought as he piloted the Cadillac off Highway 90 and past the last real town not on the rez. He looked over to Anna, curled up in the passenger seat of her car—hers, not theirs—although she let him drive it. Her brown eyes were wide with a child-like excitement.

"I've always wanted to see where you grew up, Jonathan." Her words came out in that languid fashion that he thought was the most cultured way of talking that existed. He'd tried so hard to copy her southwestern accent, to erase the clipped vowels that marked him as an outsider. But he hadn't been able to do it. He still sounded like an Indian. "To think... ." her words trailed off as her eyes got all shiny, "... I'll finally get to meet your family. They must be so proud of you."

This is not a good idea. He swallowed and tried to work his practiced smile. "Yeah. Proud." Proud that he hadn't been home to see any of them in six years. Proud that he'd only called on Albert's birthday, and even then, he'd kept it short. Proud that he'd tried not to be one of them, one of *those* Indians. "Very proud."

He couldn't even convince himself. This was a disaster in the making.

As he hit the first of many gravel roads, he snuck another look at his wife, the love of his life. She loved him. She told him so every morning when she left to work at the gallery and every night when she slipped between the sheets and he slipped between her legs. She was beautiful, delicate and refined. And she adored him. They were very happy together.

It wasn't too late. He could turn the car around and take her to a hotel and have one more night when she thought he was the most perfect man who ever existed.

But he knew that was delaying the inevitable. And the inevitable was her meeting his family. To see where he grew up. To find out what he'd been before he left South Dakota.

This is a terrible idea.

"I can't wait to meet your brother," she gushed, brushing the short hair out of his eyes for him. "I promised Cynthia I'd bring her back a picture. She's got such a crush on you, you know."

He knew. Anna was never shy about letting him—anyone—know that other women wanted what she had. Especially her older sister, Cynthia. Clearly, Anna was already planning the next wedding. "Jesse and I don't look that much alike." *Shit*. His accent was already getting harder to understand. Must be something in the air.

"Come on," she scoffed, digging around in her purse. "You're a Native American, he's a Native American. I brought a picture of Cynthia, just in case." And she thrust the snapshot of his sister-in-law in a bikini before his eyes.

You all look alike to me. That's what she really meant, like using the P.C. *Native American* somehow balanced out the subconscious racism. They were all alike.

This was the worst idea he'd ever had. But he had to go home. He couldn't breathe anymore in New Mexico, couldn't think, couldn't even create anymore. He had to come home. He just had to.

And Anna had insisted that she come with him.

She kept chatting about anything and everything—how excited she was to meet the rest of his family, how beautiful the sky was here, how tired she was of sitting in this car after three days on the road. But by the time they passed a small cluster of government-provided trailers, the Quik-E Mart where two drunks were brawling in the parking lot and the clinic where Albert had gotten a job to help cover the college bills, her silence was louder than the wheels crushing dirt.

This was about to get ugly.

They turned down the last road. Albert's house—

which was being generous—stood at the end, looking like it was being propped up by toothpicks. "You grew up... here?" She sort of squeaked out the last word, like he'd taken a pair of needle-nosed pliers and made straight for her fingernails.

He cringed. *The end.* The thought popped unbidden into his head. The end. "Yes." He made damn sure he pronounced it right too.

He wanted to reassure her that this wasn't who he really was. He wasn't the kind of person who lived here, who even knew people who lived here. But that wasn't the truth. And he couldn't bear to live another lie.

Oscar was outside, standing in front of a barrel and feeding in trash. And for every piece he fed to the fire, he took a swig out of a bottle in a paper bag. When the Cadillac came to a halt, Oscar shook his head, like he couldn't believe his eyes. The front door banged open, and Albert came out, his arms full of old paper. He didn't have on a shirt, and his pants were held up with a length of twine.

Two things happened at the same time. Rebel's gut unclenched, flooding him with relief from a pain he had only dimly been aware of. He'd known he needed to be here, needed to see his people again, but he hadn't realized just how deep the need had run. The reaction was immediate and physical. He could breathe again, for the first time in six years. He could finally breathe free.

And Anna gasped in horror.

"My God," she said, patting him on the shoulder like he was a lap dog, not a husband. He turned to look at her, knowing it was futile but refusing to believe it.

146

Her lips were curled back in disgust, like she'd stepped in dog shit. And then her eyes swiveled over to him. The adoration was gone. Instead, she looked scared. Terrified. "I just had no idea. You poor thing."

You poor thing.

She'd loved Jonathan Runs Fast, but he'd been just an idea, an abstract idea so well rendered that it had been a *trompe l'oeil*, an illusion mistaken for reality. She'd loved an idea named Jonathan.

She didn't love a thing—especially a poor thing like him.

And she never would.

"Why are you going so slow?" Madeline demanded, the wind snatching her words out of the air and bending them until she sounded like she was howling. Blue Eye tossed her head in agreement. This was way, way too slow.

Because the slower they went, the longer he could put this off, that's why. He had no reason to expect the same reaction from a different woman. None. Hell, she already knew everyone.

But that didn't stop the clawing worry.

Finally, after what seemed like milliseconds but was probably twenty minutes of trying and failing to keep Blue Eye reined in, they hit the last dirt road. He could see cars already parked haphazardly along the road. Grocery day was as good a day as any to have a party, after all. It was what Albert wanted, and he wasn't going to let a little thing like feeling lousy interrupt a good party.

He didn't want to dismount, as if staying safely up on his horse would somehow change the fate of the free world. Madeline parked in the grass behind the last car and hauled out a duffel bag half her size. Her back bowed under the weight.

Shit. He had to get off the horse. Only an asshole would let her carry that duffle around by herself. "Here. I've got it."

She came up firing even as she let him take the duffel. "You know what you've got? You've got my boots. I want them back."

"Not so sure about that," he replied, taking a long step to put him out of swinging range. This was more like it. She was pulling, and he was enjoying it. "Those were serious blisters. It wouldn't be sound medical advice to continue irritating your skin like that."

She snorted, but kept pace. A slow pace. "You're a fine one to be dispensing medical advice over there."

He smiled in spite of the dread fact that they were getting closer to the light of the fire. There was no backing out now—but then, there'd been no backing out, period, not since he'd showed up at her clinic tonight, intent on seeing her again. All of her. He had the sudden urge to take her hand, to hold onto that touch for as long as he could, just in case. *Just in case.* "Don't have to be a doctor to know that intentionally blistering your feet is not a good idea."

They passed another car. "Rebel," she said, and he heard the note of uncertainty in her voice. "How many people are coming to dinner?"

"I went grocery shopping. Anyone who needed groceries is here."

She stopped behind the third car in line, Henry's rusted-out Camaro long past its muscle-car prime. "But it looks like half the rez is here."

He couldn't help but smile at the amazement in her voice. Amazement. Not horror. And that, in itself, was amazing. "Nah. Probably only forty or fifty people."

"You bought groceries for forty or fifty *people*?"

He noticed it was taking that much longer to get to the house than normal. *So?* "In case you haven't noticed, the only grocery stores on the rez are the Quik-E Mart and the food pantry. And Nelly could eat a pound of fresh strawberries in one sitting. Besides," he added, knowing he needed to take a step forward, a step toward those strawberries but still not able to move his feet, "I wanted everyone to have reliable beef for a while."

She let that slide. And she took a step toward him, a step closer. The dim light of the fire behind her gave all those wild curls a 24-karat glow, and the moon above made her eyes gleam like the brightest turquoise. She was such a jewel, a jewel of the High Plains. "And how exactly did you do that?" Her voice dropped a notch. He could see the wheels turning. She was trying to pull again, but she was going about it a new way. New since Saturday, anyway. "Hook a rack wagon up to Blue Eye?"

Shit, it was working too. Damn intruding zippers. She was going to pull him right over the edge. "Jesse's not exactly capable of handling a stick shift right now. I took his truck. Like when you get your... supplies."

Moving with what he prayed was steady deliberation, she took another step in and then placed a single hand right over his pounding heart. Her eyelashes fluttered as she gave him the kind of look that would bring him to his knees in broad daylight. "And where did you get that kind of money?"

149

He couldn't help it. The duffel hit the ground and he had one hand on her neck, the other around her waist, and she was right where she belonged. "Somebody bought a bag," he whispered as he kissed her ruby lips. Right where she belonged. And, as she nipped at his lower lip, it was painfully, wonderfully obvious that she knew it too.

Everything that had been wrong with the world for the last five days was suddenly right. Five days without seeing her had been five of the longest days of his life. Five days with no one challenging him every step of the way, no one to spar with, no one who brought so much light into his life to look forward to. Five days that made six years seem like a three-day weekend. Five days that had been the longest decade of his life. And suddenly, with her back where she belonged, he wanted time to slow even more, so he'd never have to let go of her. He never wanted to let go of her.

Until he heard the twig snap. His head shot up so fast that Madeline didn't have time to release her hold on him. She nipped a hole into his lower lip as a dark figure stepped out from behind a van on the other side of the road.

Not again, he thought.

But it was different this time. Without the blinding flash of light, even Madeline could see that Nobody Bodine was watching them. She spun around with a much smaller squeak this time and jammed her hands onto her hips with enough force that Rebel was afraid she'd bruise herself. "Nobody! Stop sneaking up on us!"

Rebel smiled again. Nobody hadn't had to tell him she'd given him hell when he'd finally left Rebel

Monday afternoon. Nobody snapped his hat off his head as he nodded to her. "My apologies, ma'am." Then he looked to Rebel.

He knew what the man wanted. He'd known Nobody for a long time, and had gotten something like good at reading him. "She got it all ready to go out in the mail tomorrow."

Nobody crushed his hat to his chest. It was as much of a tell as he had. "Much obliged, ma'am. I'll watch the clinic tonight, then."

Madeline took an agitated step toward him, and Nobody took a parallel step back.

"You'll *what*?"

Nobody shot him a pained look, his jaw clenching and unclenching. Rebel shrugged his shoulders. *Yeah*, he thought, *whatcha gonna do about her?*

"Ma'am, I'll guard the clinic. It wasn't easy to get those things. I don't want nothing to happen to them."

Wow. Another three sentences. Something about Madeline made the normally silent man downright chatty.

This fact didn't seem to impress her, though. She jutted out her chin and said, "You mean, you aren't coming to dinner? I thought everyone was coming to dinner?" in the same kind of voice she used when another whatever-it-was broke on her. Rebel decided that was just the way she talked when reality didn't meet her high expectations. Which threw him right back over into worried about dinner.

Well, he wasn't the only one worried about dinner, although Nobody would never admit to it. "Your groceries are still in the back of the truck. Parked behind the shed. Extra carrots," Rebel added.

Nobody's horses were the most important things in his life.

Madeline elbowed him in the ribs. "You should come to dinner, Nobody. The clinic will be fine."

"Ma'am." Nobody took a deep breath. "Two of my horses died. And they shot me," he added, almost as an afterthought. No doubt about it, the dead horses were the more important of the two events. "I'll be at the clinic, just to be safe." And then he stepped back into the shadows. Rebel knew no one else would see him, no one else would even know Nobody had been here. Just Madeline. Whether he liked it or not, Nobody had to trust her too.

"Wait. Nobody, wait!" Despite her call, he didn't reappear.

But that didn't mean he was gone. "He's listening," Rebel whispered in her ear, savoring the way one of her curls danced over his nose. "Go on."

Madeline nodded. She just took it all in stride. Just another night on the rez, and she could deal. Suddenly, Rebel knew it was high time to get her up to see Albert. "Can you leave me a list of what was wrong with your horses? What were their symptoms?"

"Yes, ma'am," came the distant reply, already thirty feet down toward the shed. And then he was gone.

"Come on," Rebel whispered. "Albert's waiting."

Chapter Ten

You seem nervous," she said as they got ever closer to the house.

"I'm not," he defended. Maybe a little too quickly.

Stopping again, she shot him a look that was easier to read in the stronger light. Hell, he was lucky she was just looking at him. "You said you trusted me." Her voice was low but warm.

He swallowed. The challenge was in her eyes, and he was suddenly afraid he wouldn't be able to meet it. "I do."

Her smile was small, but it looked just right on her face. "Then trust me." And she walked into the circle of light. He had no choice but to follow.

Everyone is here. He watched a hundred different daily soap operas play out before his eyes. Current lovers avoided old ones as the people in between tested the waters. Kids played hide and seek in the shadows, never far from the fire. Tim, the law around here, was keeping an eye on Oscar and the other ones who never had enough money for food but always seemed to be able to buy beer.

It would have been funny if he wasn't, in fact, nervous. One after another, his friends—his family—called out to him from around the fire and then pulled

153

back when they realized the good doctor was at his side. He could see the confused looks on their faces as they all politely welcomed Madeline to the party—which was something, he guessed. They were looking at her, talking to her. Everyone seemed to agree that the white woman amongst them existed, although the jury was still out on whether or not she belonged.

He saw the looks people gave each other over the fire. He knew they were jumping on the nearest conclusion—the correct conclusion—that she was not just here with him, but here with him. That he'd lost his heart to another white woman, another outsider who would blow away with the breeze as soon as she was done with him, done with all of them. That their medicine man didn't want one of his own. That he was a traitor, again. That he would always betray the Lakota way.

This is not a good idea.

If Madeline noticed the tension that gripped the air, she didn't let on. She was, if anything, more friendly now than he'd ever seen her. Instead of the curt hello she used at the clinic, here she told people how happy she was to see them, asked how they were doing, and even shook a few people's hands.

And she did it while keeping an eye on him. Nervous? Hell, he was practically paralyzed. But now, his fear had switched from worrying about her reaction to everyone else's reaction. And those fears, it seemed, were a lot more justified.

"Is Albert inside?" she asked, tugging on the duffel.

Inside. More people inside. He swallowed again. It was becoming a regular occurrence. "Yeah. Come on in."

The people in front of the house parted for them.

Rebel felt the air cooling and it had nothing to do with the night. *Snap out of it*, he ordered himself. *Pull it together.*

"Oh, Dr. Mitchell." Tara was the first to notice them. She was holding Mikey in her arms. "You're... here."

"Tara, isn't it time you started calling me Madeline?" She wrapped an arm around Tara in what looked like an awkward hug and chucked Mikey under the chin. "Who's this cute little guy? How old are you, buddy?"

Mikey, for one, was downright gleeful to see the pretty white woman. Within seconds, his chubby little hand was locked onto a swath of Madeline's curls. "This is my nephew, Mikey—he's eighteen months old," Tara said, trying to pull Mikey away without pulling Madeline's hair. "My sister's son." She looked over her shoulder to her sister. "Tammy, have you met the new doctor?"

Tammy Tall Trees was a slightly shorter, slightly heavier and much quieter version of Tara. Rebel had to hide his grin as Madeline studied the two of them. He could tell she was thinking they looked a hell of a lot more alike than he and Jesse did. Helped to have the same parents. "It's so nice to meet you. Tara, I didn't know you had a sister."

Something blunt hit him in the shins. "Ow!" he snapped, looking down to see Jesse pulling the crutch back toward the couch. "What the hell was that for?"

Jesse's eyes darted between Rebel and Madeline. "You didn't bring me any chew," he said with his mouth. His eyes, however, asked what Madeline was doing here.

155

"That shit's not good for you," Rebel shot back. He lifted an eyebrow to send the message, *because I brought her*, to his brother.

Jesse looked around the room, silent except for Mikey squealing in delight at the strange hair that tickled his hands and Tammy politely making small talk with Madeline. Big risk, Jesse's surprised look said.

Rebel knew this. But he'd done it anyway. He shrugged.

Jesse wagged his eyebrows, and Rebel knew exactly what he was thinking. He made a motion to kick Jesse's cast, but Jesse cut him off at the knees. "Doctor, I'm glad you could come to see me," he said with that impish smile that Rebel fiercely hated, his eyes not leaving Rebel's face. "When the hell can I get out of this cast?"

The spell of the room seemed to shatter into chatter. Tara and Tammy roundly scolded Jesse for cursing in front of the children, Madeline shook her head at him like he was acting like the irritating little brother he really was and people met Rebel's eyes, nodding their heads.

And through it all, Madeline kept an eye on Rebel.

"Three more weeks," he heard her say. He snapped his attention back to her. "I'm sure Rebel will truck your butt in when you're good and ready."

"You have no idea," Jesse moaned in a slightly faked whine.

"Sure I do. Broke my leg falling off a horse when I was fifteen," she replied. "Now, where's Albert?"

"Kitchen," Jesse replied. "He's always in the kitchen."

With a nod of her head, Madeline motioned for Rebel to lead on. The kitchen was warm to the point of sweaty. Albert was in his normal chair, looking better now than he had when Rebel had left a few hours ago. The color had returned to his face, and the pain had eased back from his eyes. He could pass for normal.

Walter White Mouse was sitting across from him, cigarette dangling out of his mouth as he boomed laughter across the room. Irma was standing next to Terry, Tara's mom, as they made the fry bread and peeled the potatoes. Nelly was on sink duty, rinsing strawberries with her head cocked in the way that said she was struggling to understand the jokes Walter and Albert told in Lakota.

Albert looked up at the two of them, almost side by side in the doorway, almost touching. And he smiled. "*Hemaca wakta niye au cante skuye,*" he said.

"What?" Madeline's smile faltered, just a little.

Nelly turned around, half-eaten strawberry in her hand and her face scrunched in concentration. "He's glad you came, wight? That's what he said, wight, Webel?"

Thank heavens Nelly hadn't blurted out the part where Albert called Madeline *sweetheart*—as in Rebel's sweetheart. "Good. That was good, Nell-Bell." This was the most normal thing in his world, the grocery-day party, the people crowded in and around the tiny house, the traditions passing from one to the next. And Madeline was right here.

She hadn't run screaming. Hell, she hadn't even broken stride.

She belongs here, he thought, his arm itching to wrap around her waist. *She belongs here with me.*

As if he was reading Rebel's mind, Albert nodded with a smile.

After Irma got her some tea, Madeline gave the old man a thorough work-up—as thorough as she could in the kitchen, anyway. When she finished, her brow was wrinkled.

"Well?"

Her eyes settled on him, and she chewed on her lip. "Has he always had that skip in his heartbeat?"

His heart. Rebel should have guessed. "It's off?"

"It's a little irregular," she admitted. "But I don't know if that's normal for him or not. I didn't bring his file... Otherwise, he seems okay. Definitely not the flu," she added, shooting him a sharp look.

He felt the blood fade away from his face. With an ache of certainty, he knew what had happened. Albert had had a heart attack last night. A small one, maybe. One that left him up and walking. But a heart attack all the same.

He looked at his grandfather, who was telling another joke in Lakota that Tara would blush to know her daughter was hearing—and understanding. As he watched, Albert reached out and patted Nelly on the head, and then went back to his stories. He glanced up at Rebel and nodded again.

His time was coming. And he knew it.

That ache ran deep, and for a moment, Rebel felt not just nervous, but a full-on panic. Albert had made him what he was. Albert had saved him. He was a Lakota because that was what Albert had taught him. Without Albert...

The panic burned away with a certain knowledge. Albert had made him what he was, and what he was now was a medicine man, here to shepherd souls on to the heavens. He would be okay. They all would, because that was what Albert had prepared them for.

Albert looked at Madeline and his gaze darkened a little. He was worried about her, Rebel realized again. After all, she didn't know much of a good Lakota death.

The rest of the evening passed in a whirl of people laughing and eating good food, telling jokes in Lakota and telling them again in English and laughing at both. Madeline seemed most comfortable in the kitchen, helping Nelly cull the strawberries, so Rebel went back out to the bonfire alone, like he had something to prove. Some people smoked, some people drank, but he turned a blind eye to the bad parts and focused on the good. And the best of the good parts was that no one gave him any shit. In fact, several people mentioned that Albert had been expecting them a little sooner.

Maybe this wasn't the worst idea he'd ever had, after all. In fact, it might turn out to be a perfectly okay one. Rebel came in from the fire to find Madeline in an earnest conversation with Tammy, seemingly oblivious to the fact that Mikey was hell-bent on tugging on each lovely curl.

A hammer hit him in the chest. She'd always seemed so formal, so stiff around the kids at the clinic, but now? Now she was helping Nelly with the prized berries and bouncing Mikey on her knee like it was the most natural thing in the world.

Anna had not wanted children. She'd been afraid of the disorder a baby would bring, both to her world and her body. And, at the time, Rebel had been on board with that. He didn't want any more kids to grow up with the kind of confusion that kept Jesse locked between two different worlds, and he sure as hell hadn't wanted any child of his to be nothing but a dirt-poor red man to the rest of the world.

Madeline looked up at him, her eyes bright.

It didn't have to be that way, he realized. Jesse had let himself be stuck in the middle. And who the hell cared what the rest of the world thought?

And then she smiled at him, and the hammer hit him harder.

"Just the man I needed to see," she said.

His gut clenched, which left him wide open for what she said next.

"How big is Jesse's truck?"

Huh? "Standard bed," he replied as he noticed that Tammy had a huge grin on her face. "Why? What did I miss?"

"I need someone with a truck to go with me to Rapid City. I'm going to buy some filing cabinets."

He'd missed something, all right. No one had breathed a word of filing cabinets. "More than one?"

"Tara thinks it'll take at least two," she replied, and both sisters nodded. "If we had filing cabinets, I would have been able to pull Albert's file before we left. I need filing cabinets and someone to organize them for me."

"Dr. Mitchell," Tammy said, her voice barely above a whisper, "I don't know how to thank you."

He'd definitely missed something. "For filing cabinets?"

All three women looked at him like he was a tree stump. "I've decided that I need filing cabinets," Madeline said, her voice dropping well into teasing range. In front of other people. Maybe someone had gotten her a beer? "And it turns out that Tammy finished a year of a secretarial program at, where again?"

"Sinte Gliske," Tammy replied, staring at her feet.

That's right, Rebel remembered. Tammy had been following in Tara's footsteps—their mother was a huge fan of higher education—and then she'd gotten pregnant and dropped out. And with an unfinished degree and a newborn, a paycheck had suddenly become out of reach.

Until Madeline showed up. Madeline, who seemed to understand about these things. Madeline, who was going to save the world, one person at a time. Starting with Tammy.

Hell, who was he kidding? Starting with him.

"And Lord knows I don't have time to organize anything," Tara said, shooting him the kind of look that demanded agreement.

Finally, he caught on. "So you're going to test Tammy's organizational skills?"

"On a trial basis," Madeline added, smiling with genuine warmth. "It's not like we couldn't use a little more help."

"She said I could bring in Mikey if Mom was too busy," Tammy added, the embarrassment coloring her cheeks.

"Nelly can help," Tara reassured her, a sisterly arm on her shoulder.

"That's... " Well, hell. He didn't have a word. And everyone could tell.

Tara rolled her eyes as Tammy blushed even harder. Madeline notched an eyebrow at him. "Assuming," she said, the sarcasm dripping, "someone keeps paying his bills."

His mouth opened to give her what-for—*his* bills? More like everyone else's bills—but Nelly bounded into the room.

"Webel. Dr. Mitchell. *Tȟunkášila* Albert told me he wanted to talk to you. I think," she added as she scratched her head. "Maybe he said... oh, shoot."

Madeline had that same look—a little worried, but not too much—as she handed Mikey off. "We'll go check, Nelly. Thanks for telling us."

He fought the urge to grab her hand—not because he was afraid it might be the last touch, but because he wanted her to know that she didn't need to be afraid, not while he was here. But he didn't. Jesse was watching. Hell, everyone was watching as they wove their way back to the kitchen.

Walter was gone now, and Irma brushed past them with an old grin on her face. Rebel thought he heard her whisper, "Easy on the eyes, yeah?"

Madeline's back stiffened and, although he was behind her, he was sure he saw her ears shoot red. But then she giggled and patted Irma on the arm. "Those potatoes were amazing, Irma. The best I've ever had."

No, certainly not the worst idea he'd ever had.

"*Yanka*." Albert said.

"Have a seat," Rebel translated, beginning to wonder what this was all about. The kitchen was now empty; the sounds of people talking and laughing in the next room seemed faint.

Albert began to talk. The beautiful music that was Lakota flowed out of him like an old, well-loved song, one that Rebel never got tired of hearing. He began to translate.

"You are a good doctor," he said, doing his level

best to get the spirit, if not the letter, of Albert's words right. "You do much good in this world."

Madeline squirmed in her seat, like she'd never had to just sit and take a compliment before. "That's sweet, Albert, but you don't have to—"

Albert's hand snapped up and cut her off at a speed that impressed even Rebel.

"He's not done yet," Rebel chided her. Bad form to interrupt one of the most senior members of the tribe, after all.

"Oh," she said, blushing even harder. For a second, Rebel got lost in the sunset pink that gave her skin the look of first true love. "Okay. Sorry."

After a pause that carried a lot more weight than normal, Albert began again and Rebel translated. "You have made your mother and father proud."

Madeline made a little noise as her hand flew to her mouth. "What?"

Albert nodded. "It wasn't that they lived or died, it's how they lived and died," Rebel translated, keeping a close eye on her. The blood was draining from her face at an alarming pace. "A good life and a good death are all a man can ask for."

Albert turned those eyes to him, the eyes that had watched him walk away without judgment when Rebel had been too young and stupid to know what he was leaving. The eyes that had watched him crawl back without contempt when he'd realized he could never be who the rest of the world wanted him to be. He knew Albert was talking to both of them.

So it was in the world. A true Lakota warrior didn't fear death, didn't hide from his true path. And Albert had always followed his true path. "Today is a good day to die," Rebel said to his grandfather in English.

Albert nodded, the crinkles around his eyes telling Rebel he was pleased the younger man had finally remembered their truth. "*Apetu kile waste ekta te*," Albert repeated in Lakota.

"I don't... understand." She was slouched down in her chair, like the weight of her world was resting full on her shoulders, and her hands were shaking. Just like her voice. "I don't understand."

Albert stood, steadying himself on the table until his legs caught up with the rest of him. Then he leaned over and kissed Madeline on the cheek. "I'm glad you came." In English, Albert's voice had a distinctive rasp that was missing from his Lakota. "I hope you stay." And he shuffled off to take a tired Mikey from his mother's arms and rock the baby to sleep. While he still could.

"I don't understand," Madeline repeated after a long moment, her hand touching the spot Albert had blessed with a kiss.

"You don't have to understand." It was going to be all right, that much he knew. "You just have to believe."

"Believe what? Believe Albert knows something about my parents?" She shook her head, and when her eyes met his again, he saw some of that fierce, analytical look in them. "What did you tell him?"

"Nothing." He couldn't help crack a little bit of a smile. "I told you, Albert is a powerful man."

Her glare was just strong enough to let him know that she considered him lying to be a distinctive possibility, but weak enough to say that she hadn't ruled out another option. Even if she didn't know what that option could be.

The confusion was all that was left. She looked like she might cry. "I don't... I just don't understand, Rebel. It doesn't make any sense."

He looked out to the living room, to where Albert sat on the part of the couch Jesse wasn't sprawled out on. Mikey was half asleep in his arms, and Nelly was curled up under his free arm, rubbing the baby's tummy as Albert hummed a lullaby. He glanced up and caught Rebel staring. He made a shooing motion with his hand. His meaning was clear—go on, we're all fine here.

They were all fine. Madeline was not. He looked at the shaken woman in front of him, seeming far more delicate than she ever had, including heat stroke. She needed him.

And he needed her.

"You want to get out of here?" His question was met with a silence that bordered on stony. He could throw a million things at her—she'd accomplished her goal of checking on Albert, had complimented Irma on the potatoes and had even managed to squeeze in giving Tammy a job, however temporary. She was tired, she had to work tomorrow, the moon was shining—anything and everything would have been a good reason to walk out of Albert's kitchen and away from her exposed vulnerability.

He kept his mouth shut and waited. Couldn't push her. A woman like Dr. Madeline Mitchell needed to pull. She was that damn good at it.

"With you?"

He let the question settle in the air for a minute

longer. "If that's what you want." Something in her face changed, something that took it from chilly to amused without moving a muscle.

Damn, she was beautiful. And even if she didn't understand, she was still here. He couldn't help it. Three condoms in his wallet were proof of that. Leaning forward, he whispered, "If that's what you *need*, Madeline. What do you need?"

Oh, she was going to let him sweat. That much was clear when it looked like she bit her cheek to keep the smile hidden and tried to glare at him. She couldn't lie to him. She just had no idea how bad she was at it.

Sighing, she looked around the kitchen, then peeked out into the living room. "Everyone seems okay." Her voice danced across his ears. She turned to face him and there was that challenge again, the glacier he wasn't near done climbing. "I guess I'm done here. Will you carry the duffel back to my Jeep?"

She couldn't lie to him. He could only hope she wasn't lying to herself.

Chapter Eleven

The air, colored with smoke and moonlight, did little to clear the weird fog from her head. Yes, Albert doing that medicine man thing had freaked her out, but just a little. And the part where he spoke English for only about the third time? No big deal. For all she knew, he'd been practicing those two lines. A special thank you from a special man. That's all. She should have been thanking him. She'd had dinner at his house. Not a big deal at all.

What was a big deal, however, was her shocking inability to get her damned mouth shut as she watched Rebel carry her duffel. She was only vaguely aware of the fact she was swaying in the breeze, even though the air was still. The muscles in his forearms clenched and unclenched as he picked up her duffel like it was a bag of cotton balls and carefully set it in the trunk. Those muscles weren't the only things clenching and unclenching. Her muscles—between her legs, across her chest—that she knew she had, anatomically speaking, but had never really had much personal experience with, were doing strange things. Things that hurt in a bizarre, good way. Things that demanded attention, a very certain kind of attention.

And what was a huge deal was the way he leaned

against the side of the Jeep, arms crossed and that know-it-all smile that drove her nuts during daylight hours doing its damnedest to melt her in the moonlight.

Things clenched again. God, it hurt. And there was something in his smile that promised the rest of the evening would be wonderfully pain free.

She was not just going to throw herself at that smile. A woman had to have her principles, even if she couldn't quite recall what those principles were at the moment. "Thank you," she managed to get out without melting. Lost in a fog of confused thoughts and muscle spasms, the first thing that surfaced was supplies. He'd said he had supplies. "For helping me with that."

"You're welcome. And you're doing it again," he replied as he slid one hand under her hair. In less than a heartbeat, his fingers were wrapped around her neck, pulling her closer.

The warmth spread like a fever from her neck all the way down. So what if they were within earshot of everyone? Parts of her—oh, hell, who was she kidding?—*all* of her wanted him to touch more than just her neck. Just thinking about how close she'd been to an honest-to-God, one-handed climax a mere five days ago was enough to make her want to do bad, bad things. Her muscles clamped down with a spike of pain. "Doing what?" That's what she came up with? Excellent. He was outflanking her within earshot of the party.

"Ignoring what you really want." His lips found the same spot he'd practically devoured just a few hours ago, and much more than just a few isolated muscle groups spasmed. "What you really *need*."

God, what was she *doing*? She wanted him, but she didn't want to want him. Not like she did. "What if I don't need what you think I need?"

His lips, already moving against her skin, curved into a smile. She could feel it just as surely as she could feel the heat pooling in spots he'd already touched. Spots that would kill for another touch.

When he spoke, the reverberations followed the fever south. "What if you do?"

An unexpected thumb flicked over her nipple, and her knees buckled. She opened her mouth to tell him to stop, to tell him that they couldn't, that Nobody or even Albert would pop up and turn on the lights and honk horns and then she'd never be able to look anyone in the face again because she couldn't admit to anyone, most especially herself, that he was the one person in this world she needed. All that came out was a whimper that sounded like he was hurting her, when what was hurting was that frustrated orgasm that was begging, just begging, to be unleashed in the middle of a dirt road.

He caught her in a hard kiss, which only made the pain that much more acute. Another whimper clawed its way out of her throat, but this time, it was matched with a moan from deep in the back of his throat. "Can you drive?" he all but growled at her.

"No." She couldn't even shake her head. It hurt far too much.

"Keys?"

With unresponsive hands, she swatted around at her pocket until she somehow got them out. "But— your horse?"

He flung the passenger door open and backed her

into it with another kiss that rendered her incapable of doing a damn thing to stop him. Then he turned and let out a whistle that was in serious danger of shattering glass.

The results were immediate. Blue Eye came cantering up so quickly that Madeline was sure the mare had been watching them—again. *Voyeuristic horse*, she thought limply. *Go away.*

"Go home," Rebel said sharply. Blue Eye nudged him with her head. He said something in Lakota, which must have been the same thing, because Blue Eye shook her head and then trotted off into the darkness. Rebel watched her go before he turned around and shut her door. Seconds later, the car was barreling down the road.

She knew she lived about twenty miles away from where she thought Albert lived, but Rebel took the roads with a white-knuckled speed that took away what little breath she tried to grab. And then they were squealing to a stop in front of her studio cabin and she couldn't get the seat belt off fast enough, so he did it for her.

God, she'd been horny before, needed the release of a good, old-fashioned climax to make everything all better—hell, Saturday was a prime example. But even with that recent memory still seared in her mind, she could honestly say it didn't compare to the hot, heavy weight between her legs that pulsed with spasm after painful spasm. She could barely freaking walk.

Rebel pulled her out of the car and then she was up against the door and all that heavy weight was riding something equally hot and a whole lot harder.

"Mad-e-line," Rebel growled into her neck,

rocking those hips that never stopped into her with each and every syllable. "My Madeline." But they didn't move away from the car.

He was making her crazy, plain and simple. He was intentionally *not* giving her what she so desperately needed because—because—because he was waiting for something, she realized. He was waiting for her.

She shoved him back, trying to buy enough space that she could say something—anything—without losing what was left of her mind. "Rebel." It came out thin and weak, but at least she hadn't whimpered, right?

"Madeline." His chest heaved with the effort. Her medical mind couldn't help but note that his pupils were completely dilated, his skin flushed. At least she wasn't the only one suffering right now.

"Supplies?" One word at a time was, apparently, all that was happening right now. Verbally, anyway.

He whipped his wallet out of his back pocket. "Three here. Nine back at camp." But still he hung back, waiting.

Waiting for her.

Three here. Would it be enough? "I… " God, she wanted him, but the words were stuck somewhere between the last whimper and the next one. Nothing else came out.

"Tell me." He moved in close again, but instead of another scorching kiss, he touched his forehead to hers. His body trembled. Was he nervous? "Tell me what you want. What you need, Madeline." She saw his Adam's apple bob. "Please." It wasn't a question. It was a prayer.

What she wanted *was* what she needed. She couldn't pretend that wasn't the truth, and she was damn tired of trying. She surrendered to that truth; the answer came easier. "You." That was all she had.

That was all it took.

She didn't know how she got from the car to the bed. She didn't remember walking, but neither did she remember Rebel carrying her. She lost her ugly sneakers and socks on the porch, her top by the door and her bra by the table. The next thing she knew, she was flat on her back and Rebel was peeling her jeans and panties off her in one smooth motion.

The cool air hit all of her hot spots—her hottest spot—and the shiver rocked her at the same time another spasm did. She convulsed so hard the whole bed squeaked dangerously.

Not that she cared. What she cared about right now, at this very second, was Rebel undressing. Her clothes might have come off in a flurry, but his were going much slower. *This man*, she thought, stuck somewhere between amusement and irritation. *He drives me crazy.*

The shirt was unbuttoned first, and she managed to keep her little noises to herself when all those muscles were laid bare again. She'd seen that before. But the pain of holding it in had her eyes fluttering, and she almost missed the best part.

God, he was so good with his hands, and he wasn't even touching her. Just watching him undo the buckle and then the button fly was enough to bring tears to her eyes.

Oh, it hurt, hurt so deeply that the pain took over and left her unable to do anything, not a single thing a mature,

172

experienced woman would do in a situation like this. She couldn't suggestively offer to remove those jeans for him, couldn't tell him that she'd roll the condom on and a whole lot more, couldn't even say that she'd never seen a man as physically gifted as he so clearly was.

He wasn't circumcised. Bigger than Darrin was too, to say nothing of Bryce and his immaturity personified. Bigger, but not *too* big.

The pain rippled out from her center and threatened to rip her in two. It hurt so bad that she started to moan.

"Wait for me," he scolded. And then he had the condom on and was spreading her legs out as far as they would go. He crawled between them, the bed shuddering as first one knee, then the second hit the sheets.

Come on, she thought, surprised at her own impatience. She was splitting in two, right down the middle. Only he could make her whole again, and he didn't seem to be in a huge hurry.

Come. On. Please. But the words wouldn't come

"My," he grunted as flesh hit flesh without a moment to spare. "My Madeline."

And then he was inside her, and she couldn't tell if he just made her that much wetter than she'd ever been or if the condom was extra lubricated, but he slid in with no resistance.

Everything spasmed in a blinding flash of pleasure that erased any trace of the pain. Her muscles clamped down on any and every part of him she could touch. She tried to bite back the scream and managed just to bite his shoulder.

And then she was empty.

And alone.

For a hysterical moment, she was afraid she'd dreamed the whole thing, the most terrifyingly real wet-dream she'd ever had. But then her eyes decided to focus again and she saw that he was sitting on his heels, digging around for something on the floor.

What was he doing? Getting dressed? *Leaving?* One fucking thrust—literally—and that was it?

What had she done?

"Rebel?" Excellent. Even to her own ears, she sounded like she was going to cry. Hell, if he was leaving, she really would break in two.

Then he stood and turned, and she saw the two condoms in his hand. "I—sorry, Madeline," he said, his voice in that low growl that had gotten her into this position. "I just—so sorry, babe. But give me a minute." And he crawled back into bed, back between her legs, back to where she was still slick and wet. "Just a minute."

The light bulb went off when his mouth found one breast as his hips began to move again, and she felt as foolish as she could while still experiencing this much arousal. Technically, that was a premature ejaculation.

"Been so long," Rebel murmured as he moved to her other nipple. He licked, then sucked in a deep breath. The cool air rushed over the wetness he'd left on her skin, and she shook. Then his mouth fell on her again, like she was the perfect tip of a soft-serve cone and he was hungry. "You were so… " Another lick, another breath, another shaking shiver. "I wasn't ready." He reached down between her legs and hit the spot that hadn't split in two, hadn't healed whole yet. "I'll be ready this time."

She opened her mouth, wanting to tell him that it was okay, no really, it was—words she'd said before, on a semi-regular basis to Darrin. Words she'd maybe come to believe just a little too much. But she didn't get the chance before those hands were being so very good to her. And nothing came out of her mouth.

As one, then two fingers rubbed in and his thumb rubbed out, the spasms shook her again and again. But this time, they didn't hurt. This time, the spasms were nothing but warm waves of satisfaction, each leaving her more limp than the last.

She felt so good, so much better than she'd ever felt. He hadn't left her—no, instead, he'd come back with reinforcements and a promise of more, better, best. Neither of her previous lovers had ever come back for her. No one had ever given her what she wanted. No one had ever even tried to guess what she really needed.

Rebel did. And he was going to do it again.

The minute must have been up because he sat back on his heels and rolled on the second condom. Then he grabbed her legs and tucked her knees up under his arms.

"What—" What, what? Just admit that she had no idea what he was doing? That she'd never done anything more adventurous than the standard missionary?

He froze. She could feel him, just inches from being back inside her. "You trust me?"

Well, hell. She was in no position to argue otherwise. And she wanted him. She could only hope it wouldn't be too weird. "Yes."

"Then trust me." With her legs still captive to his arms, he leaned forward, plunged in, and—and—

Light whiteness flooded her system, again and again, until she thought she would burn up from the heat. She wasn't doing anything—anything but holding onto those biceps for dear life. He was doing it all, and, oh, God, he was doing it all so much better than she'd even allowed herself to think. Each stroke in was much tighter around him than even that first thrust. Each pull back hit something new inside her, something she was certain she'd never known was there before. And through it all, Rebel's hips kept pace with the low moaning of her name, the sound of pure sex on the wind.

"Mad-e-line," he repeated, over and over, leaning down and thrusting harder and harder until he couldn't say anything.

Until she couldn't keep the scream inside. As it flowed out of her, everything—her mind, her hands, her legs, her everything—clamped down with enough force that even Rebel couldn't stroke his way through it. But maybe he didn't need to, because his head shook down, surrounding her in black silk, and he shuddered as she held him still.

And then they collapsed into each other, panting.

He didn't say anything, She felt like she should be saying—doing—something, but what? Thank him for the amazing orgasm? *Thank you*—please. It would sound like he'd washed her car or something. Tell him he was the best she'd ever had? Shit. Could that get any more trite?

Tell him she loved him?

Did she love him?

Rebel rolled off her, which was a condom-driven necessity, she knew. But she wanted to hold on to him in an irrational sort of way that had nothing to do with proper usage of prophylactics. Even as he sat on the edge of the bed, she kept her hand on the small of his back until he stood and headed for the bathroom.

Yes. Right. She needed to get cleaned up too. Using the bathroom after intercourse helped flush the system, reducing urinary tract infections. She knew that, had told countless teenaged girls that.

But she didn't want to get out of the bed, most especially if he got back in it.

She didn't have a choice. "Your turn, beautiful," he said as he walked around her cabin, art in motion.

And still, she couldn't say anything for fear the wrong thing would come out, starting with, "Will you still be here when I get out?" and ending with, "I love you." She couldn't tell which one would be worse. She only knew they'd both come out wrong.

She hurried, thinking, *please be there, please don't leave*, even as she was fully aware she was being ridiculous. He'd already sent that horse home. He wouldn't get far, right?

She came flying out of the bathroom faster than she knew was prudent, but she couldn't help herself. When it came to Rebel, she was increasingly unable to help herself, she realized.

He was on the bed, thank God, the sheet draped just so around his waist and nothing else. "I haven't slept in a bed in a long time." He was half asleep, she realized, his accent a whole lot thicker than normal. "If it's okay with you... "

"Stay, stay." Finally—she'd not only said something, but given the smile that managed to tug his lips up, it had been the right something.

She slid in next to him, and his hand draped over her waist until it was nestled between her breast and the bed. His skin, pressed along her entire back, felt cool against hers. "Madeline," he murmured in her ear. "My love." And then his body relaxed and his breath evened out.

My love.

She lay there a long time, feeling him twitch through dreams of God-only-knew-what, repeating those two words over and over.

My love.

His.

Rebel stood in the shower. Well, it was supposed to be a shower, he guessed. He remembered that the British had once called the first bathrooms water closets, back when he cared enough about British art to take three whole classes on it. That's what her bathroom was, a water closet. The concrete shower floor was a step down from the bathroom floor, which led him to suspect someone had cut a hole in the floor to wedge this thing in here. He had no idea what kept her pipes from freezing in the winter—but then, she probably didn't, either. He had just about a foot and a half of elbow room, front and back, so he kept banging into the caddy full of smoothing shampoos and taming conditioners Madeline had hung over the showerhead.

But the water was hot, so he had nothing to complain about. It was a piss-poor shower, but it beat the hell out of the one he didn't have. And, after all, he thought with a shake of his head, his hair would be smooth after this.

He grinned again. Maybe he should have awoken

her before the shower. He'd thought about it for a long time this morning after the birds started singing. But, frankly, he probably needed a day or two to recover from last night. His groin muscles felt like they'd run 26.2 miles by themselves, although his dick was not complaining. Well, maybe just a little. Besides, she'd been too pretty to wake up.

Madeline liked to sleep on her back. When he'd woken up this morning, the sheet had been down around her hips, leaving the canvas of her flesh bare for him to study. She had faint tan lines around her wrist and neck, but not on her face, which was most likely explained by the different lotions with various SPFs she had crammed around the bar sink in the bathroom. The hair below her belly and on her arms was pale and faint, just catching the morning light that filtered through the window above the kitchen sink, giving her a little bit of an ethereal glow.

Her mouth had been open, just a little, and the corners had curved up with a delicateness that seemed at odds with the toughness with which she normally carried herself. Add in that natural blush that gave her cheeks a hint of rose, and she looked like a woman who had gotten exactly what she wanted in bed.

He hadn't picked up a paint brush in a long time, not since he'd left New Mexico, but he was unexpectedly itching to paint her, nude like this, something between Titian and Marilyn Monroe. A beauty for the ages.

He found himself staring at that sink of lotions and makeup. Maybe a third of what Anna had constantly cluttered up their apartment bathroom with. The bathroom said low-maintenance.

179

But it didn't say no maintenance.

Wrapping himself in the only towel he could find, he tiptoed out. She was on her side now, but her eyes were still closed and, after a minute of watching her, her chest still rose and fell evenly. So she wasn't a top-of-the-morning kind of person. *Or maybe*, he thought with proud grin, *she's just a little more tired than normal.*

Nothing some coffee couldn't fix.

Except that meant he'd have to make some coffee. He stood in front of the contraption and tried to remember how to make coffee in something that didn't involve an open fire. Well, first, a man had to locate the various parts.

He had his head poked under the sink, trying to find a filter or something, when the coffeemaker above him beeped, startling him so that he hit the back of his head on the counter. The coffee was brewing automatically. *How about that*, he thought, staring at the darn thing. Who knew? Coffeemakers that made their own coffee.

Sure, this cabin was cramped, but really, it wasn't too bad. Hot water, automatic coffee pots, soft bed with a soft woman in it. It was the kind of thing a man could get used to, especially when the winter winds began to blow.

But if he got too used to this, then that would mean no more tents, no more rivers, no more forests. And, as low maintenance as Madeline seemed, she didn't strike him as the kind of woman who would give up automatic coffee, hot showers and soft beds on a permanent basis.

His gut sank a little.

He heard the bed squeak at the same time she said, "Good morning."

Yeah, it had been good, right up until reality smacked him in the face. He couldn't bring himself to turn around and see her right now, because an ethereal beauty like her was just that, ethereal. So light and delicate that she would float away on the breeze.

"Your coffee makes itself."

She giggled. "You didn't know that?" The bed squeaked again. Sounded like she was standing now. "Coffee does that now. I'm beginning to think you have a predilection for towels."

"Pink's not my color." Yeah, right, this was all normal. *Normal in that temporary, short-lived kind of way*, he thought as his gut took another turn south. "Sorry. It was the only one I could find."

Maybe not normal. She didn't say anything, and it didn't sound like she was moving either. And still, he couldn't turn around.

"Rebel?" All traces of light-hearted banter were gone now, and he heard the worry, loud and clear.

And then he remembered murmuring *my love* last night.

"Is everything okay?" she went on, sounding smaller and smaller.

Shit and double shit. Not only was this whole thing doomed, he was dooming it a whole lot faster by being an A-number-one asshole. "Yeah, yeah." *Suck it up. Suck it up and take it like a man.* He turned around.

Triple shit. Madeline—his Madeline—was standing two feet from him, that sheet wound around her as she clutched the front with one hand. Her hair was wild, curls springing out in all directions with

181

happy abandon, which made the confusion in her eyes that much more painful. She looked like something out of a Degas painting, the form and the function of art embodied with the soul of a woman.

God, it hurt to look at her.

Then, right before his eyes, she was gone, and Dr. Mitchell was standing before him. One hand jabbed onto a hip, and the confusion was erased with furrowed brows and set lips. "Look," she began, and he only heard a whisper of tremor in her voice, "if this is about last night... " But she couldn't finish the sentence without closing her eyes, like she was bracing for the worst.

Not last night, he wanted to tell her. Not last night. This morning. The world was a different place in the light of day. "I was just thinking we should get going. Nobody's waiting on us at the clinic, you know."

Eyes still scrunched shut, she nodded. "Sure. Yeah." Then those ice-blues opened, and Madeline was right there, scared. Of him. Of what he would say. "Will I... " She took a deep breath, squared her shoulders and started over with a hell of a lot more bravado than he was expecting. "Will I see you again tonight?" like he was scheduling a check-up, not like he was her lover.

Shit, he hadn't even gotten to tonight. The list of things he had to do today began to run through his head like a Rolodex at top speed. Steinman at the gallery wanted five more bags before the Christmas season. He needed to take the rest of the groceries to the elders who had no way of getting to the party last night. And then there was Albert. "I have to check on Albert and start on the sweat lodge." That was the top of the list. Albert couldn't wait.

That look would have been tearful if she hadn't been so mean about it. She was doing it again, ignoring what her body was saying. "Of course. I know you're not used to being at certain places at certain times. You're quite busy." She turned away from him, that sloped shoulder filling the room with cold. "I'll be ready in twenty minutes, if you can wait that long."

The unspoken words—if not, he could just walk his ass out of here—hung in the room long after she shut the bathroom door with enough force to shake the jerry-rigged walls.

He'd waited six years for a woman like her.

He knew he'd have to wait for forever to find another one who even came close.

After a drive that gave new meaning to the word *chilly*, they made it to the clinic by 7:40. And the whole time, Rebel was trying to figure out what the hell he should do and getting nowhere.

He felt like the best course of action would be to go into the sweat lodge and ask Albert about it, but the lodge wasn't for him. It was for Albert. That's what he had to remember, he decided as she parked the Jeep. Right now, he had to focus on Albert. Madeline would be here long after Albert had crossed on over.

"I don't see him," Madeline said in that same pissy tone of voice. "I thought he said he was going to be here, guarding the place."

Rebel was going to owe an apology to Tara and Clarence for getting Madeline into this state. He didn't have much left after the grocery run—only a couple hundred bucks. Maybe if he gave her the money left over from the bag? That would still be enough for some supplies, wouldn't it?

"Just because you can't see him doesn't mean he's not here."

On command, part of the wall separated from the shadows on the west side of the building and Nobody stepped into the sun.

Madeline gasped a little but kept her composure. She just took it all in stride, he thought again, and his gut ached a little more. He'd never find another woman like her.

"Morning, Nobody."

Nobody tipped his hat. "Ma'am."

Madeline looked at him like he was a teenager and curfew had been about twelve hours ago. "Did you have a quiet night?"

"Yes, ma'am."

She let go a weighty breath. She hadn't seemed the least bit worried about potential vandals last night, but she still seemed relieved. "Did you write a list of symptoms like I asked?"

Nobody fished something light brown out of his back pocket. "Yes, ma'am," he said, handing it over.

"A paper bag?"

Rebel bit back the grin as Madeline's scowl deepened. Later, he'd apologize to Nobody, too. Hell, at the rate he was going, he was going to owe the whole tribe an apology for unleashing the mad doctor on them.

"All I had, ma'am," Nobody replied, managing to look sheepish about it. Then his head snapped up and he stared off down the road. "How long will it take?" he asked as he began to edge back into the shadows.

"Four to six weeks," she replied, looking a little concerned. "Where are you going?"

"Someone's coming," was the only answer she got before he was gone.

Seconds later, Clarence's truck rattled around the corner. "Nobody was never here," Rebel whispered as he too took a step away from her. Madeline stiffened at the motion.

Which was ridiculous, after all. They'd left together last night, and were standing here, together, at the clinic before eight in the morning. A man would have to be an idiot not to put one and one together, and Clarence was no idiot.

But all Rebel could think was that this wasn't going to last, because she couldn't give up a house and he couldn't give up the stars, and when it ended—which, at the rate he was screwing it up, was going to be sooner rather than later—he wanted her to be able to hold her head high.

He was going to hurt her, and she was going to take a chunk out of him that he wasn't sure he'd ever get back, all because he hadn't been able to swear her off. He would get what he deserved.

"Morning, Doc. Morning, Rebel," Clarence said, his eyes shifting between the two of them. He must have caught a whiff of Madeline's cold shoulder, because he made straight for the clinic. "I'll, uh, just get that coffee going."

Rebel heard her make a guttural noise that sounded a hell of a lot like she was growling. *So much for holding her head high*, he thought as she swung those cold shoulders and colder eyes to him.

"You're still here." She sounded pissed and

185

confused, but not even a little bit happy. "Is there something else you wanted?"

What he wanted was for the world to go back to the way it had been before she'd come here and taken everything he'd worked so hard to become and tossed it all on its ear. What he wanted was to be beholden to no one and nothing, to come and go as he saw fit.

And what he wanted was another night in her arms, to kiss that perma-scowl away from her face and to plunge into her body again and again until she screamed his name and drained him of everything he ever had to give.

And, more than anything, he wanted those two things to be the same thing. But they weren't and would never be, and the sooner they both saw that, the better off they'd be.

Then he remembered the filing cabinets. If he helped her get her filing cabinets, that would count for something, right? "Did you want me to go with you to get some filing cabinets this weekend?"

She stared at him like he'd asked her how she liked Tupperware. He saw her swallow once, then again as her eyes narrowed into fine slits. *Here it comes.* And he had it coming.

"You do what you want. I know you always do."

And she left him alone in the middle of the parking lot.

Chapter Twelve

Madeline let her hair stay curly, although she wasn't exactly sure why. She could come up with a couple of perfectly good reasons if she thought about it hard enough. Getting out the door was a hell of a lot easier when she didn't have to fry her hair one lock at a time. Everyone had already seen it, and showing up with straight hair would probably set more tongues wagging.

She could look in a mirror now and not shudder at the sight of her mop. It was kind of pretty, she had to admit, especially after she started wrapping each curl around her finger to set it, as per Melonie's long-distance instructions. She liked it. After all these years, she finally liked her own hair.

But, solid as each of those reasons were, they weren't *the* reason. *He* was the reason, damn it. She just couldn't figure out if she was hoping to woo Rebel back with it, or torture him some more by letting him see and not touch.

Because he was never going to touch again. Period, end of sentence.

God, what had she done? Screwed up, that's what. She'd screwed up in a highly old-fashioned kind of way, losing her head and a whole lot more to a smooth-talking, untamed bad boy. Plus, she'd slept with a—well, he wasn't exactly a patient, but he paid the bills. More like a client. She'd slept with a client, and had put the entire financial health of the clinic on the line. If Rebel stopped paying everyone's bills, the clinic would go under faster than the *Titanic*. She only had so much money to work with, and her selfish *wants* and *needs* had put the clinic and the wellbeing of the entire damn reservation in danger of sinking.

And for what? For a one-night stand? So what if one night with Rebel had been mind-bogglingly good? So what if she was suddenly unsure if she could live without that kind of personal attention, that kind of shattering release? So what if she felt whole again? So *what*? He'd made it perfectly clear how he felt the morning after. Hey, thanks, she was a swell kid, maybe he'd call her some time. A one-time deal. It wouldn't happen again, and she was all the more fool for even having believed it might. He'd sworn off women. He'd said so himself.

Against her will, she still tingled at the thought of *it* happening at all.

A week passed. A long week. A week that had her sitting on her porch at sundown, drinking wine until the sky went as dark as she felt.

And, of course, Rebel hadn't shown up during the week. She'd hoped—against her will—that he would show up on Thursday to mop the floors and that she might be able to figure out what she'd done wrong so she could try to fix it, but no. Instead, Nobody Bodine had just appeared in the waiting room and began to empty the trashcans without a word. Her blood had boiled. Rebel wouldn't even face her. He sent his lackey instead.

So she'd driven herself to Rapid City and coldly flirted with the office-supply stock manager until he'd loaded the cabinets for her. Strangely enough, Nobody had been waiting in the shadows for her Monday morning and had gotten both of them out of the trunk and unpacked in the corner of the waiting room Tara had cleaned out before Clarence showed up.

She wanted to be mad at the big, silent man, but there was little good in that. It wasn't Nobody's fault Rebel was an asshole, and besides, Madeline was still a little afraid of him. So they kept their conversations to pleases and thank yous and yes, ma'ams, and the world kept on turning. People still got sick, the sun rose and set, and she ran out of iodine again.

Her world kept right on turning.

Without Rebel in it.

Bambambam.

Madeline shot straight up in bed, her heart pounding. What the hell?

Bambambam.

Someone was pounding on her door at—she rolled over and looked at her clock. 12:47 in the morning? Someone was pounding on her door at 12:47?

By the third round of pounding, she was up and out of bed, shrugging into her summer-weight bathrobe as she dug around the island drawer for a knife. Just in case.

"Who is it?"

"Madeline?" the muffled voice shouted. "It's me. Open up!"

Me? Me who? Grabbing the biggest knife she could find, she attempted to shake the last of the cobwebs from her head and tried to place the voice. For a heart-stopping second, she was certain that Darrin had shown up, driven all night to beg and plead for her to come with him, come home back to Ohio, back where she belonged.

The thought terrified her.

Knife at the ready, she opened the door a crack. A shaft of light spilled out of the doorway and right onto Rebel.

"It's me," he repeated, but without all the shouting this time.

Her mouth fell open. What was he doing here, standing on the steps of her porch? No, he wasn't just standing. He was *swaying*, for God's sake, hips swaying from side to side like he was a cobra and she had a flute. Her heart did that weird lurching thing again, and for a split second, she was not only glad to see him, but really regretting not sleeping in something a whole lot prettier than a tank top and flannel shorts.

Rebel cleared his throat, breaking her spell. "Is that a knife?"

She looked at the knife, a big santoku that she rarely used because it didn't come with a can-opener attachment. Jeez, it seemed even bigger in the pale light. And then she realized that perhaps she wasn't as awake as she'd like to think.

Rebel took a step back. "I, uh, I need you."

"Really?" Damn, she really wasn't as awake as she wanted to be. She was hoping for a cool, don't-give-a-shit attitude, and instead, she sounded like a hopeful teenager. She tried again. "Is that so?" There. That was better.

"Could you put the knife down?" Well, at least he sounded properly cowed. Next time he'd think twice before angling for a late-night booty call.

She glared at him as best she could, but he didn't seem dangerous. At least, not any more than someone in those jeans normally did. "What do you want, Rebel?" She honestly couldn't tell what she hoped he would say.

Keeping one eye on the knife, he answered, "Albert. He's, well, I think he's having a heart attack."

She froze. A heart attack. That irregular heartbeat hadn't been normal, and she'd been so wrapped up in her selfish little world that she hadn't followed through like she should have.

"Come with me," Rebel said, keeping his voice low and cautious. "He wants to see you."

Albert needed her. The paralysis snapped and suddenly she was a whirl of motion. She raced back into the house, grabbing her pants and throwing her keys at Rebel at the same time. "Here. Get the Jeep started."

By the time she got a T-shirt pulled on and her sneakers scooped up, he already had the Jeep parallel with the porch. She didn't even have the door shut, and they were off.

"What are his symptoms? How long has he been having them?" she asked as she tried to cram a foot into a sneaker while the Jeep bumped over the gravel.

"He can't move his left arm at all this time."

"*This* time?" No, she had to have heard that wrong. That would mean that not only had Albert already had a heart attack, but Rebel had known about it. And done nothing.

Rebel nodded, looking far calmer than she felt, because she felt like she was about to lose it. "The first time, he just fainted. The second time—"

"The *second* time?"

"Madeline." Was he scolding her? "I need you to calm down."

"I need to have you arrested for elder abuse," she snapped back. And she'd thought he was just a danger to her mental health? Damn it all, the man was a menace to society. "You intentionally withheld medical treatment from a man suffering from cardiac arrest? I swear to God, Rebel, if you weren't driving, I'd punch you myself."

"I didn't withhold anything. I didn't even realize he'd had one the first time, and I brought you to see him that evening. Remember?" He looked at her out of the corner of his eyes. "Remember?"

She could not remember ever being this mad. It was one thing to be furious when Rebel wouldn't tell her his name or how he paid those bills. But this was different. This was a matter of life and death, and he was acting like the mere mention of her one-night mistake would somehow make it all better. "Yeah, sure, I remember. I remember you sweet-talking your way into my bed and then acting like I'd trapped you the next morning. I remember you not showing up for days on end, and I remember you not bringing Albert to the clinic after the second one. I would certainly remember it if you had brought your grandfather to see me because he had chest pains."

"You don't understand."

"I don't understand? Fuck you, Rebel. I understand perfectly. I understand that Albert's had three heart attacks and if he dies, I understand perfectly that it'll be because of you. I understand that you'll have killed him."

The Jeep squealed to a stop so hard that she just missed banging her forehead on the dash.

"You. Do. Not. Understand." The way he said it, like not only did he believe it, but he'd fight to the death for it, whatever it was.

It scared the hell out of her. "Jesus, Rebel!"

"Albert is *dying*," he went on, ignoring her. Just like he always did. "He refused to *let* me bring him in after that first time. He forbid me from *getting* you the second time. I haven't left his side in days because I've been trying to convince him to let me take him to the hospital. He is dying, Madeline. It is his fate, and he is ready. What you don't understand is that it isn't the end. That's not what we believe."

His gaze was steady, his voice even. She could see the steady beat of blood through his jugular. He was telling the truth. Or thought he was, anyway. "So what do you believe? If he's given up, why are you pissing me off in the middle of the night?"

Everything hard about the man got something closer to gentle. "You've got to believe me, Madeline. He didn't want you to worry, that's why he kept quiet."

Lord, not that, not the special way he said her name that was his and his alone. Not when she was so mad at him. "So why now?"

"He wants to say goodbye." He must have seen something in her face that he took as an invitation, because he reached over and stroked her cheek. "This isn't the end, Madeline. It's just the next step."

She lurched away from that touch. No touching, none. Period, end of sentence. "I don't believe you. I want to see him for myself."

"Done." And they were off again, barreling down roads she could barely see.

When they got to Albert's house, Madeline was

surprised by the number of cars there. Not as many as had been at the party the other night, but still, there were maybe ten. Rebel sped past all of them and nearly parked on the front step.

"Should I even bother to ask you to carry the duffel?"

"If it will make you feel better," was the only answer she got before he hauled it out.

In they went. The first thing she saw was that Jesse wasn't occupying the couch any more. Instead, he was leaning against the door. "Doc, I'm glad you're here," he said, the strain in his voice more notable than it had been in Rebel's. He appeared almost upset.

"What's going on, Jesse?" Not that she particularly trusted Jesse—he seemed like the textbook definition of irresponsible—but she needed a viewpoint different from Rebel's, and Jesse lived here.

"He's been holding on for you, I think, but he's fading." He sort of pivoted to Rebel. "I was afraid you wouldn't get back in time."

Rebel set the duffel down and then pulled a small bundle out of his shirt. "I'm ready," he said, cutting through the crowd and kneeling down next to Albert.

Madeline recognized most everyone here. Walter White Mouse was sitting with two older men in a far corner, chanting and lightly beating a drum. Tara was here, holding a sleeping Nelly on her shoulder. "Doctor, I mean, Madeline." She was somber, but she didn't sound upset. "It's his time."

God, what if Rebel had been telling the truth? What if Albert hadn't let him come get her? What if he didn't want to be saved?

What if he died?

Suddenly, the lump in the back of her throat was huge and oppressive. Rebel was on his knees, holding Albert's good hand in his and speaking in a low, soothing tone. Irma was behind Albert, wiping his head with a damp cloth. No one was acting like a crime—a murder—was occurring before them. And no one in the room was upset or mad or even confused about what was going on. Just her.

Rebel looked to her, his eyes wide and knowing. "Come," he said, still speaking in a low tone. "He's been waiting for you."

She dug out the nitroglycerin pills. "Albert, take one of these. Please," she added when she got down to his level.

He let go of Rebel's hand just long enough to wave the vial off. "Don't worry," he said in English, which just about knocked her on her butt. But between the accent and the slurring that indicated he might also be having a stroke, he was almost impossible to understand. "It's okay."

Then he switched to Lakota, which seemed less difficult. Rebel began translating. "It is a good day to die," and every head in the room nodded in agreement. "We will meet again on the other side." Then he looked at Rebel, and patted his face. "I am..." Rebel's voice faltered a little. Albert repeated it, so Rebel kept translating. "I am proud of you, my son. You will be happy when you find your own way. No one else's."

The lump in her throat got bigger, and no amount of swallowing was budging the damn thing. Why wasn't Rebel more upset by this? He'd said it himself—Albert made him everything he was. Why

195

wasn't he fighting for his grandfather? Why was he just *letting* him go?

Then Albert looked at Madeline. "Don't worry," he said in English again. "It's okay."

God, she didn't want to let Albert go. He was just a kind old man, a rock of goodness in this strange place, who seemed a hell of a lot more worried about her than he was about himself. She didn't know if it was proper to touch him or not, but she didn't care. She ran her hand down his face. "Thank you, Albert." She wasn't exactly sure what she was thanking him for, but that didn't matter. What mattered was Albert. And he'd wanted her here, like she was a part of the family.

The room was silent except for the steady sound of the drumbeat from the corner. The three men there kept chanting, the sound growing louder and louder as Albert's breath got shallower and shallower.

No! No, she prayed. It wasn't too late. She lurched forward to begin chest compressions. She could save him. She knew she could.

Rebel latched onto her arm. "Let him go, Madeline." He was doing it again, using that calm voice. "It's his time."

She tried to shake him off, but he wasn't having any of it. "This is ridiculous!" she hissed. "He's dying!"

He tightened his fingers as he hauled her to her feet and backed her away from Albert. "We all die," he said in her ear as he stood her next to Tara. "Today is as good a day as any."

"Here," Tara whispered, and suddenly Madeline found herself holding the dead weight of a sleeping kindergartner. "Thanks."

Damn it, she was trapped, and all she could do was watch Albert's breathing get slower and slower. Rebel lit something on fire and held it near Albert, but the old man didn't move, except to draw in another breath. The seconds between one breath and the next stretched as time got blurry. No matter how much she blinked, the whole world just got blurrier. She could barely breathe, her throat was so closed up.

Albert's chest rose. And fell.

And didn't rise again.

The chanting from the corner peaked in a jarringly happy crescendo as Rebel did something she couldn't see. The world had gotten too blurry, and all she could do was clutch Nelly to her chest because she needed to hold onto someone, someone real and solid and still breathing. Even asleep, Nelly felt like the safest person in the world right now.

Time stayed stretched. People started to move around, some of them even coming up to say things to her she couldn't understand. She could tell they were talking to her, but the words all came out garbled. Maybe she signed the death certificate, maybe not. She didn't know. Nothing anyone said or did made any sense.

Rebel was next to her, prying her arms away from Nelly. Madeline clung briefly, but then Tara was there, taking her child back.

"Thank you, Madeline," Tara said, She sounded like she was whispering at the end of a great tunnel. "Thank you for everything."

For what? *Everything*? She hadn't done *anything*, nothing she should have. She should have made Albert take the nitro pill and done chest compressions and mouth-to-mouth and gotten the man to a damn hospital. She should have *tried* to save him. But she hadn't—she'd just let him die.

She'd just let him die.

She opened her mouth to say as much, and nothing came out but dead silence.

Rebel was still next to her. She thought he seemed upset too, finally upset. One arm was around her shoulders, and she found herself in a firm hug. "Don't cry," he whispered, so low that no one else could hear it. "It's okay, babe."

Not cry? What the hell? This was like some horrible, first-person version of *The Twilight Zone*, where doctors let people die and no one cried.

"It's not okay," she managed to get out. She sounded like she was choking. "He's gone."

The arms around her tightened. "You need to get out of here?"

Maybe she nodded or said yes or did something—she couldn't tell, but then they were moving, his arm still holding her shoulders to his chest, still holding her together as the clear air hit her in the face. "We're going, babe," he said a little louder now. "Almost to the car." But then he pulled up short.

She blinked, and blinked again, and the world un-blurred enough that she could see a dark shadow separate from a car.

"A good death?" Nobody Bodine asked.

She did *not* know what was going on. A good death? What the hell was that?

"Yes. He went with peace." Rebel answered like he knew exactly what Nobody was talking about, which only added to her Twilight Zone sense of things. "It's good you were here."

She couldn't be sure, but it looked like Nobody was somehow embarrassed by this statement. And then he turned to her. "Ma'am." And he was gone again.

Nothing. She understood nothing about any of this, but she was pretty sure Rebel had been telling the truth earlier. Albert had been calm, not agitated, not scared. Certainly not a prisoner in his own home. And Rebel didn't seem like a murderer. He seemed like, well, a medicine man taking care of his people. His grandfather.

She was the one who'd been wrong. Completely, totally, wrong. About everything.

Especially Rebel.

"I'm so sorry," she choked out as Rebel put her back in the Jeep.

"Don't be." How could he sound so normal, so calm even after watching his grandfather die? "It's okay, Madeline. It really is."

"But you let him go. I let him go." Saying it out loud made it all the more horrible to her own ears and, in the enclosed privacy of her Jeep, she began to cry. "I didn't do anything—nothing I should have. You didn't let me."

"You did everything you needed to," he countered in that damningly calm voice again.

For the second time that evening, she thought about punching him, just to get some sort of reaction out of him.

"He wanted you there. He wanted to say goodbye, to say not to worry. What else was there to do?"

"You—I—we let him go, Rebel. I didn't even fight for him. I didn't even put up a fight." The tears came harder now, choking up her words and making the world one giant blur. "I failed."

He sat quiet while she sobbed. Strangely, it didn't help her feel any better. Instead, she felt like she always had back in all those advanced math classes she'd had to take because she was just smart enough. She knew there was something she *should* be understanding, something she was fully capable of understanding that was right there in front of her, but she couldn't get it. She was just spinning her wheels in the mud, and that upset her all over again.

"Sometimes, you have to let people go." The car stopped, and she was surprised to see that they were in front of her dinky cabin. It looked lost and forlorn in the woods. Alone.

God, she didn't want to be alone. She was tired of being the person people needed for one moment, one crisis at a time. And as soon as that crisis had passed, they went on their way without a look back at her. She didn't want to be the person everyone needed and no one wanted anymore. Not anymore. "What about me?"

His eyes found hers, and she saw. She saw who she really was reflected back in those endless black eyes. Someone whose two halves could make a whole. *Please*, she found herself praying. *Please.*

"What about you?" It came out soft.

Please. "Will you just let *me* go? Without a fight?" *Please.*

The blackness ended as he looked out the windshield. She saw his hands flex around the wheel.

The shame was like a sledgehammer right down the middle of the two halves that would never, ever be a whole. The pain was so intense that she could only feel it in a disembodied kind of way, like it was someone else breaking to bits in the front seat, not her.

Another night with Rebel, another screw up. Of course he'd let her go. His own wife had walked away, and he'd never gone after her. His wife. And who was she? Who was Dr. Madeline Mitchell? Nothing but a stupid white woman who'd thought she could do a little good in this world, one patient at a time.

She couldn't even cry. She could for Albert, because she'd lost him forever. But she had nothing left to lose. Least of all herself.

Suddenly, Rebel was out of the car, moving silently through the night. Her door flew open, and he lifted her out and cradled her to his chest.

"Rebel?" But he didn't answer, and he didn't set her down either. Instead, he carried her across the cabin threshold like she was a new bride, not an utter failure of a woman.

He didn't let her go, not when he kicked off his boots, not when he sat on the bed and held her even tighter, and not when he kissed her. "My Mad-e-line." His voice shook almost as much as his hand when he stroked her cheek. "You don't understand."

"I don't understand anything." Least of all why he was stroking her hair and kissing the tears away from her cheeks. Why he was peeling the T-shirt off, then her tank top. Why he was laying her out on the bed, then taking her jeans off. Why he was stripping off his own clothes as if they were on fire, and why he was rolling on a condom.

"I don't understand anything," she whispered again as he found his way back inside her, each gentle thrust tying all the little shards of her back together until she stopped caring about understanding anything, anything but the way he held her legs, the way he

201

wrapped her hair around his fingers, the way he kissed her like forgiveness was on her lips.

She didn't understand, but her body did, and it shuddered around his until she cried out, the relief at being wanted, really and truly wanted for who she was, not what she did so strong that it crested over the orgasm. The waves of release left her unable to do anything but hold on for dear life as he moaned her name to a finish against her neck.

He pulled out, but he didn't leave her. He rolled onto his back, pulling her into his arms and running his fingers through her hair. She clung to his chest, warm and solid and there. He was there. With her.

She couldn't ever remember being this tired, not even when she was pulling a thirty-six-hour shift in the E.R. Then, she'd just been physically tired. Now, she was emotionally drained on top of being exhausted. And Rebel's warmth was fast lulling her into sleep. But she fought against it because he hadn't answered the question, the one question that held her world in the balance.

She had to know. "Please." The effort to get the word out was just enough to send her rushing toward the inky darkness of sleep.

He sighed as he stroked her hair, the motion hypnotizing her. It sounded like surrender to her fading ears. "I will never let you go, Madeline. I couldn't, even if I tried."

Never.

She drifted off, feeling wanted and loved for the first time ever.

Feeling whole.

And she knew he'd still be there in the morning.

Chapter Thirteen

Rebel sat on the edge of the bed, waiting. He didn't want to wake her up, but the coffee had already made itself, Blue Eye was pawing around outside and Albert wasn't getting any deader. He needed to get going before the sun started racing across the sky.

But he didn't want to wake her. It was easier to ignore the complications of his reality when her eyes were closed, her hand tossed over her head as her chest rose and fell, one perfect breast exposed for his eyes only. Like a composition, her form was balanced in a perfect function of femininity.

A loud clomp came from the front of the house, followed by another. The floor trembled under his feet. Damn. His reality could *not* be ignored, not when Blue Eye was standing on the porch. If he didn't get his ass in gear, that mare would be inside in minutes. Madeline didn't like horses in the clinic. He was sure she wouldn't want one in her cabin. Short of him just leaving, he couldn't imagine a worse way for her to wake up.

He leaned over and kissed her, fighting the urge to let his hands get underneath the sheets and do the waking for him. Instead, he just licked her lips until she startled beneath him. Slowly, her eyes opened.

Man, he hated to wake her. Her eyes were still bloodshot from too much crying and too little sleep, and the way she scrunched them shut made him think she was working on a hell of a headache. Still, she kissed him back as she touched his cheek, like she was making sure he was real and not a dream.

"Good morning, Madeline."

Her eyes cracked open again with a tired smile. "Hmph. What time is it?"

Damn reality. Always complicating things. "Almost six thirty. I need to get going." For a second, she just looked at him, like he'd said something in Lakota instead of English. Then her eyes closed again as she turned her head away and pulled the sheet up high. She looked like he'd slapped her in slow motion. Always easier to jump to conclusions when she wasn't awake yet. That had been his problem last time. She'd started jumping and he'd just let her go. This time, he wasn't going to make things worse. Not if he could help it. "Have you ever gone camping?"

Eyes suddenly wide, she turned to look at him. "Not really. Why?"

That was better. At least she didn't look like he was wounding her again. "It's Saturday."

"And?"

"I've got to take Albert to the funeral home in town. And while I'm there, I'll need to get a few more… supplies."

She still looked confused, but at the mention of condoms, she managed a small grin.

"But I don't have anything to do tomorrow, and I'm under the impression the clinic is closed on Sunday."

The relief crept over her face like a sunrise after a stormy night. "Your impression is correct."

"If you want," he said, fighting the urge to kiss that sunrise smile, "I'll come back for you tonight."

"So we can go... camping?"

"Just for the night," he said, feeling way more hopeful than he really had a right to. One night of camping was a hell of a lot different than one week, one month, or even one year of camping. But he hadn't lied. He couldn't let her go, and he'd hold onto her for as long as she'd let him. And, judging by the look she was giving him—sleepy and awake and coy and knowing all at the time—she might let him hold on for a while longer. "You won't have to walk it this time."

She took a deep breath, and he wished she hadn't covered up with the sheet. Well, there'd be time for that tonight.

"How could I refuse an offer like that?"

"I was hoping you wouldn't. Pack light—and a swimsuit is optional."

She hit him with the pillow just as another ominous thud came from the front door. "What the—"

"Blue Eye," he said, catching another kiss. "I really do have to go."

"Go then," she replied, pushing him off the bed. "But come back."

"I will." He leaned down and took a quick kiss. "I promise."

The image of Madeline, bare shoulders and bright smile, stayed with him on the brisk ride to Albert's. But it wasn't enough to make his reality any less complicated.

Jesse was sitting on the front step, his cast jutting out in front of him. He looked like hell that hadn't even been warmed over.

"Hiya, Rebel." Somehow he managed to sound worse than he looked. "I, uh, got a sleeping bag into the truck. I couldn't get... Albert," he said, like the name was shards of glass in his mouth. "In. By myself, I mean."

"You doing okay?" *Nothing like an obvious question with an obvious answer*, Rebel thought. But he was just as responsible for the living as he was for the dead. And Jesse was still living.

"I... " Jesse looked to the sky. Rebel dismounted and sat on the step.

"I thought I hated him," Jesse said, and Rebel waited. Jesse wasn't known for introspection, but this sounded serious. "He loved me. I wasn't even his own family, and he loved me anyway."

That much was true. "He was your family, Jesse."

"You're the only family I've got now." Jesse sounded in serious danger of breaking up.

Rebel looked at him. His first instinct was to remind him not to cry, because true Lakotas did not cry over their dead. If Albert's spirit saw Jesse crying, he would worry, and a worried spirit wouldn't move on to the afterworld.

But Jesse needed another reminder that he wasn't a full Lakota like he needed another broken leg. No, what he really needed was to finish growing up. Albert was gone, and Rebel couldn't babysit him the rest of his life. Not if he wanted to hold onto Madeline for as long as he could. "What the hell are you talking about?"

"What?" Jesse jumped, like he'd been asleep and Rebel had dumped a bucket of water on him.

"You have a family, or did you forget? Tara, your woman? Nelly, your daughter?"

"Yeah, but—"

"You know what Albert did for you? He raised you because you didn't have a father, the same thing he did for me. You want someone else raising your kid?"

Jesse began to squirm. "No, but—"

"No buts. It's your turn to be the man."

Jesse squirmed, looking like Rebel had issued a life sentence. He dropped his gaze to the ground. "Albert—he told me, after you left to get her—" Amazingly, Rebel didn't hear anything but sorrow in Jesse's voice. All the sneer that used to color his voice any time he talked about Madeline was gone. "After you left, he said you would *see* something. He told me you'd tell me what to do, Rebel."

Jesse looked up at him, and suddenly Rebel was nine and Jesse was four again, and they'd been alone all night, all alone until Albert had come to get them. He'd taken them home and then, three days later, taken them to their mother's funeral. Jesse had been so little, younger than Nelly, too young to really understand that Mom had died face down in a ditch outside a bar. All he had known then was that Mom wasn't coming back. Rebel remembered standing next to the pine casket, his arm around Jesse's little shoulders, and Jesse looking at him with watery eyes—not crying— because Albert told them they couldn't. Mom was going to have enough trouble getting past Owl Woman without the tears of little boys pulling her back. "What are we going to do, Rebel?" Jesse had asked in that little-kid voice. "What are we going to do now?"

"Don't worry. I promise I'll take care of you," was all Rebel could say then. "We'll do what Albert tells us to."

It was a promise he'd kept—maybe for too long. Then, now—it was the same. Even though Albert's spirit had gone on, his will was still strong. Albert had made Rebel who he was. Now, it seemed, he wanted Rebel to do the same for Jesse.

The problem with this plan, however, was that Rebel had had no such vision, no flash of the past that gave clues to the future. Even if he had, he doubted a vision would have been specific enough to get Jesse's ass moving.

Which only left one option. Faking it.

He rubbed his eyes. Pretending he'd had a vision went against just about everything he believed. But Albert had laid out the path. It was up to Rebel to walk it.

Rebel sat back down, staring out into the warming sky. This was a unique opportunity—not only could he tell Jesse what to do, there was a decent chance the man would listen. For once.

What the hell. "I saw… " How best to get Jesse to man up? "I saw a vision. Your hair was white with age and you walked with a staff." Which was probable, so not quite a make-believe lie, right? As Jesse nodded, Rebel's mind scrambled for a future Jesse could hold onto. "Your family was here," he added, sweeping his hands around to show Albert's house and land, "and you were cooking the venison your grandchildren had hunted for you." Also probable—after all, he and Jesse had done the same thing often enough. Jesse would take comfort in the familiar.

"Really?" Rebel snuck a glance at him, afraid Jesse wouldn't believe his little white lie any more than Rebel did. But, to his surprise, Jesse looked thoughtful. Introspection was odd on him, but that didn't make it bad. Hell, he might even get used to it. "My grandchildren?"

"Yes." Shit, he didn't want to get any more specific—specifics were easy to prove wrong, even if it took another twenty or so years to do it. "Your family, Jesse. The family you make is the family you have."

Something about his own words rang in his ears. He'd spent six years making his tribe his family, and that had been enough. *Had* been, but it wasn't now. A man couldn't hold a tribe at night, couldn't watch a tribe sleep in the morning, couldn't swim in a river with a tribe. A man could love his tribe, but he could only be *in* love with a woman.

He was in love with Madeline.

"How do I do that?"

The longer he sat here, trying to get Jesse to see the light, the more time it would take him to get back to Madeline. "Get a job, Jesse. A real one. Even a job at the Quik-E Mart. Pick your daughter up from school, read her stories at bedtime and kiss her mother every night. It's not hard. You just have to do it." Jesse's head sagged again. Rebel was just about done being the medicine man—a plastic shaman—right now. He was just about to become the big brother. "It's what Albert wanted."

"It did make him happy when Nelly came over. I read to her a lot then."

"You keep the house." Sure, a house would be nice. A house would be something Madeline would like—more than a tent, anyway. But this wasn't where he belonged. Jesse needed a place to belong. "I need to get going."

Jesse's mouth was open, but when Rebel looked at him, he snapped it shut. Rebel kept the smile off his face as he stood. Jesse struggled to his feet. "I was going to go through his stuff, get it organized for the giveaway. If that's okay with you."

"That'd be good." A small step toward responsibility was still a step. "And thanks for getting the sleeping bag ready."

"I know he's dead, but... " Jesse shrugged, but he looked pleased with the compliment. "I wanted him to be comfortable."

How about that, Rebel thought long after he'd gotten on the road to town. There was hope for the twerp after all.

By the time Madeline's little cabin came back into view, the sun was on the other side of the earth, marching toward night with unwavering certainty.

He wished he felt the same certainty. Well, he did. He was certain he was in love with Dr. Madeline Mitchell. But he wasn't some kid anymore, convinced that the ideal love would triumph over all. He'd made that mistake once. He wouldn't do it again.

Which left him with that unsettling feeling of uncertainty, and he was pretty sure no message from the past—real or made-up—would guide him toward his future path. All he had was Albert's final words. Find his own path, no one else's.

Hell was knowing what Jesse should do at the same time Rebel had no idea what he was supposed to do.

But then he saw her, and all his uncertainty about tomorrow and the day after melted into certainty of what he was going to do right now. Her hair was pulled back in a loose knot, and she was wearing that pink shirt he loved to take off her. Then he spied them, underneath her jeans.

She had on his mocs.

His blood warmed under his skin. To hell with later. Right now, he had a beautiful woman waiting for him. Right now, he had Tanka saddled up. Right now, he was just going to be in love.

Right now, life was good.

"I was beginning to wonder," she said as she stood, picking up the small backpack at her feet. He dismounted and found her in his arms, hugging him tight. "How are you?" She sounded worried.

"Better, now that I'm here." He kissed her, but quickly. Lingering was for later. "Ready?"

She held him for just a second more, then turned to Tanka. "Hello there. Who are you?"

"Madeline, this is Tanka. Nelly rides him a lot."

"You brought me Nelly's horse?" Even in the dimming light, he could see the sharp look she shot him as she let Tanka sniff her hand. "Oh, ye of little faith."

"Show me what you got, then."

It wasn't that he doubted she could ride—she'd done just fine bareback—but he wanted to see for himself that she really knew how to handle herself on a horse. He wanted her to ride with him. To be with him.

211

Backpack on her back, she slung her right leg over Tanka's back with authority. "Cowboy, you're on." And she was gone in a cloud of summer dust.

"Hey!" With him? He grinned. Or in front of him?

He tore off after her. Even through the dust, he could see she was having the time of her life. She rode like an old pro, head down, arms pumping with each stride. She was holding the reins in two hands, not one, but Tanka was going flat out anyway. *Oh, yeah*, he thought, giving Blue Eye her neck. She looked damn good on that horse. He shouldn't think dirty thoughts about watching her bottom rock as Tanka galloped, hell for leather. But it had been a long day, and he hadn't had a hell of a lot of sleep. Madeline—on horseback, at top speed—was just what he needed.

He wanted to stay behind her just to enjoy the view, but she was following the road left when they needed to go right, over the hill. Tanka was good, but Blue Eye was better, and in less than three strides, he was in the lead.

And they headed home.

By the time his hill rose up over the river and he slowed Blue Eye to a trot, he wasn't tired anymore. Instead, his blood was pumping, flooding him with a heat that sure felt like certainty. Damn, she was beautiful, she was amazing in bed and she could ride. Man, could she ride.

"Woohoo!" Madeline trotted ahead of him and then circled back, wearing the biggest smile he'd ever seen. "That was—wow! Can we do that again?"

"Maybe in the morning."

She looked at him, wanting to argue, but then something about her changed. "Long day."

212

The horses were walking side by side now, slowly but steadily heading back to camp. "Very."

"Did you get everything taken care of today?"

"I think so." He'd given Jesse a gentle kick in the butt, taken Albert to the funeral home, spent four hours in Super-Mart buying things for the giveaway and ordered cake for the funeral. On about three hours of sleep.

She didn't say anything as they made it to camp. She didn't say anything as they unsaddled the horses or spread the sleeping bag out on the sand. She didn't even say anything as she handed him logs for the fire. It wasn't until the fire was going that she turned to him. Her hands found his chest, and she kissed his cheek. "So, you take care of everyone?"

He hadn't thought of it quite like that. "Yeah, I guess." The buttons on his shirt began to give. He didn't know where she was going, but he liked where she was heading.

She laid his chest bare, leaned over and bit down around his nipple. Heat poured from her mouth onto his bare skin and he shuddered. Grinning, she looked at him through thick lashes. "Who takes care of you?"

All that heat began to melt the parts of his brain that did the thinking. "What?"

"You take care of everyone. Even me." His belt was gone, and his jeans were down. She was undressing him, just like he'd undressed her on that hot afternoon by the river. He could remember her being dazed, in a hazy way. Hazy, dazy—all he really knew was that he was hot. That she made him hot. "What I want to know is who takes care of you?"

His mouth felt stuck in the open position, which was a damn good thing when she kissed him.

"You," he managed to get out.

His hat went flying, and she pushed him down onto the sleeping bag. His back hit the stump, but that was okay. He had a full view of her.

"Then let me take care of you."

She let her own hair loose. It sprang free, and he began to sweat. No part of his brain was functioning right now. All he could think was this beautiful woman—his beautiful woman—was going to take care of him.

The fire blazed brightly behind her, cutting her silhouette out of the dusky night as she undressed for him. Everything was red-hot—the fire, the woman, his dick—especially his dick. He tried to lean over to grab his jeans and get the condoms in his back pocket, but she used her foot on his shoulder to push him back against the tree stump. "I told you, I'll take care of you," she scolded. He could hear the smile in her voice as she finished shimmying out of her jeans.

He was burning now, burning from the outside in, the inside out. She fished out the condom, and with that crisp efficiency that made her such a good doctor, rolled in on his aching dick. Her hands lingered, which drove that hot ache up into his gut. He groaned. He couldn't take much more. Hell wasn't this hot.

"I promise," she whispered, her voice thick with the same kind of heat that was burning him through and through. "I promise I'll take care of you."

She straddled him, and then all of her warmth and wetness was surrounding him as she whimpered his name every time she rose and fell on him. He caught a breast in his mouth and sucked hard. Her noise went from a whimper to a scream in a second, so he sucked harder. The fire in his blood went from red-hot to clear blue as she took care of him, again and again. In his mind's eye, he was watching her ride the horse. Up, down, up, down, faster and faster until he couldn't tell who was going to win this race. She knew how to ride, all right. She knew how to ride with him.

She slammed her hips down onto his and, in a white-hot moment, he emptied everything he ever had into her. Her head whipped back as she ground down even harder, and then she collapsed against his heaving chest. He'd won, but she hadn't lost. Everyone was the big winner here.

"Better?" she murmured into his neck as she kissed his still-hot skin.

"Mad-e-line." It was all he had left, and even that wasn't much.

"I love you too."

Good. She knew. That was all that mattered.

Sunday was nearly perfect, Madeline decided. Rebel made something that looked like biscuits but tasted a whole lot better in a big, cast-iron pot over the fire. Even the coffee seemed to be a little more special. After that, they went on a long ride, winding through parts of the High Plains that seemed still untouched by human hands. Rebel showed her where he camped in the spring and fall and then took her down a deep valley to see a herd of pronghorn grazing in the tall grass. After they got back, they went for a dip in the river and then made love under the shade of trees. Sated, they dozed through the hot part of the afternoon.

Hell, if she'd known how much fun camping was, she'd have done it years ago.

215

Her wheels began to turn. The cabin would be cramped for a while, sure, but maybe between the two of them, they could find enough money for a new place. And on the weekends, they could head out to the open range and rough it. It could work. They could be together. It was insane, she knew. She'd only been here for two months. But after staring down the throat of a life of Darrin-based boredom, she wanted to hold on to all the honest-to-goodness excitement that was being with Rebel. She didn't want to let go, either.

Still, by the time they mounted up to head back to the cabin, she could tell something had changed about him. He was quiet again, and he kept looking at her not like she was going home for the night, but like she was leaving. Like she was leaving him. Like he'd looked at her that first morning.

He was making her nervous. But she refused to give into some sort of hysterical panic. Last time, it hadn't even been about her. It had been about Albert. And he'd already come back for her, right? Right. Focus on the positive. "I had a good time camping," she started, breaking the silence as they walked the horses back to her house.

"Yeah?" Did he sound a little hopeful?

"Yeah. I think that would be fun on the weekends—at least when the weather's nice."

"Yeah." The hope was gone, and he sounded dangerously close to something like depressed.

Did he not want her to go camping with him? Lord, this man drove her crazy. But she resolved not to get ahead of herself and ruin the day. "How about you? Do you like the cabin?"

His answer was a long time coming. "It's pretty

nice. I could maybe stay with you a night or two a week."

A night? Or two? She swallowed. That sounded ominous. "Oh. I thought… " She caught herself before she got her foot too far into her mouth. She thought he couldn't let her go. She thought she took care of him, and she knew exactly how well he took care of her. She sort of thought he might be able to love her, crazy white woman and all.

Perhaps she'd thought wrong.

They rode the rest of the way back to the cabin in a tense silence as she tried to figure out what was going on exactly. This wasn't a one-night-stand kind of thing. He'd gone way out of his way to make her a part of his family and to explain his customs—especially the ones that made the least amount of sense. He'd made her moccasins—moccasins she was wearing right now. He'd made breakfast, for God's sake.

So what the hell was it?

She half expected him to just tip his hat and ride off into the late afternoon sun, but he dismounted with her and then took her hand as they walked up onto her porch. She let him, because holding hands was holding onto something. For all she knew, it might be the only thing, but it was something.

He stopped in front of her door, like this was the end of the first date and he was nervous about the kiss. "My Madeline." His voice said it all. He wasn't coming in. He was leaving.

"Stay," she said, surprising even herself. So much for that foot in the mouth. Well, hell. Since she'd already shoved it in there, she might as well keep on going. "Why won't you stay here with me?"

217

He closed his eyes and touched his forehead to hers. "A piece of me will always be here with you."

"I don't want a *piece* of you, Rebel. I want *all* of you. Even the parts that make me crazy."

"I... " He tightened his arms around her, like she'd said what he wanted to hear and didn't want to hear at the same time. "I can only give you the one piece." He found her hand and pressed it to his chest. She could feel his heart strumming along beneath the skin. "I don't have anything else left to give."

"What does that mean?" Was he dumping her, or what?

His raised his mournful eyes, and she saw a sadness that she didn't think was hers. It was his. "I can't leave the land, and it's not fair to ask you to give up indoor plumbing."

Her mouth opened and shut without her approval. So that was it. She'd just assumed he'd move in with her—that he'd *want* to move in with her and live in a real house and have a real life with her. But no. He wasn't going anywhere.

It felt like he'd tied a lead sinker to her heart and made a long cast out to the middle of the river. He was right, of course. It was one thing to go from the Mitchell Mansion to a studio cabin, but it was a whole other thing to go from a cabin to a tent on a permanent basis. "So what do you want to do?"

A little bit of hope crept into his eyes. "We could do what we just said. A night or two during the week, camping on nice weekends. It's not perfect... " He kissed her forehead. "But I can't let you go."

Her heart sank even farther. She'd had no idea that those words were so open to interpretation, but clearly they were. She'd interpreted them to mean something damn close to *I love you.* This was the problem with not speaking the local language. The interpretations were always open. "And you can't stay."

He nodded as he smoothed a curl away from her face. His mouth was saying one thing, his body something completely different. Maybe that was her problem. She'd been listening to the wrong part.

"I'll understand if that's not enough for you. But you'll always have a piece of me."

One piece. What the hell was she supposed to do? Love him when he was here, miss him when he was gone? Damn it. Damn it all. She was going to miss him no matter what. And if she couldn't do that, couldn't live half in his world and half in hers, then she wouldn't get to love him at all.

One piece. She wouldn't be able to avoid him. Every time he popped up at the clinic, she knew she would fall apart all over again, all because she wouldn't settle for one piece.

She took a deep breath, hoping to clear her head and instead just breathing in his smell—the smell of horse and man and river and sun, all blended into a perfect musk—until she knew she couldn't live without any part of him. Even if she couldn't have all of him. "Will you stay the whole night? When you come?" Because if she woke up with him, she could pretend that there was something normal about all of this. If he wouldn't be there when she woke up, then she couldn't. She couldn't just be a booty call.

His arms tightened a little more, until she thought he would squeeze her right back into bits again. "I want to wake up with you, Madeline. You're beautiful when you sleep. Just beautiful. And I'll even make you breakfast, as long as the coffee makes itself."

That was it—that was as good as it was going to get. Not perfect, but good enough. She smiled, just a little, and he smiled back. And maybe, just maybe, by the time February rolled around, he'd change his mind. "There'll always be a mattress here for you."

His smile got wider. She could still see the sadness at the edge of his eyes, but it was tempered now. He almost looked normal as he said, "Would you go to a funeral with me?" like he was asking for a second date.

It wasn't going to be perfect. After setting up when he'd come get her for Albert's funeral and extracting a promise that he'd swing by the clinic before then, just so she could see him, she kissed him goodbye, watched her cowboy ride into the sunset, and went in to open a can of soup for dinner.

It wasn't going to be perfect. But then life never was.

Chapter Fourteen

So it wasn't perfect. Madeline had never needed anyone the way she began to need Rebel, and it took her more time to get used to the sensation of longing than she was comfortable with. She went to sleep most nights craving his arms around her waist, his breath on her cheek. She woke up most mornings missing the sight of him parading around the cabin in her pink towel. When he came into the clinic, she had to fight the urge to haul him into the supply closet and kiss the hell out of him. Definitely not perfect.

But that didn't make it bad. After a few weeks, they settled into an easy routine. When he came for her Friday nights, she practically swooned at the sight of him riding up in the summer sun, leading Tanka for her. With every weekend she spent camping, she got more comfortable with no fans, no automatic coffee and no hot showers. She still missed an enclosed toilet, though, but for two days at a time, she was willing to trade that for long trail rides and campfires. When she came home on Wednesday nights, he'd be sitting in her recliner on the porch, waiting for her. God, how she loved the sight of him there, waiting for her. They'd make dinner together and then spend the night wrapped in each other. She loved him with everything she had. And all the while, she counted the days until the first snow fell.

Madeline was pretty sure everyone knew she and Rebel were sleeping together now. Tara started greeting him by saying, "Hiya, Rebel. Madeline's in the back," or in the closet, or with a patient. Clarence seemed to wink a lot more when Rebel was around, and Tammy was prone to quiet giggling when Rebel would make Madeline blush—which he continued to do with alarming frequency. But no one, not even Nobody, said anything. The medicine man sleeping with the doctor was just another day on the rez, apparently.

The clinic wasn't perfect either, but it kept going. She began to get used to Nobody Bodine just appearing and disappearing at closing time, and he picked up on how she liked things arranged pretty quickly. One corner of the desk at a time, Tammy got the files organized, and then took the initiative to work up some new patient forms. Madeline cut Jesse's cast off while Tara held one hand and Nelly the other. She delivered four babies, only one of which was premature and showed signs of fetal alcohol syndrome. More people came through with flu-like symptoms, although she still had no lab results to prove Rebel right or wrong. Some people paid some bills. It was just enough. And Rebel still showed up at unexpected times to translate or drive someone home.

A few times, Rebel came for her in the middle of the afternoon. Someone was sick, too sick to even be carried in. She'd never considered house calls a part of her professional world, but wasn't that what she'd done for Albert? Plus, it made her look at Rebel in a new light. When he took her to see someone who was sick—dehydrated, weak, bloody diarrhea—she realized more and more that he wasn't trying to practice medicine, and he wasn't trying to kill people. And what's more, he trusted her. When she couldn't get a frail old man to respond to the anti-diarrhea meds she now kept stocked in huge quantities, and he died in spite of her best efforts, Rebel was waiting on her porch that night. They sat in the recliner for a long time, discussing their different versions of heaven as the sun set on another day. He didn't even reprimand her when she got a little teary, but instead kissed her tears away. The next day, he brought in another new patient with the same symptoms. He had faith in her. She was beginning to realize that the feeling was mutual.

Maybe it was ridiculous, but she started to think of them as a team. *The yin and yang of the White Sandy Clinic and Hospital*, she thought with a smile as she hooked up another IV one day. He was good at the bedside manner thing, the caring and understanding thing, and the translating thing. He literally spoke the language. And she was good at the medicine. She knew what to expect now, what her patients could realistically be expected to afford and, beyond that, do. She began to understand on a fundamental level what Rebel and Nobody had meant by a good death. She began to understand what Rebel meant when he talked about being right with the world.

She began to understand what it meant to be a Lakota. As much as an outsider could, anyway.

July had long since turned into August when Rebel woke her up with a hard shake one Thursday morning. Immediately, Madeline knew something was wrong. Instead of wet hair, a pink towel and languid laziness, he was already dressed, and he was moving so fast he was almost a blur of agitation. "What's happened?"

His eyes snapped up, and she saw his terror. "Are you okay?"

She was not the one having a panic attack right now, but she doubted he would see the humor in that. "Yes, fine." She looked at him more closely. His pupils were dilated and he was breathing so fast that he was almost hyperventilating.

"What's wrong?" she asked more carefully.

He began pacing, the heels of his boots hitting the wood floorboards so hard she was afraid he was going to take the whole house down. "I—I don't know. Something. Something's wrong. I don't know what."

"What did you see?" She'd only seen him go into a trance once since the night of Albert's party, and all he would tell her when he snapped out of it a few minutes later was that Jesse really would have gray hair, which made him laugh and laugh. But this was different. This was no laughing matter.

"It was the same thing—the same thing I saw before you came here. The horse was sick, the people—" He shuddered, almost as pale as she was. "The people were all dead. And you—" He stopped—really stopped. He didn't even blink as he stared at her with wild eyes.

Her blood went ice cold in her veins. "What about me?"

"You—I think it's you, but I don't see you, just footprints in the snow—you tried to save them again, and it was too late. They were all dead." He spun on the balls of his feet and grabbed her by the shoulders. His hands were downright chilly. "It's not like these things happen in repeats. This means something. Something's wrong."

Irrational relief flooded her system. She forced herself to take a breath, forced the air to move through her lungs. It wasn't like she would have really believed he'd seen her dead—would she? Of course not. That was just not possible. But he was frantic. One step at a time, she thought as she said, "Have you talked to your brother?" in her calmest voice. She'd taken Jesse's cast off three weeks ago. According to everyone, that meant it was just about time for him to hurt himself again.

His eyes widened with dread. "Can I use your phone?"

Madeline dressed quickly as Rebel called just about everyone in the phone book. And everyone had the same thing to say. They were fine. Everyone was just fine.

"I'm coming with you," he said as she got her keys. He clutched her in his arms, and his current of terror shot through her.

Damn, in this state, he'd probably scare everyone, even Clarence. For the first time, she wished Albert was still here, not because she missed the old man, but because she was pretty sure he was the only one around who could talk Rebel down right now. But she was also pretty sure that telling him to go home and get over it—whatever *it* was—would push him right over the edge. "Okay. Come on. But I'm driving."

On the way in, he grilled her. Had more people been getting sick recently? No, the number of people experiencing flu-like symptoms had been holding steady. Had she heard any chatter from the medical supply people? No, nothing.

"How about the samples?" He was a little calmer now, but the terror that had held sway earlier was now becoming a laser-like focus on finding something—anything—that was actually wrong. "You said four to six weeks, right? It's been six. Have you heard anything about them?"

"No. I had Tara call a few weeks ago and nothing." Open Diagnostics Laboratories was no different from the rest of the world. *The White Sandy is a non-entity to them*, she thought with disgust. Some days, she felt like she needed to sacrifice a chicken or something in order to get the ball rolling.

His lips disappeared into a thin line. "We need to know. What if that's it?"

Part of her wanted to tell him to snap the hell out of it, because everything was fine. He'd just had a bad dream or eaten something he shouldn't have, or maybe he was having a nervous breakdown. Nothing was wrong, and he was starting to freak her out.

But another part of her knew he wouldn't just make something like this up. That part of her knew that it didn't matter how much or how little she believed in his visions or the spirit world or any of the Lakota stuff she didn't understand. What mattered was the fact that he did believe.

"I'll call the lab myself when we get to the clinic, okay?"

He nodded even as he shot her a disapproving look. She must have sounded unconvinced. "You think I'm nuts."

The giggle was out before she could stop it. Lord, what she wouldn't have given for a little more coffee. "No, I know you're nuts. But," she added quickly, "it's clearly important to you. And you're important to me. So I'll call." Calling was one thing, though. Convincing was another thing. How the hell was she going to do that? What she needed was some backup. Her wheels began to turn.

"Okay, good," he said, seemingly not the least bit insulted. "Just to be safe. Just to be ready. Just in case."

By the time she pulled up next to the clinic, Rebel was considerably calmer, and that made her feel good in a new, different way. She had the sneaky feeling that Albert, wherever he was, would be proud that she'd talked Rebel down all by herself.

First, she called Melonie. If she was going to exert a little pressure on the lab people, she needed to know as much as she could. Melonie was an expert at getting people to do what she wanted them to do *and* making them think it had been their idea in the first place. Melonie had never needed the Mitchell sneer.

"Open Diagnostics?" Melonie said with a yawn, even though it was almost eight in Columbus. "What for?"

Sheesh. Madeline had been up for over an hour already. "Just look them up online. Where they're located, who the manager of the lab is—see what you can find and call me back in fifteen minutes, okay?"

"Whatever, Maddie."

"Melonie, this is important."

There was a long pause. "Does this have anything to do with a cowboy? Or an Indian?" At least she sounded more awake now. "Well?"

227

Madeline rolled her eyes, which was wasted on the telephone, but old habits die hard. "Both," she finally admitted.

"Two men? Maddie!" She gasped in melodramatic shock. "I had no idea."

This whole conversation was rapidly spinning out of control. "*One* man," she said through gritted teeth over the sound of giggling. "Now, can you help me out or not?"

"Ooh, I gotta meet this guy. I'll call you back in ten."

Hanging up, she turned to find Rebel looking almost normal—for Rebel, anyway. Something close to his normal wolfish grin was on his face, and he was lightly shifting from one foot to the other. But the strain was still written large across his face.

"You look like you could skin a cat right now," he said.

She rolled her eyes again, which made him laugh. "You haven't met my sister."

"But I will."

Her heart jumped like it was playing hopscotch. In the month they'd been doing this not-perfect thing, neither one had said anything else about any part of the future that didn't involve a trip to Rapid City on the weekend. But that—meeting her family—that sounded a whole lot like long-term planning. February could not get here fast enough.

But they still had to get through this week.

She couldn't just stand here and stare at him, so she got to work. She got the coffee going, checked to see if Nobody had gotten everything out of the autoclave, and then, because she didn't know what else to do with herself, she began flipping through the files Tammy had put in immaculate order.

Which was a mistake, because her back was to the phone when it rang, and Rebel picked it up before the first ring was done.

"Clinic, this is Rebel speaking." His grin was more wolfish all the time. He looked just like he had on her first day here. Heck, Madeline half expected him to go mix up some plaster at this rate. "How may I help you?"

"Damn it, Rebel." She lurched at him and tried to grab the phone, but he neatly sidestepped her. "Give that to me."

"Why, yes, I am a cowboy *and* an Indian, thanks for asking. And you are? Melonie Mitchell." He sounded like he was selling used cars. "You must be Madeline's sister. It's so nice to talk to you. I've heard *so much* about you."

"Rebel!" She managed to catch him by an elbow, but he twisted so she couldn't get to the phone.

"Did you like the green bag? You did?" That man had the damn nerve to wink at her. "Yes, I made that. Your sister must love you a lot, because she dropped a couple of grand on that. How much did you spend on her present?"

That did it. She elbowed him in the gut and managed to get a hold of the phone cord. "Do you want me to call the lab for you or not?"

"I love it when you fight dirty," he whispered before returning to his conversation. "You'll have to come out and visit sometime, Ms. Mitchell. Oh, okay. Melonie. I'd *love* to meet you in person. That'd be great. Yes, she's here." Finally, he held the phone out to Madeline. "It's your sister."

"I know that," she snapped, grabbing the phone from him. "You'll regret that later, mister."

"Promises, promises."

"Maddie. Who was that?" Melonie's breathless wonder pulled her attention away from *that man.*

"The pain in my ass," she grumbled. Rebel blew her a kiss from across the waiting room. She could not figure him out right now. Manic depressive, maybe? "What did you find out?"

"Does he look as good as he sounds?" Excellent. Now her sister was gushing.

Part of her wanted to say, no, he looked way better than that, but she'd rather eat nails than say that in front of him, and that wasn't the point, anyway. "Focus, Mellie. The lab. What did you find out about the lab?"

A hushed silence cascaded down the line. *Oh, shit*, Madeline thought. Here it comes. "You're *sleeping* with him? Oh, my God, Maddie. You really are. Is he good?"

As soon as she got off this phone, she was going to lose it. Possibly before then. "Melonie."

"Better than Darrin?"

"*Melonie.*" Count to ten. *One, two, three...*

"Wow, that good?" She whistled in appreciation, a sound that hammered itself right between Madeline's eyes. "I am *so* coming out there to see this for myself. Does he have a brother?"

Seven, eight, nine... "*Melonie!*" Across the room, Rebel snickered.

"Sheesh, and I thought getting laid would make you *less* uptight. All right, all right. Fine. The lab. Open Diagnostics is headquartered in Baltimore.

They're a publicly traded company on the NASDAQ whose stock price is up $0.33 this year alone."

"And?" Baltimore. She dug a pencil out of the desk and wrote it down.

"The director of the actual lab is a little troll named Leon Flagg."

"Mel, be serious." She wrote it down, and then added *troll* after it.

"I am serious, Maddie." She sighed in frustration. "This would be so much easier if you had the Internet out there."

"I don't need the Internet. I have you. Why is Leon Flagg a troll?"

"Aside from the name?" Melonie snickered, and for a brief second, Madeline was homesick. She actually missed her little sister, irritation and all. "Well, he is. From his Facebook page, he seems about five feet tall and two hundred pounds, with red hair that looks like he stuck his finger in a socket. I friended him," she added with another giggle. "Not only has he already accepted my request, but he's already sent me a slimy message."

The feeling of homesickness grew, just a little. Madeline had never gotten on social media—never had the time—but back in Columbus, finding out that the director of the lab at Open Diagnostics was a troll named Leon took less than fifteen minutes. Out here on the rez, it would have taken her weeks to dig up that kind of information. Madeline looked at Rebel, which was no help. She doubted the man even knew what Facebook was. "Really? What'd he say?"

"Oh, the usual. If I'm ever in the Baltimore area, he'd love to show me a good time, etc. etc. etc. Total slime ball. Which is good."

On the other hand, out here on the rez, one didn't just randomly friend slime balls for fun. A little insulation was a good thing, Madeline decided. "How's that?"

"Maddie, I have no idea what's going on. But you need this Open Diagnostics to process something for you? Something they're in no hurry to do?"

Hell, even if Melonie knew what was going on, she still probably wouldn't have any idea. Madeline barely knew what was going on, and she lived here. "Right."

"So," she said, like Maddie was that stick in the mud again, "horny trolls are easy."

"Melonie…"

"Call him up. Pretend to be me. Promise that if he processes your stuff, you'll make it worth his while when you come to Baltimore next time. Easy."

"What?" Promise some troll a good time? She'd rather tell Melonie there wasn't a man alive who was better than Rebel—in front of him, no less.

"Trust me, it'll work. You can't scare him over the phone with that sneer of yours, and bribery works best in person." Melonie really did sound like she knew what she was talking about.

Especially the part about the bribery. Madeline shuddered. "I don't think I can do that."

"Okay. Fine. I don't care what you tell him. Promise him something medical, I don't know. And I'll unfriend him as soon as you're done."

"No, wait." So Madeline wasn't exactly in touch with the modern world these days. But even she knew that was a bad idea. "Wait until I get the results, okay? Then *unfriend* him or whatever."

"Good plan." Hey, score one for Madeline. "I couldn't get his direct extension, but I got the lab number."

Madeline wrote the number down and then repeated it back, just to make sure she got it right.

"You've got it. And Maddie?" Suddenly, Melonie sounded quite serious. "I hope whatever it is turns out okay."

"Thanks, Mel. I'll let you know." She hung up and stared at the phone.

"So that's what *artistic* and *unfocused* sounds like," Rebel said, keeping a safe distance on the other side of the waiting room.

"What is your problem?" Madeline glanced at the clock. 7:32. She had time to chew him out and call the lab before Clarence got here—but not much. "Are you trying to piss me off? I'm trying to help you over here."

"I'm sorry," he said, not looking the least bit apologetic. "But you're cute when you're mad."

Maybe Melonie was right. She couldn't scare anyone over the phone with the Mitchell sneer. But in person was a whole different matter. She fixed him with her hardest glare. "Who are you calling cute?"

He had the nerve to smile at her. She was going to have to work on that sneer some more. She was getting soft out here.

"I really am sorry, Madeline. But you were worried. It's... " He trailed off, his eyes caressing her face until she felt the kind of warmth they normally reserved for after-dark conversations. "It's easier when you're mad at me."

"Men," she grumbled. He didn't mind scaring the hell out of her, but he didn't want her to worry? She

233

picked up the phone and began dialing. "Horny trolls and mystic cowboys and silent Nobodys. The whole lot of you."

He laughed again.

In short order, a bored-sounding receptionist had her on hold, listening to the worst sort of Musak—easy-listening instrumentals of formerly groovy sixties hits. The effect was mind numbing.

She fought the artificial mellowness and focused on her notes. Leon Flagg. Horny troll. Be like Melonie. What would Melonie do? Melonie would flirt shamelessly. Madeline hated flirting shamelessly. But a girl had to do what a girl had to do.

"Flagg," a surprisingly squeaky voice croaked into the phone.

Lord, she was going to screw this up. "Leon?"

"Yeah?" He sounded cautious. Good. He was already off guard.

"Leon!" She tried to sound like Melonie did when she just loved some piece of art—or the artist who made it. Rebel winced. "It's me! Melonie!"

Rebel's head jerked back in surprise. That old feeling of satisfaction grew in her chest. She was single-handedly outflanking two men at the same time. And that was exactly what her sister would do.

"Melonie?"

"From Facebook? I just got your message!" She was forgetting something… Oh, yeah. She giggled.

The line was quiet, then Leon was in her ear again. "Why, hello there, Melonie." Was he was hiding under his desk? "You've got quite a sexy voice. It's almost as hot as your picture."

Her stomach turned, which wasn't helped by the

confused look on Rebel's face. She forced another giggle out. "I'm just so glad I got a hold of you. I was hoping you could help me out."

"Is that so?" She was losing him. He sounded more clinical this time around. "With what?"

Time to creatively bend the truth. "Oh, it's just the weirdest thing." All of her sentences were suddenly ending on an up note, like everything was a big question. "My sister needs some things processed and she asked me to find out what I could about the lab." She swallowed her revulsion. "And I found you online and, wow, you know? Redheads! That's why I friended you!"

Rebel made a gagging motion, but at least he did it silently.

"Is that so?"

Excellent. She had his full attention again. "You know, I was planning to visit Baltimore this fall . . ." Because, because—oh! "because there's going to be this art show I wanted to attend." She managed another giggle. "If you could get those samples processed for my sister . . . I'd love to make it up to you when I'm there." Ugh, she was going to gargle with bleach after this. Anything to get the horrible taste out of her mouth.

"Honey, I'd love for you to make it up to me," he said in what Madeline could only assume was supposed to be his hot n' heavy voice. "What does your sister need? A friend of yours is a friend of mine. Especially if you bring her with you."

Wrong didn't begin to describe this conversation. "Really? Oh, Leon!" How the hell did her sister pull this off? "My hero!"

"You just let Leon take care of it, honey." Did he honestly think this was sexy? Eww. She was going to take a bleach bath after this.

It wasn't easy to keep up her fake Melonie-ness while getting out the important information on the samples, especially not with Rebel sitting over there, glowering in disapproval. But in ten minutes, she had Leon eating out of her hand. "How long will it take?" she asked, trying to sound gushy.

"Three days, honey. I'll have them ready for you Monday morning. Of course, if you wanted to come pick them up yourself, say this weekend... I'd love to get a jump on things. If you know what I mean."

Blech and barf. This was the last giggle. She couldn't pretend any more without throwing up. "I'll be waiting, Leon. Goodbye." She turned to see Rebel pouting. She'd never seen him pout before. It looked unnatural on him. "What?"

"What the hell was that?" He might look pouty, but he sounded nothing short of furious.

She felt like she was unexpectedly walking across a huge sheet of glass—in stilettos—and the whole thing would shatter with the wrong step. "The lab will call with the results Monday morning."

This news brought little change to his face. She thought she saw a flicker of approval, but it was gone before she could be sure. "You lied."

"Melonie told me to." Excellent. She sounded childish or worse—whiney. She regrouped and tried again. "You're the one who wanted the lab results." Like that whole disgusting episode was all his fault. He might like it when she was mad at him, but she couldn't say the same thing. "Besides, it's not like I'm ever going to talk to that troll again." The expression on his face didn't change. "What?"

"I didn't think you could do something like that. I

didn't think you lied." He had the nerve to look hurt. "Anna…"

Beneath the ice that had her frozen to this spot on the floor, she felt a simmering rage build. What the hell did his ex-wife have to do with any of this? "And you think I lie to you too?"

He looked at the ground and sort of shrugged his shoulders. "No…"

That was the loudest maybe she'd ever heard. The rage went from simmer to roiling boil in a flash. "You listen to me, Rebel Runs Fast. A girl's got to do what a girl's got to do. No one wants to do anything for anyone on the White Sandy. This is what it takes to get the medical supply place to stay open late, to get filing cabinets loaded, to get lab results in a hurry." She thought she was shouting, but she didn't give a shit. He opened his mouth to say something, but she didn't give him the chance. "I would think that you, of all people, would understand that sometimes you have to be the person everyone wants you to be, not the person you really are." His head jerked like she'd slapped him. Good. She was hitting a nerve. "And I've got news for you. I will not stand here and be made to feel the sinner just because I'm trying to help you and your little visions out, understand? If you don't like how I get things done, well, there's the door."

Her words settled around her in the silence that followed, and she realized what she'd actually just said. She'd mocked his visions. And told him to leave.

And now he was just looking at her, his face staggered with shock.

Damn it all to hell, she felt like she was going to throw up. The regret from her little speech whipped around the self-loathing from Leon the Troll until there was nothing left but gut-shaking revulsion. She wouldn't blame him if he did walk out that door. And if he walked out, well, would she really have anyone to blame but herself? She closed her eyes and took a cleansing breath, which didn't help much.

Which meant that when Rebel spoke, she was completely unprepared for what he said. "Hiya, Clarence."

Madeline's eyes flew open to find Clarence filling the doorway, looking cautiously at the two of them.

"Hiya, Rebel." He cleared his throat. "Doc." His brow furrowed as he looked at her, as if he was asking if everything was okay.

It was a question she could not answer, not now, and maybe not ever.

"Catch you later, Clarence," Rebel said, patting the big man on the shoulder as he walked out the door.

She watched him go, and then went and threw up in the bathroom.

So much for not perfect.

Chapter Fifteen

Rebel crouched in the sweat lodge, trying to clear his mind. He needed to get right with the world, but at this exact moment, he was anything but right.

He was starting to think he'd been wrong.

He poured another ladle of water over the stones and braced himself as the steam smacked him in the face. Man, he needed this. He needed something, anything to fill the void Madeline had left in his chest for the last three days. And a good sweat was the best option he had right now. Hell, who was he kidding? It was the only option.

Settling back into his spot, he worked on being still. It didn't come easy today, but then, today was Saturday, and he was out of the habit of being still on the weekends. Starting with his feet, he tensed and relaxed every muscle in his body. Calves, thighs, butt cheeks, stomach, shoulders, biceps—each muscle in turn tightened and then went still in the wet heat of the lodge.

Except for his mind. His mind was already tense, and no amount of effort on his behalf could relax the gnawing sense of wrongness that had followed him like a cartoon dark cloud for days now.

Shit, what was he doing? He should be in a river, holding a beautiful woman who loved him while the water washed him clean. Instead, he was sitting in a claustrophobic sweat lodge during the hot part of a Saturday afternoon with Jesse, Walter White Mouse, Burt Speaks Loud and, for once, Nobody Bodine. He should be glad he was here to make sure Nobody was included. He was actively doing his job as medicine man to the tribe. Jesse was thinking about a job, Walter was praying his plumbing kept working, Burt was worried about Irma and, well, he didn't know what had drawn Nobody out in broad daylight. But that didn't matter. He was here for his friends, his family. He should be glad he was doing his job well.

But he wasn't. All he could think about was Madeline. About how she'd looked like she was drinking four-day-old coffee when she'd been making all sorts of phony promises for some strange man. About how, when he'd opened his own fool mouth when he knew full well he should have kept it shut, she'd looked like he'd said he'd laced that coffee with arsenic. And, more than anything, about how she'd come up swinging, her face twisted as she spit her words out like they were weapons and he was the target. *"There's the door."* The words had sliced him down the center. He, of all people, should know about faking it. And she hadn't been faking that.

Shit, what had he done? She'd jumped to a conclusion—that he didn't approve of her actions, of her—and he'd just gotten the hell out of her way as she went over the edge of the cliff. He knew that sentence had started with an *if*. If he couldn't handle it, there was that door.

He'd wanted to tell her she had it all wrong. He hadn't thought she was whoring herself for him. It wasn't about her at all, really. The disgusting truth of the situation was that for ten minutes, she'd reminded him of Anna. *Anna.* Madeline had used deception as a last line of defense, at his bidding, and even that had just been empty promises. Not Anna. Flirting had always been her weapon of choice, and she wielded it as only a true master of the art could. Madeline had purred, "*Leon,*" at the end of the conversation, and all Rebel had heard was Anna breathing, "Jonathan," the first time they'd met. The first time he'd worn a sport coat and a bolo tie because that was what the gallery owner wore. The first time he'd felt like a fake.

As Madeline did her best for him—*him*—all he could think was *the end.*

The end.

Walter was chanting—Walter chanted a lot—but the sound was anything but soothing. Instead, each note was taunting him, reminding him that he was here with a bunch of sweating men and not there. With her.

And for what? Because she'd done exactly what he'd asked her to? He'd demanded results, and she'd done everything she could think of to give him just that. He'd deluded himself into thinking that the little world he'd made with her in it was above the reach of the outside world. He, of all people, should have known that would never be the case. He couldn't exist only in this world, and he'd already failed at the outside world.

"Find your own way." Albert's voice pulsed into the void between each chanted note.

Odd, Rebel thought, his head snapping up. He didn't feel like he normally did when he was in a vision. He could still see the inside of the sweat lodge in the dim light, still hear Walter going on and on.

Nothing else had changed but the clear sound of Albert's voice.

In English. He was serious about it. For the life of him, Rebel couldn't tell if he was having another *little vision* or not.

"I cannot see my way, *Thunkášila*." All he could see was the stricken pain on Madeline's face. The pain he'd made her feel.

The chanting was unbroken. No one else reacted to his statement. Had he spoken out loud or not?

"Find your own place." Albert sounded more insistent this time.

"I don't know where my place is," he replied, quieter this time. If he was talking to a spirit, there was no need to shout. And if he was delusional, well, he didn't need to shout at himself. "I've lost my path."

And that was the big difference. When Anna had walked away, he'd let her go because a part of him was relieved that he didn't have to pretend any longer. He was sad to see her leave, but a new path— medicine-man-in-training, beadwork artist, loyal grandson—had been right there in front of him. All he had to do was walk it. He had done so gladly. It had been an honest life.

And a lonely one. He hadn't realized how damn lonely he'd been until Dr. Madeline Mitchell had shown up, the outsider barging into his small little world. He'd never lied to her, never felt like he had to. Who he was had always been good enough for her. Even when she found out about the parts that weren't really real, she'd never demanded anything more from him. Instead, she challenged him, excited him and, more than anything, loved him for who he was.

He was Rebel Runs Fast. And he loved Madeline Mitchell.

"I am proud of you, my son." Rebel could almost see Albert nod his head, that warm smile on his face as he fried venison for dinner. Albert had always been proud of him, even when Rebel had given him nothing to be proud of. Like now. Nothing to be proud of, walking away from her.

He tried to tell himself he hadn't just walked away. He just hadn't wanted to continue that conversation in front of Clarence. But that didn't have a damn thing to do with the fact that he hadn't gone to her house last night, hadn't come for her this morning. He'd let Anna go, but he'd walked away from Madeline. He was being a coward. It left a bad taste in his mouth.

Unexpectedly, time stopped. He couldn't hear Walter. He couldn't hear Albert. He couldn't even breathe. In the total stillness that gripped him, he saw nothing. Then Madeline appeared, and he felt his gut unclench. *Home*, he thought as she got out of her Jeep and grinned at him. He was sitting on a porch, waiting for her. Where he should have been last night. Where he should be. The scene barely finished materializing before his eyes before it was gone in the steam.

Where he should be.

The damp heat filled his body as he sucked in air. The warmth burned through his uncertainty, his confusion.

His path was right there in front of him.

He just had to walk it.

It wasn't dignified, but Madeline waited for him. She sat on the porch for the third undignified night in a row, her eyes scanning the hills and valley until the night sky made it more obviously pointless than it already was.

He has to come back, she thought for the millionth time. He couldn't let her go—he'd said so himself, over and over, until she'd had no choice but to believe him. Until she'd had no choice but to fall in love with him. He had to come back. He had to come back for her.

She'd seriously considered going looking for him this afternoon. The sneakers had materialized on her feet, three bottles of water had stood at the ready on the counter and a floppy bucket hat had appeared in her hand.

But she hadn't made it past the porch. Instead, she'd stood there for almost an hour before she gave up and sat in the recliner. What would she have said if she'd found him? I'm sorry I did what you wanted? I'm sorry I got results? I'm sorry you overreacted? Please take me back?

She couldn't do it. He'd made his position plain, and Madeline Mitchell did *not* beg. Waited? Yes. Pined? Just a little. Begged? No. She had one shred of dignity left, and she clung to it fiercely. She didn't need him. She didn't need anyone. People needed her. That was how it worked before, and that was how it would work again. She just needed a little time to readjust, that was all.

Still, she waited.

Saturday night settled over the land with the same relentless darkness that had left her all alone on Thursday and Friday night. Again, he hadn't come.

She had to face facts.

He wasn't coming. Not for her.

Only five weeks to go until she broke the last guy's record.

The phone's ring cut through a dreamless sleep. Go away, Madeline thought as she rolled over. Nothing good could come from the phone ringing at... She propped open one eye. At 2:13 in the morning. Nothing good at all. She closed her eye again, willing the phone to stop ringing. It certainly wasn't Rebel—he'd never called her, not once. He didn't even own a phone. Which meant someone needed her, and right now, she didn't want to be needed outside of normal business hours.

But the phone kept on ringing with determined insistence. *Damn it*, she thought as she sat. This better be good.

"Madeline?" The voice was faint, but familiar.

"Tara?" Nothing good at all. Her brain kicked on in seconds. "What's the matter?"

Tara began to cry. "We're sick, Madeline."

Her stomach fell like a lead balloon. Tara didn't get sick, and Tara didn't cry, and Tara most definitely didn't call her at 2:13 in the morning. Not unless it was really bad. She was up and out of bed, pulling on her pants as she said, "What's wrong?"

"Nelly... " She was interrupted by the sound of vomiting.

Nelly. Nelly was sick, and Tara was throwing up. What the hell had happened? When Jesse had dropped Nelly off at the clinic at closing time last night everyone had been fine. Not even a headache. *Don't panic*, she told herself. Maybe it wasn't that bad. "Tara, where are you?"

"Oh, oh, Madeline," Tara wept. "She's so sick, and I'm sick, and Mom... "

"Can you make it to the clinic?"

"I don't... " The vomiting sounded louder this time. "I'm so sorry... "

Oh, no. Her totally together receptionist was hysterically, violently ill. "I'm coming, Tara. Where are you?"

"I'm so sorry... it's so late," Tara blubbered. "But Nelly... "

She pulled the receiver away from her ear just long enough to get her shirt on. "Tell me where you are. I'm coming, Tara. I promise."

"My house. Down the road from the Quik-E Mart. Oh, hurry, Madeline. Please."

She was out the door in seconds. *Come on*, she prayed as she powered up the cell and peeled out. *Just a few bars. That's all I need.*

"What?" Clarence demanded in a tired-but-super-pissed voice.

She'd have to apologize later for waking him up. She didn't have time for pleasantries now. "It's me, Madeline. Tara says everyone's sick. I'm going to pick them up. Can you meet me at the clinic?"

Clarence was silent for a moment. *Come on*, she thought. *I need you right now.* "That flu?" he finally said.

"Maybe it's not the flu. Maybe it's something else." Suddenly, Rebel looked more than delusional. He looked *right*. He'd been off by about four days, but something was wrong. Very wrong.

"I'll be there in... " The static crackled and Clarence was gone.

Didn't matter, she thought as she took another corner too fast. The Jeep fought for traction as she skidded, but then the tires gripped road again. Adrenaline poured into her system. Clarence was coming. She was going to need some backup.

Suddenly, she wished she knew where Rebel was, and it had nothing to do with her selfish wants and pitiful needs. She needed someone who could handle sick people, who knew his way around the clinic, who people trusted. Tara had always been a good third to Clarence's second, but it was obvious she was way past that point right now. And, given how terrifyingly sick Tara had sounded, Madeline was afraid she might need someone to start praying.

She needed a medicine man. She needed Rebel.

She slowed down just enough to call Albert's number. She'd never gotten around to deleting it off the phone, and now she was thankful for that. From what Rebel had said, Jesse was keeping the house. And Rebel had said there was always a floor there for him. Maybe she'd get lucky and both men would be there. Two birds with one call.

No one answered. Damn it all.

The dim light of the Quik-E Mart blinked in the distance. Not much else was around here, and the all-night convenience store stood out like a sore thumb. She looked past the fluorescent glow. Hopefully, someone in the house had been able to get a light on or a door open or something that would tell her she was at the right place.

There. A door was open, and it looked like someone was waving a flag or something. She breathed a sigh of relief. The last thing she wanted to do was waste time by busting in on non-sick strangers who just might have shotguns lying around.

The Jeep squealed to a stop. She grabbed her duffle as Mrs. Tall Trees called out to her. "Doctor, please hurry!"

"What happened?" The duffle weighed a ton, but right now it felt like nothing. She hauled it into the house in seconds flat.

Mrs. Tall Trees wavered until she made it to a chair. She was green around the edges, and the sickly sheen of sweat was only making her look worse. And she was the one who was up and moving.

Bad, bad, bad. Then Tara lurched into the small room, and Madeline realized just how bad it was. She made her mother look like the picture of health. Tara's hair had vomit in it, and she was sobbing as she blindly groped for the couch. "Nelly… " she moaned, sounding far weaker than she had on the phone.

"Where?"

"Bathtub," Tara managed to get out before she stuck her head between her legs.

She had no time to waste, but she couldn't afford to be stupid. She snapped on a pair of gloves and a surgical mask. Whether or not it was the flu, she couldn't afford to catch it. "Tara, Mrs. Tall Trees, get to the car. We're going to the clinic."

The women groaned as they began to move. Good. At least they were still ambulatory. She headed for the bathroom, steeling her mind for what was waiting for her.

God. She'd worked on people cut from auto wrecks, dug bullets out of abdominal cavities, and seen more than her fair share of bodily fluids. But nothing could prepare her for what she saw.

Nelly was in the tub, her eyes half closed as she shook under the steady trickle of water. She didn't have any pants on, but Madeline could see that pants, at this point, would have been useless. The girl was covered in her own diarrhea and vomit. Black was smeared all over her legs and backside, and Madeline knew that meant one thing and one thing only. Nelly was bleeding internally. The stench was overwhelming, even through the mask.

Shit. Literally and figuratively. How long had Nelly been sick? Internal bleeding made plain old diarrhea look like a walk in the park. The flu wouldn't do this, not this quickly.

For a painful second, Madeline wanted to crumple down next to the tub and cry as she tried to clean the child. This wasn't just a patient, a collection of symptoms to be dissected and treated. This was Nelly, the beautiful, happy little girl who played with babies in the waiting room and practiced the alphabet by helping organize files. It physically hurt to see her like this.

But that second was short. Screw the past tense. *Nelly is a beautiful, happy child,* Madeline thought like she was picking a fight. *Is.* She could lose it later. Right now, she had to keep it together or she'd lose so much more than her composure. She felt Nelly's forehead as she found a pulse. Nelly managed a small moan. She was hot, but her heartbeat wasn't exactly moving at an even pace. Double shit. She was in shock. She'd lost too many fluids too fast.

"Nelly, honey, we're going, okay? Just hold on, sweetie. We're going in just a second." She jerked the shower curtain off the rod and ran outside. Tara and her mother were leaning against the car, holding each other up. As far as Madeline could tell, they were just vomiting with great regularity. She flung open the back seat door and spread the shower curtain. "Tara, get in back." What was her mother's name? Terry. "Terry, you get in front." She jammed the key in the ignition and rolled all the windows down. "Try not to throw up in the car. I'm going to get Nelly."

God, she'd only been outside for a minute, two tops, and Nelly was worse. Her body began to twitch, and her eyes were rolled back in her head. "Shit," Madeline said as she grabbed the towels. If the bleeding didn't get her first, the dehydration would finish the job. The girl's eyes fluttered as Madeline turned the water off and draped two towels over her naked body. "It's okay, honey," she murmured as she lifted Nelly out. "I'm going to get you in the car, and then I'm going to get you some water, okay?"

"Mmmm."

Oh, thank God, Madeline thought. She's still in there.

"Mom's in the car, honey. I'm taking you right there." The towels wouldn't hold for long, but she had to run an IV *now*. No one could afford seizures, not if she was already this weak.

Madeline laid Nelly out on the backseat. Tara was still crying, but when Nelly made a throaty little whimper, she made a visible effort to pull herself together. "Baby," she said, sounding almost as shaky as Nelly looked. "Madeline's here. Madeline'll fix it."

"I promise, Nelly," Madeline added, praying to God it was a promise she would be able to keep. She ran back into the house and grabbed the duffle. Thank heavens she kept the thing stocked for any emergency, even one like this. There was one lonely bag of normal saline in there.

Quickly, she ran the IV, again taking comfort when Nelly managed a small whine. "I know, honey." She had a couple of smaller gauge IVs back at the clinic, but at least she'd been able to run this one. She turned to Tara and her tone sharpened. "No matter what, you hold this bag over your head, you understand?"

"Yeah." Tara sounded a little more focused. Good. Anything was better than nothing right now.

And they were off. It wasn't like there was a tremendous amount of traffic on the rez to begin with, but at three in the morning, there wasn't another car around for miles. Madeline took the roads at top speed, still wearing the mask and gloves. As she drove, she mapped out her game plan. Nelly would need the anti-diarrhea meds and something to stop her from throwing up—Zofran would be best—and enough electrolytes to fuel an elephant. That had to be first. Tara looked horrible, but neither she nor her mother appeared to be in any real danger.

Danger from what? That was the question she needed the answer to. Tara and her mother had the same basic symptoms everyone else had been having for months, and those symptoms were still consistent with some sort of virus. Nelly had the same symptoms, but magnified to the tenth power. A stomach virus wouldn't knock out the defenses of a healthy, well-fed child in just over twenty-four hours.

But a bacteria or a parasite might.

"Terry," she said. Mrs. Tall Trees was the least sick of the three. "Did you all do anything different yesterday? Eat anything different?"

The older woman took a hitched breath and covered her mouth with her hand. Finally, she said, "We just went to the church picnic."

"What did you eat?"

"Steak." Her voice wavered at the mention of food. "They had steak. It was a fundraiser for the new school." Then Terry lurched forward and stuck her head out the window.

Steak. Cattle. Not the flu.

Damn that man. He was right.

The list of things that could do this wasn't long, but the differences between a campylobacter and a cryptosporidium were crucial. Campylobacter was a bacterium and responded to the right drugs. Cryptosporidium was a parasite that just had to be waited out.

Nelly didn't have time to wait.

Madeline had a couple of courses of erythromycin at the clinic, and maybe one or two doses of tetracycline. But a lot of these bacteria were resistant, and if it was a parasite, it wouldn't do any good anyway.

She glanced in the rearview mirror as she crested the last hill. Tara was keeping the IV up by resting her arm over her head, and Nelly wasn't convulsing. She'd have to chance the antibiotics, she decided. She couldn't risk Nelly until she got lab results first thing Monday morning.

Monday seemed a hell of a long way off.

She pulled up in front of the door and unlocked the clinic. Where the hell was Clarence? She couldn't wait on him. "Tara. We have to get her out of here and onto a bed. You have to carry the bag, okay? Can you do that?"

252

Eyes closed, Tara nodded. And then shook her head no. "I... " She threw her head out the window and vomited. Madeline grimaced. At least Tara kept the bag up, but how the hell was Madeline going to get Nelly out of the car?

And then the most magical sound of all reached her ears.

Hoof beats.

She looked up to see Nobody Bodine flying in low and fast, with Rebel hot on his heels. Appearing out of nowhere in the dark, they looked like two out of the Four Horsemen of the Apocalypse. Any other day, she'd be wetting her pants at the sight of dark riders bearing down on her like they were coming in for the kill. Not today. She'd never been so happy to see them in her whole life. Behind them, headlights shone. Jesse, she realized. Three out of four wasn't bad.

Focus, girl, she scolded herself as Rebel and Nobody dismounted at dead runs. Jesse's truck squealed to a stop behind them. So they weren't trained medical professionals. They were able-bodied men, and they were what she had to work with. "Nelly—we've got to get her out of the car and into the clinic."

That was all she had to say. Rebel opened one door, Jesse the other, and together they extracted Nelly and Tara. Madeline grabbed the saline bag and they made it in.

"Wash up—now," she ordered both men. "Strip off anything that got slimed. Wear hospital gowns if you have to. We can't let this spread." The men nodded silently and peeled off their shirts.

Any other day, she'd love to just sit back and watch three of the finer chests on the White Sandy duke it out for the title of the hottest hunk. But today—hell, it was still tonight—wasn't any old day. "Gloves and masks," she added as she hooked the bag up to the pole. At least she wouldn't have to worry about that anymore.

"Little help here!" Clarence shouted from outside. Nobody and Rebel looked at each other, and then Nobody sprinted for the door. He reappeared seconds later, carrying Tammy. Clarence was right behind him, with Mikey in his arms. "Sorry I'm late, Doc. I stopped to check on these two, and they weren't doing... so... good." His voice trailed off as he looked at the carnage the clinic had quickly devolved into. "Shit." He sounded impressed.

Stick with me, Madeline thought, although she wasn't worried. Clarence had seen combat, and everyone here still had all their limbs. "Clarence, get Nelly on the oxygen and then you're on IV duty," she ordered, like she was quarterbacking the big play. "Nobody, cleanup duty. Jesse—" But Jesse wasn't listening to her. He was standing over his daughter, brushing her sweaty hair away from her face. *Okay*, Madeline thought. Two able-bodied men and Clarence. "Rebel, come with me."

Everyone moved. The clinic was silent except for the sound of retching. Mikey and Nelly were in the hospital beds, while the three Tall Trees women were sprawled out on the exam tables. In less than a minute, the smell of bleach filled the air. Mikey yelped in pain as Clarence ran the IV. *A good team*, she thought as she and Rebel headed for the stock closet.

God, she hoped it was campylobacter or E. coli or something like it as she began to pull what few items she did have off the shelf. "Shit," she muttered again as she grabbed the suppositories and the antibiotics and piled them into Rebel's arms. She had enough for the Tall Trees family. How many other people had been at that picnic? Would Nelly be able to keep it down long enough for it to work?

"What?" he asked.

She paused, suddenly aware that he was here when she needed him—when Nelly needed him. His face was calm and focused, but she could see the worry in his eyes. "I think you're right. But we can't wait until Monday—she's in shock, and I've got to stop her symptoms from cascading." At the mention of shock, Rebel got that fierce look, the one he wore when he was going to do battle. She'd seen it more than enough, starting when he shooed Walter White Mouse out of here and ending with the phone call to Leon Flagg. Except this time, he wasn't battling against her. He was battling *with* her.

"I'm going to do antibiotics, just in case. I don't have a hell of a lot of the anti-diarrhea meds. We'll just have to keep pumping her full of electrolytes."

He nodded as she hauled out the box of half-normal saline. She had the sinking feeling they were going to use the whole thing before much longer. And all the vials for samples. It was going to take time to get them back from the lab, but if this really was some contaminated beef, she'd need all the proof she could get.

"What else can I do to help?" Rebel asked.

She looked at him and all her regret—the slimy phone call, losing her temper, not going to look for him—melted into gratitude. "Pray," she said simply and headed out to her patients.

The night got better and worse at the same time. Within half an hour, Nelly's system was responding to the fluids and the intravenous antibiotics. She even managed to keep the Zofran down for a bit. After checking Nelly's file—easy to find since Tara had organized everything—Madeline made the executive decision to hook Nelly up to one of her precious pints of blood. She couldn't tell how much the girl had lost, and she was pretty far down on the total fluid count for a girl her size. Warding off shock meant hitting it with everything she had, and she had a bag of B+ blood. The result—a five-year-old girl with two different IVs running into her plus an oxygen tube—was almost as unsettling as finding her in the tub, but Madeline didn't have time to dwell.

Jesse donned the mask and gloves and then put himself on cleanup detail, giving his daughter a sponge bath and holding the bedpan for her when she threw up. Madeline felt proud of him, although she didn't have time to stop and think beyond that. Even though he was a toddler, Mikey hadn't been as far gone as Nelly was—he'd been a mess, but at least he hadn't been bleeding. He only had one IV, and that was doing its job. And the three women all managed to keep their antibiotics down. All good things. She'd gotten to them in time.

But they weren't the only ones who were sick. Before long, Madeline was in real danger of running out of IVs. She already had people lying on the floor and sitting in the waiting room, with the patients who could stand acting as human IV poles. Rebel had taken over Tara's job, answering the phone and pulling files while Nobody made pass after pass of the place, trying to stay one step ahead of the mess. She thought Jesse was washing down all the kids, but she couldn't be sure.

They were barely keeping their heads above water. The clinic got more and more crowded as people dragged themselves in. Everyone was throwing up, which was bad enough, but the diarrhea seemed to be hitting the kids the hardest. And the story was all the same. Everyone who was sick had gone to the church picnic. Everyone had eaten steak.

For Madeline, each hour had been the same as the one before. Sick people, not enough space, not enough supplies. She felt vaguely like she was stuck in a movie—everyone had had the fish, the pilot was ill and was there anyone on board who could fly a plane? That was just the exhaustion talking, she knew. It had all started to blur in a mess of vomit and saline and bleach when she looked up and saw it was seven in the morning. Dawn had happened at some point, which meant it was morning in Columbus.

It took three tries before Melonie answered the damn phone, but when she heard Madeline's voice, she didn't even whine about the ungodly hour. The woman was an Internet-stalking genius. In twenty minutes, Madeline had the home phone number of the owner of the medical supply place in Rapid City. She didn't have time to do it Melonie's way, so when the owner, one Mr. Hubert Terstrip, told her he couldn't possibly make it to the store today because it was Sunday, she broke out the Mitchell sneer with enough force to make half the waiting room recoil in fear.

She sure as hell wasn't going to let a little thing like Sunday keep her from containing this mess. "If I lose a single patient because you didn't get me what I needed," she shouted, not caring who heard her, "I'll sue your ass back into the last century and then, once you're there, I'll sue it again. And I'm talking class action, Mr. Terstrip. Hordes of lawyers, all wanting a piece of you, for years. By the time I'm done with you, you'll be begging to open the damn store on Sunday and give me what I need."

Even Rebel backed up a step. Well. At least the Mitchell sneer was working again, even with a surgical mask covering her mouth. She'd have to remember this version of it the next time she needed to put that man in his place—but that wasn't today. She waited.

"Fine," Mr. Terstrip said, sounding anything but happy about it. "But I'm not going in before nine, you hear me?"

"Fine. Nine it is. I'm sending an associate," she replied, feeling the sneer crack just a little into something that might be a smile. Rebel's eyebrows knit together in suspicion. She nodded, and he nodded back. Rebel was the only one who could do it right now. "He'll pay with my credit card."

With a snarl, Mr. Terstrip hung up.

"Supplies?" Was she insane, or did she hear a little joke in his voice as he dug out a pen and a piece of paper?

She snatched them out of his hand and chose to ignore whatever double entendre he may or may not be slinging at 7:46 in the morning on less than four hours of sleep. "Can you do this?" She needed more of everything—dextrose, saline, IVs for both kids and adults, more Zofran for the kids and lots and lots of antibiotics.

"You can count on me," he replied as she dug out her card.

"Can I?"

Over the top of his own mask, he gave her a look that said, "Oh, come *on*," and she mentally winced. This was not the time or the place to get into that again, not when she needed his help. His help, she reminded herself. Not him. "I can cover four, okay?"

"Thousand?"

Damn, she hated it when he got mildly bug-eyed. Him looking freakish made her feel freakish. "Do the best you can."

Rebel got himself back under control. After all, Madeline reminded herself, he'd been up for hours on heavens-only-knew what kind of sleep too. He took the list, read through it once and held out his hand for the credit card.

She paused for a second. This was unfettered access to her back account. But then, he'd already had unfettered access to her body. Was this any different? And she was desperate. Behind her, the wet sound of projectile vomiting hit her ears. Desperation in a nutshell. She gave him the card, and he tucked it in his back pocket. "If he gives you any crap, you have my permission to beat the hell out of him."

He caught her eyes and held her gaze for a long moment. She tried to read his eyes, but all she could see was something that might be admiration, professional respect.

"I'm going," he said, his voice low and suddenly intimate.

"Go, then."

With a nod of his head, he turned and stepped over patients on the floor.

But come back, she added silently as Jesse's truck peeled out of the parking lot.

Come back.

Chapter Sixteen

Normally, it took Rebel about an hour and fifteen or twenty minutes to get to Rapid City. Today, he made it in under an hour, which, unfortunately, left him with seven minutes to sit in the Terstrip Medical Supply parking lot and figure out how he wanted to handle this. Madeline had gone in with both barrels blasting, but he wasn't Madeline. And he'd never met any of these people, so he didn't know what was coming. Who would he need to be? Rebel or Jonathan?

As he debated, he looked around. He'd never been on this side of the city. When he came in, he stuck to the gallery neighborhoods and the Super-Mart strip malls. A corner grocery that looked like it catered to Mexican immigrants was up the block and a manufactured-home sales lot was across the street. Terstrip Medical Supply took up most of a whole block all by itself. Together, they gave the place a desolate, industrial feel at nearly nine on a Sunday morning.

He wondered what time the grocery opened. No one had eaten anything since he'd shown up, and Madeline probably wouldn't let anyone eat anything that had already been in the clinic for fear of cross-contamination. But everyone would need something to keep going, or they wouldn't be any better off that the patients. His stomach managed a small growl in agreement.

At exactly nine, a smooth black sedan with dark windows pulled into the lot and an ill-tempered man who looked dressed for church got out and slammed the door. His comb-over ruffled in the slight breeze as he stalked up to the door, unlocked it and wrenched it open.

He'd have to go in as Rebel, he decided. Nothing about Terstrip said he could be flattered into anything right now. He followed Terstrip into the store.

"Well?" Terstrip snarled, his lip curling up in distaste. "Who the hell are you?"

"Jonathan Runs Fast. Dr. Mitchell sent me to pick up the supplies." No need to give this man more to glare about. He held out the list.

Terstrip looked at him like he'd taken a dump in the middle of the sidewalk. "You're an *associate*? You look like a dirty hippie. A *girl* hippie."

So much for politeness. He knew it didn't have much on Madeline's sneer, but he didn't have to look mean. He just had to look a little dangerous, so he smiled. Terstrip froze. Smiling always threw people off. "I'm just here for the supplies."

Unfreezing, Terstrip scooted behind the counter. Gun or baseball bat? Rebel hoped baseball bat. They were a lot easier to dodge than bullets. "You dirty Indian, you'll probably just steal the stuff, try to get high or something. I outta call the police on you, on all your kind."

To hell with *looking* dangerous. He was feeling a whole lot of dangerous. Terstrip started to duck under

261

the counter, but Rebel moved before he could get anywhere and had the man by his Sunday-best lapels. "Too bad that they'd never find me. You know Indians. We all look alike. But they would find *you*."

"Take your hands off me!"

That's better, Rebel thought. Proper fear. Terstrip started to stink with it.

"I'm just here for the supplies," he repeated, aiming for more menacing this time. Too bad he hadn't brought Nobody. Nobody could do menacing like, well, nobody. The man was a professional at it. Rebel was a rank amateur in comparison. However, Terstrip didn't know it. His eyes widened even more. "And then I'll leave." He let go of the man and got ready to dodge lumber.

"What's going on in here?"

The sound of a soft voice whipped him around to see a petite woman with big, artificially blonde hair standing in the doorway. She had the kind of sweetheart face that said she'd turned a lot of heads back in her time, Even now, her generous curves were still a sight to appreciate.

He felt a sigh of relief try to escape. A woman like that—even if she was married to this asshole— was someone he could handle with his eyes closed. He whipped off his hat and let Jonathan's eyes do the talking for him. She blushed. Oh, yeah. He knew how to handle a pretty woman. "Ma'am, I was just *thanking* your husband for opening up for us today." He let his accent drawl on a little. Most every woman he'd ever met had a secret thing for a tall, dark, mysterious stranger. "The clinic has just been flooded with sick children."

A manicured hand flew to her mouth. "Oh, goodness, what happened?"

Rebel stepped away from the counter, just in case Terstrip took advantage of this distraction and tried to bash in his brains. "Ma'am, we were at a church picnic, and most everyone got food poisoning. My niece… " He drifted off. It didn't take much work to get choked up. He'd tried real hard not to think about what Nelly had looked like when Madeline found her, because she'd looked terrifying enough when he'd pulled her from the back seat of the Jeep. In that crystalline moment, he'd seen the sickness had come, but not with the silent, sterile whiteness of his smallpox vision. If he didn't get the hell out of Dodge, and soon, Madeline would be fighting a losing battle with a death of moaning and retching and shit that reeked to high heaven. And he didn't have to be a medicine man to see that Nelly would be first. "The children are suffering, ma'am. The doctor needs more supplies or we might start losing them… "

Mrs. Terstrip looked like she wanted to hug him. "Oh, you poor thing. Church picnic, you say?"

You poor thing. The words scraped over his ears like steel on flint. *No*, he yelled to himself. *You've got her where you want her. Just reel her in, and then you can go.* "Ma'am, the St. Francis parish on the far side of the White Sandy reservation." He didn't have a problem with Catholicism on the whole—they did good work and educated a hell of a lot of people who otherwise wouldn't get anywhere, like Tara. However, they'd only added classes in Lakota culture to the curriculum a year or so ago. That was why Tara and Tammy and whole bunches of people didn't speak the language. While it was true that he hadn't been at yesterday's picnic, he'd gone to one or two in the past. "It was a fundraiser for a new school," he added, trying to sound mournful. "I've got the money to pay for the supplies, but I've got to hurry. My niece... she's only five, ma'am."

"Oh, goodness." This time, she did touch him. She patted his arm with sympathetic sorrow, but Rebel couldn't help but note that her touch lingered for about two seconds longer than it should have.

A girl's got to do what a girl's got to do, Madeline's voice whispered in his ear. He gritted his teeth through the appreciative smile he was favoring Mrs. Terstrip with. *And sometimes*, he silently replied, *a man's got to do what a girl asks him to.* He realized that no matter how hard this was for him, it had been a thousand times harder for her, but she'd done it anyway, for him. He saw exactly what kind of first-class jerk he'd been. Later, after the dust had settled and everyone was out of the woods, he owed her the biggest apology ever. He, of all people, should know about faking it. Like he was doing right now. "I do appreciate you took time away from your own worship to help us out." *This is it*, he thought. Going for the kill. "You truly are doing God's work today."

Her hand was now resting on his biceps, and, given the warm weight of it, she was about ten seconds from squeezing. "Bless your heart," she said, her eyes watering.

"Kathy!" Terstrip snapped from behind Rebel, making them both jump. "What the hell are you doing? This man is a criminal."

"Don't be ridiculous, Hubert." Any trace of the

caring-mother figure disappeared in a heartbeat. "You heard him. He needs his stuff." She let go of Rebel and marched back to her husband. "Why are you just standing around? Go on, get moving."

Mission accomplished, Rebel thought as he kept his victory grin to himself. As the two of them traded snipes behind the counter, he wondered what would be the best, least dangerous way to make it up to Madeline. Flowers weren't enough, and she rarely wore jewelry. While he tried to come up with something that would convince her to take him back, he found himself looking out the front door at the manufactured-home lot. There, gleaming in the morning sun, was a pristine white house on cinderblocks. The porch ran the length of the house and was wide enough for some chairs. Or even a recliner.

The vision he'd had in the sweat lodge yesterday—although it felt like a lifetime ago—floated back through his mind and seemed to merge with the house he was looking at. He saw himself sitting on that porch in the early evening sun as Madeline pulled up in the Jeep. He saw her get out and rush up the porch, where he met her with a kiss. He saw the two of them settle back into the recliner and watch the sun finish setting.

He saw home.

Shaking back to reality, he glanced back at the Terstrips. Hubert had a couple of boxes on a wheeled cart.

"Is there anything I can do to help?"

"No!" Hubert shouted, no doubt afraid that once behind the counter Rebel would start stuffing painkillers in his pocket. "This will take about half an hour. You can wait in your truck."

"Hubert!"

"I'll be back," he called over his shoulder as he headed across the street. *Open*, the neon sign in the sales office announced.

His path was right there in front of him.

He just had to walk it.

By the time he got back to the clinic, it was almost noon. Nobody was outside waiting for him, and silently they offloaded the boxes. *Damn*, he thought as Madeline tore into the first one like a hungry animal, *she looks like hell*. He couldn't see a lot of her—she had on that mask she was making everyone wear, her less-than-pristine doctor's coat and gloves covered her arms, and she even had on one of those shower caps doctors wore in surgery. The only things he could see were her eyes, but that was enough to worry him.

The bags under her eyes were so purple that he was afraid for a moment someone had been beating up on her in his absence, but he quickly realized she was just that tired. Her eyelids weren't even making it past half-mast, which gave her the air of being permanently pissed.

He didn't want her to be pissed at him. "Madeline—"

Her head jerked up. She may look exhausted, but behind those lids, her eyes were still sharp—sharp enough to stop his apology in its tracks. He almost bit his tongue.

"Did that ass give you any trouble?" she said under her breath to him as he ripped open the box of IVs.

Wrong conclusion, again. The relevant conclusion, but still the wrong one. And he couldn't do a damn thing about it right now. "Nothing I couldn't handle. I've got the receipt." *Both of them.*

She shot him a sharp look but let it slide. "Hang on to it. We don't have time to file anything." She scooped up a few bags of saline and IVs and went right back to work.

That's right. They didn't have time for filing and talking and apologizing and making up. They had work to do.

So he got to work.

"I think we've turned a corner," Madeline said, the weariness dripping off each word as she chugged a Gatorade outside. Something about electrolytes, she'd said when she'd sent him to clear out the Quik-E Mart of all its sports drinks. Rebel thought she sounded worse than she did when she'd come looking for him during the hot part of the day. "Some of these people can be just as miserable at home." She turned to look at him. "Do you want to be the chauffeur, or should we send Jesse?"

We. There was still a *we*. She'd been too tired to notice it, no doubt, and there was always a chance that she'd meant *we* in a medical-professional sense. But she was looking at him when she said it.

"Jesse." Rebel didn't want to leave, frankly. He wanted to keep close to her. She looked like a drowned rat. Plus, he was tired. In addition to the Rapid City run, he'd made peanut butter sandwiches—outside, away from the germs—for anyone who wanted one and tried to keep up with the patient files—although he knew Tara would probably have a cow once she started feeling well enough to see what he'd done to her carefully organized system. He'd called the priest at the church and Tim, at Madeline's request. He'd burned sage and said prayers with anyone who wanted him to, which had been nearly everyone, despite the number of practicing Catholics in the clinic. When people felt that bad, it didn't matter who was praying for them, as long as someone still cared.

In addition to his medicine-man responsibilities, he'd gone over Madeline's Jeep—inside and out—with bleach and a scrub brush. He suspected she owed someone a new shower curtain because they sure as hell weren't getting that one back. He'd burned it in the trash barrel, along with the steady supply of contaminated medical waste. He was probably single-handedly jacking up the pollution rate for the rez, but Madeline had been explicit, and he trusted her when she said to burn everything.

All in all, it had been one hell of a day.

It wasn't like Jesse hadn't also been pulling his weight. Both hospital beds had two kids lying toe-to-toe in them. Madeline didn't want to put the little ones on the floor if she could help it, and Jesse took it upon himself to keep the kids as clean and as calm as he could. As he sponged down kid after kid, he told the old stories that Albert had raised him and Rebel on, of Iktomi and Manstin, turtles and bears. He held hands when an IV had to be moved or a shot given, and he didn't complain once about being puked on. Albert would have been proud. Rebel sure was.

Still, someone had to be the driver. He headed into the clinic to delegate. "Jesse, Madeline says Tara and Tammy and Terry can call go home. Can you take them?"

Jesse looked at Nelly, who was sleeping fitfully. "She stays?"

Nelly was still hooked up to two IVs, although Madeline had taken her off the oxygen. "For now. I'll keep an eye on her, okay? It won't take long, but we've got to get some of these people out of here."

For a second, Jesse looked like he normally did, pouty and whining and angling for the easy way out of everything. But then he squared his shoulders, his eyes gleaming with a new purpose. "As long as no one dies on me… "

Rebel couldn't help but chuckle. "I don't think Madeline would send them home if she thought they were going to do that."

Jesse leaned over and kissed Nelly's forehead through his mask. Rebel never thought he'd see the day—Jesse being a real father to his daughter.

The situation seemed to have stabilized. Madeline began discharging patients with a fervor that struck Rebel as religious. Everyone went home with a four-week supply of antibiotics, explicit orders to finish all four weeks and some Imodium.

Finally, they were down to four kids and two elders still on IVs, which meant that for the first time in a long time, everyone was either on an exam table or a bed. Jesse had returned from one of his runs with bags of chips, candy bars and soda from the Quik-E Mart and handed them out like he was Santa. Nobody was making another pass of the place, using his mop as a crutch. The man was a night owl to begin with, but even he was slowing down.

By comparison, they were the ones in good shape. Madeline was... well, Rebel wouldn't say collapsed at Tara's desk, but she was damn close. Her gloved hands were propping up her masked face, but even with all that, her head was only four inches off the desk. She looked like a zombie in a lab coat.

"You should go home." Rebel crouched down next to her, wanting to put his arm around her shoulders and hold her until she was safely off to dreamland. He was pretty sure that wasn't the best course of action right now. Zombies were unpredictable, and he sure as hell didn't want his head bitten off. Not to mention they both needed a bath in the worst sort of way.

Her head didn't move, but her eyes found the clock on the wall. He followed them and saw that it was eight. The sun had just about finished setting outside. "That was a bone-crushing twenty hours of triage." She sounded like she'd been crushed, all right. Flatter than a pancake.

"Go home, Madeline," he said more gently. He couldn't help it. He inched closer to her. "Get some sleep."

This time, her head did move. With what looked like a hell of a lot of effort, she swung it around and fixed him with a look that was pure stubbornness. "Clarence first."

"You," he said more insistently. She couldn't be serious—but everything about her said she was.

"No," she replied just as insistently. "I'm staying until the lab calls. I have to know if we did the right thing."

Rebel felt like she'd slapped him. Because of her, not a single person had died today. Not even Nelly.

270

How could she think she'd been wrong? He caught the frustrated shout before it got out. She was jumping to conclusions again. But this time, he wasn't going to let her go. "*You* did the right thing." His arm twitched, like it wanted to grab hold of her all by itself. He fought to keep it still. "All you."

The stubbornness melted into something else as her eyes crinkled. Damn it, this mask thing was seriously impeding his ability to read her, but he thought she was smiling.

"I couldn't have done it without you, Rebel."

"We make a good team, don't we?"

The crinkles disappeared into an unreadable blankness. "I was under the impression that *we* didn't do anything anymore."

He swallowed. He didn't want to beg—and he really didn't want to beg in the middle of the clinic, the smell of bleach and sage and barf still strong in the air—but he would if he had to. "That's not the impression I was operating under."

She blinked, her eyelids moving at two different speeds. Damn it, this was not the time to be having this conversation, not when she was dead on her feet and they still had kids hooked up to IVs. Here he was, trying not to be a jerk, and he was still screwing it up.

He waited for some sort of reaction from her for a minute, but got nothing else but a few more off-kilter blinks. "Come on," he said, getting to his feet and pulling her to hers. "I'll take you home."

Unexpectedly, she jerked her arm out of his hand and spun back to the beds. "Clarence," she said in that boss-of-the-world voice she'd been using all day. "If you go home, will you sleep?"

"Hell, yeah," was the muffled reply as Clarence lumbered in from the stock room with an armful of clean sheets.

"Go home, get cleaned up and get some sleep. I want you back here at eight tomorrow morning."

Rebel caught her arm again. "Madeline, what are you doing?"

"I told you," she snapped, sounding victorious. "I'm not leaving until I get those results. Clarence?"

The big man's head rolled in their direction. "Yeah?"

Madeline turned to Rebel. He thought she was smiling again. "Take Rebel with you. Make sure he gets a shower too. I don't want to see either of you here for twelve hours. Do I make myself clear?"

Painfully. Rebel was tempted to growl at her, but he should have known. What Madeline needed was to get some rest, but Dr. Mitchell had overruled that basic need without missing a beat. Second nature. "I'm coming back for you."

Her eyes flashed, and in spite of the insanely long day, he felt a spark of heat from her. "Not until eight, you aren't. And if you show up before then, I'll—" Rebel fought the grin. She was too tired to even make a proper threat.

"Don't hurt yourself." He stepped around her and, nodding his head for Nobody to follow, went to talk with Jesse. "She's ordering me out."

Jesse managed to raise his eyebrows, but gravity was too much for him. By the time he said, "This a reoccurring habit?" his eyebrows were already back where they'd started.

Rebel managed a good-enough glare. Actually, now that he thought about it, he was beat. A hot shower and a flat surface—he thought Clarence even had a couch—sounded mighty nice right about now. "I want you two to stay here with her. Sleep in shifts, let her get as much shut-eye as possible. I'll be at Clarence's. I don't care what she says—something goes south, you call us quick. Got it?"

"No one gets past me," Nobody said, and despite all those bone-crushing hours, he still managed to pull off a damned convincing menace.

"And that's how I want it." Rebel shook both men's gloved hands. "Take care of them."

"Rebel." Jesse fixed him with a pretty convincing stare of his own. Not bad for a little twerp. "You can count on us."

"Yo, Rebel! Get the lead out!" Clarence was already out the door.

Rebel stopped by the desk on his way out. He wanted to kiss her, even if that meant just pressing his masked lips to her masked cheek. But he didn't even get that chance. Ice-blue eyes rimmed in red looked up at him.

"Jesse and Nobody will keep an eye on things. Try to get some sleep, Madeline."

"Go." It was an order.

"I'm going."

But I'm coming back, he thought.

I'm coming back for you.

"Can't this hunk of junk go any faster?"

"And good morning to you too, sunshine," Clarence said, not even bothering to take it personally as he fiddled with the radio. "She's not going anywhere. Keep your pants on."

273

They both knew which *she* Clarence meant. Rebel forcibly snapped his mouth shut and waited for the big man to put the pedal to the metal.

Finally, the truck picked up speed. *Shit*, Rebel thought. Blue Eye would leave them in the dust. They weren't going to make it by eight, and to Rebel, each minute after that was a shot through the heart.

Madeline. He had to get to Madeline. He'd never seen her less pretty than when she'd kicked him out of the clinic last night—shower cap, red eyes, exhaustion rolling off of her in waves—but even then, she'd been a beautiful angel of mercy. She hadn't just tried to stop the sickness, she'd succeeded. She'd stopped the whatever-it-was dead in its tracks. Even if he hadn't been in love with her, he would have been brimming with the kind of gratitude that can only be earned the hard way. He owed her everything—including that apology. And now she needed him, and he needed to be there for her.

"Can I ask you a question?" he heard himself ask as he mused on his angel of mercy.

"Hoo boy," Clarence said under his breath. "What?"

"Do you like her? Madeline, that is?"

"Sure. I like paychecks."

"Not like that." Maybe he needed a little more sleep, because he wasn't doing a bang-up job of saying what he wanted. "Do you *like* her?"

Clarence shot him a look out of the corner of his eye that said, *watch it*. "Yeah. I like her. Not like you do, though."

Rebel rolled his eyes.

"Why do you ask?"

Rebel pressed on. "She's a good doctor? You like working with her?"

"Yes, okay? She's a damn good doctor—or did you blink out last night?"

"You wouldn't mind working with her on a more permanent basis?"

The silence filled the truck's cab as the miles squeaked past. "Is that what you're thinking?"

"Yeah." Permanent. Permanent like a house with a porch. Like a wedding. Like forever.

He'd tried forever once before, but if he was really honest with himself—and there was no time like the present—he'd known then that it wasn't *forever* forever. This was different. This really could be his forever—if she didn't order him out. Again.

"We could do a lot worse than her—and we have. But I doubt we could do a whole hell of a lot better," Clarence finally said. He sounded almost like he was lost in thought. "You think she'll go for it?"

The clinic crested over the hill. Jesse's truck was still out front next to her Jeep, and he could see both Blue Eye and Nobody's horse off in the distance. Two other cars filled out the lot. From a distance, it looked like a normal Monday.

Normal for the rez, anyway. "I don't know," he replied in all honesty.

"Well, if she don't, try not to piss her off so much that she bails. She's supposed to stay for another year and a half."

The vote of confidence was underwhelming, but then Clarence had busted in on them when Madeline had jumped right off the cliff of conclusions. The fact Clarence hadn't already punched his lights out was probably as good as it was going to get. "I'll do what I can."

The truck pulled to a stop. Even though he'd been itching to get here, he sat for just a second, bracing himself for whatever version of doctor-lover-zombie was waiting for him. Knowing her, she'd refused to sleep much, if at all. She wouldn't have wanted to miss anything, or she wouldn't have trusted Nobody and Jesse.

He was betting it all on zombie. Big time.

Four people were sitting in the waiting room, looking miserable but not deathly. Madeline was sitting at Tara's desk.

Sitting, he quickly corrected himself, was too strong a word. She was slumped over, nose-to-nose with the desk in a way that didn't look like she'd moved a lot recently.

"Madeline?" He got no response, not that time or the next three times he said it, not even the last time, when he nearly shouted it in her ear.

Nobody sidled up next to him and nodded to the waiting people.

"How long?" Rebel asked.

"Ten minutes. I, uh, told them they had to wait." He looked down at Madeline, and Rebel was surprised to see real concern in his eyes.

Rebel nodded. Clarence could handle the new people. "Good thinking." He looked back to Madeline.

Nobody's head ducked. He actually looked embarrassed. *The man must be exhausted*, Rebel thought. He never looked embarrassed, especially during daylight hours when someone might actually see him.

"She wouldn't sleep. She just sat there, staring at the phone," said Nobody.

That was an apology, Rebel realized. And staring was an overstatement. She was sleeping with her eyes open. "It's okay. I'm gonna take her home and put her to bed. Can you get home okay? Do you need a ride?"

Nobody's shoulders stiffened. "I can stay."

"You've been here for thirty-two hours. So have Madeline and Jesse." Speaking of, where was Jesse? Rebel stepped out of the waiting room and found Jesse in a relocated waiting-room chair, looking like a Slinky gone haywire. He had one hand on Nelly's arm, the other on a different kid's arm, and his legs looked like jelly left out in the sun too long.

"Jesse," Rebel said as he nudged jelly legs with his boot. "Wake up. Go home." And then, feeling a whole hell of a lot like boss of the world, he added, "Take Nobody with you. Both of you get a shower and some sleep. Or else."

Jesse started, rubbing his eyes with the back of his hand. "Huh? Oh. Rebel."

"Go home," he said again, pulling Jesse to his feet. "Clarence is here. We'll keep an eye on Nelly."

"Oh. Yeah. Home." Jesse slapped his face twice and shook out some of the cobwebs. "Uh, Nobody, you coming?"

Nobody managed to look inconvenienced, which was enough to make Jesse pale. Jesse didn't know Nobody, after all. When it had been them against the world for the last thirty-two hours, that had been one thing. But in the light of day, Nobody was still more or less an unknown.

Rebel shot Nobody the strictest look he had, which turned out to be enough.

"Thank you kindly," Nobody said as he slipped out the door ahead of Jesse.

Two down, Rebel thought with a mental sigh. *One to go.*

As he crossed the room, the phone rang. The sound froze him in his tracks for a second, but when the phone rang again and Madeline made no movement to answer it, Rebel found his feet and ran to pick it up.

"Clinic, this is Jonathan," he said, hoping and praying that this was the lab. If the lab called, he could take her home. Everything would be okay.

At the sound of his white name, he swore everyone in the clinic turned and stared—even Clarence. But if it was the lab, he didn't want to scare anyone off with Rebel.

"Uh, yeah, this is Open Diagnostics," a high-pitched male voice cut through the static. "I'm calling for a Madeline Mitchell."

"Dr. Mitchell is with a patient," he lied. He'd heard Tara say it enough. "She is expecting your call and told me to take a message. If she has any questions, she'll call back."

"Can't you get her? You're talking to Leon Flagg here. I *head* the lab."

Oh, Leon! Madeline's fake giggle floated back to him. His hand clenched in a fist as if it thought it could punch the asshole out over the telephone line. "I'm sorry," he replied, amazed at how smooth and un-homicidal he managed to sound. "She's performing a procedure... " Yeah, sure. If you called slack-jawed staring a procedure.

"Yeah, yeah. Well, you tell her that what she's

278

got there is a nasty little double infection there, campy and E. Coli. You tell her that I've never seen concentrations so high. Where the hell did she get that sample?" Suddenly the high-pitched voice dropped a notch or two. Leon was impressed. "Because levels like that of those two things together would kill a man inside a day, no question."

"E. Coli? Campy?" He didn't know what the hell it was, but he wrote it down anyway. At least he'd heard of E. coli. Then he looked at Madeline.

Instead of the zombie, she was staring at him, her bloodshot eyes wide with recognition. So he didn't know what campy was. She did, and that was all that mattered.

"You know, campy. Campylobacter jejune?" Leon sighed. "Can I talk to someone who knows what they're doing?"

He tried to phonetically spell campylobacter, just in case Madeline wouldn't remember this conversation when she woke up. "I'm sorry, sir, but everyone is helping with the procedure." Leon snorted as a new thought occurred to Rebel. Madeline had made him call Tim last night, and Tim was the law around here. She'd been treating the campy outbreak like it was a crime scene—but the hard proof was with Leon. "Will the lab be sending out a full report?"

"Yeah, yeah, don't get your panties in a bunch. We'll finish it up and have it in the mail by the end of the week."

That was probably as good as it was going to get—unless someone started offering sexual favors. Rebel shuddered at the thought. "Is there anything else I should pass along to Dr. Mitchell?"

The pause was too long. "Well, I would love to meet the doctor herself. Do you know if she'll be coming to Baltimore anytime soon? Maybe with her sister?"

If he thought he *could* punch a man through a telephone wire... "Like I said, the doctor will call if she has any more questions." And he hung up the phone as fast as he could before he said something that would get their lab report lost in paperwork limbo.

"Campy. E. Coli. Campy." Madeline was repeating to herself, so softly that it sounded like she was just breathing. "Campy."

"Yeah. That." He pulled out the chair she was sitting in and crouched down in front of her. "Is that good?"

"It's... a... bacteria." She was averaging one completed blink an hour, and each word seemed to take about half of what she had left.

"And you gave everyone antibiotics." She'd done the *right* thing, as she'd put it. She'd made the right call.

"Yeah." Her head moved, and he saw that her eyes—still wide—were all shiny.

She was about to start crying.

He had to get her out of here. She was done, toast, stick a fork in her, and anything else she said or did right now would only come back to embarrass her. "Clarence. The lab said it was campylo-something and E. coli."

"Shit," the big man whistled to himself. Some of the kids giggled—the sweetest sound he'd ever heard. "Campy. I'll be... " Clarence shot a warning look at the kids, "... darned." They all whined in disappointment.

Rebel didn't like being the only one in the room who didn't know what was going on—it was a foreign feeling, to say the least. But he couldn't care about that right now. "Listen. I'm taking her home and putting her to bed."

Clarence looked at him, at the kids in the beds and at the new, pitiful patients. Rebel thought he seemed a little anxious. Talk about a foreign feeling— Clarence never looked anxious.

Rebel sighed as he pulled Madeline to her feet. Her knees buckled, and he was forced to sweep her off her feet in full view of everyone. What the hell. If things were going to be more permanent around here, this was as good a place to start as any. "Give me an hour or so to get her cleaned up. I'll come back." She wouldn't miss him while she was passed out. He just had to be there when she woke up.

"Thanks, man," Clarence called after him as he carried Madeline out to her Jeep. She didn't even flinch when he whistled for Blue Eye to follow them.

And then he took her home.

Chapter Seventeen

Madeline had the nagging feeling she should be doing something—something besides chasing a rabbit down his hole. She'd been having strange chase dreams the whole night, but as she lay in bed in the limbo of not awake and not asleep, the only one she could remember was of Alice in Wonderland. She'd been wearing her costume from trick-or-treating when she was seven, but she'd chased that damned rabbit all over the rez. That was all she had, though. Alice in Wonderland and something to do.

God, what was it? She knew she had something she needed to get up and do, but her eyelids were not responding. Nothing was responding. She tried to say something—tried to tell herself to get out of bed—but she couldn't even manage a mumble. And attempting to swing her legs out of bed was even less productive. No, it seemed she had no choice but to lie there and continue drifting.

Still, that *something* itched at her—if only she could remember what it was. *That does it*, she thought with growing impatience. *I am waking up. Right now. That's an order.*

Which, actually, didn't turn out to be *right now*. Even concentrating all of her effort, waking up was more like climbing underwater stairs in the dark. A long set of underwater stairs.

Finally, her eyelid—just one, the left one—opened. An amber glow made the ceiling of her little cabin look like a magnificent dome of some cathedral. The brightness of the room popped the other eyelid open for her. An amber glow? The sun didn't hit this side of the house until late in the evening. Her heart picked up the pace, which was enough to get the rest of her moving. She managed to get her head turned to the clock. What the hell time was it?

6:10. As in, 6:10 in the evening. As in, 6:10 at *night*.

She swung her feet over the bed and shook her head. It didn't help. She should be doing *something*? Holy hell, she should be at *work*! She'd slept through work? How did she sleep through the *entire day*? It was Monday, for God's sake. It's not like she could just... sleep... through...

Monday. The lab.

And from there, her brain filled in the blanks like it had just been waiting for the word *go*.

The phone call. Nelly, sick. Everyone sick. Rebel and supplies. Jesse and Nelly. The phone call.

She kept coming back to that call. As her eyes did their best to operate at the same speed, she was fully aware that she might have dreamed the whole thing. But she had the word *campy* ricocheting around her brain. Campy. If it had been campylobacter, then she'd done the right thing. And everyone would be okay.

She pinched herself, but nothing changed. Except that she noticed the straw cowboy hat hanging off her dining room chair, and then the pair of black cowboy boots next to the door. A mug, still steaming, was on the table. She managed to get on her feet and took a cautious sniff. Tea. Warm tea.

She wasn't alone.

"Morning, Madeline." The voice coming from the front porch made her jump. That was why her ceiling looked so lit up. The front door was open. "Or should I say evening?"

Rebel was here. Rebel was waiting for her.

She bent over to pick up her mug and noticed that she was wearing a T-shirt—and nothing else. It barely skimmed her thighs. Her hands flew to her hair—it was a gnarly, knotted mass of scratchy craziness that made Medusa seem well-styled. There was no doubt about it. She'd gone to bed with wet hair.

Rebel was here, and she was wearing nothing but a T-shirt and had funky hair. It was dinner time on a Monday, and she couldn't remember leaving work.

What the hell was going on?

There was only one way to find out. But she was doing it with her pants on.

A few minutes later, she cautiously crept out onto the porch, mug in hand. Her head hummed in protest as the full force of the sunset hit her, but she ignored it. Instead, she focused all her attention on the man on her porch. Rebel was kicking back in her recliner, his bare feet up on the railing as he watched another jeweled sunset settle over the land. He had a mug of his own in his hand, and his hair hung loose around his shoulders.

The sight of him tried its hardest to take her breath away. In the amber glow of light, he was hot. Unfairly hot. It wasn't right of him to look so damn good, all proud and noble and intelligent and caring and out-and-out sexy on her porch. Getting her all worked up for nothing didn't do anyone any good anymore.

"What are you doing here?" Excellent. Bitchy. Well, maybe that beat swooning or confused babbling. She could at least pull off bitchy. She went with it. He didn't have a right to look that good on her porch. He'd walked away, remember? He'd walked right out the door. Waiting for her on her porch—like he always did on Friday nights before they went camping—that was just being cruel.

"Waiting for you to wake up." His eyes didn't leave the sunset as he sipped at his tea.

She supposed she should count her lucky stars he was waiting *outside*. "Why?"

"Wanted to make sure you were okay." Finally, he looked at her—all of her. His eyes started at her bare feet and worked their way over her jeans, then the T-shirt, to her insane mop of hair. Her nipples tightened under his gaze, and she wished she'd taken the time to put on a damn bra. Finally, he settled on her face, and a slow grin took hold of his mouth.

She knew that look. He liked what he saw, and he wanted to see some more. She tried to cross her arms over her pointy chest and just missed dumping tea down her front. "Well, as you can see, I'm fine." Which was patently not true, but to hell with him.

"Sure are," he drawled with another once-over.

Okay, it was now officially past the time that she took control of this situation and got to the bottom of all this. "What happened? How long have I been asleep? How did I get home? Is everyone okay? Why didn't I go to work today?"

285

Sarah M. Anderson

The grin faded away. "I didn't think you'd remember all of it."

"Well, start talking." Keeping one hand over her traitorous breasts, she took a sip of her tea. The sweet warmth rolled down into her stomach, so she took a bigger sip. Her brain already felt perkier. He did make good tea. "What's going on?"

"Everyone's fine. You *were* at work today, until just after eight thirty this morning, when you passed out after I got off the phone with the lab. I brought you home, got you cleaned up and tucked in, and went back to help Clarence. The kids are all fine," he repeated with more insistence this time.

She hadn't dreamed it—any of it. Well, maybe just the Alice in Wonderland part. "You got me *cleaned up*?" That sounded bad. That sounded like being naked—in the shower—with him. That sounded like he'd put her in a T-shirt—and nothing else.

Damn this man. All of him. Even the parts that took care of her.

"Trust me, you needed a good scrubbing, but you weren't exactly up to it yourself. Don't worry. I already took care of your clothes. Clarence washed them for you at the clinic."

A good scrubbing. And he took care of her clothes? She hadn't been wearing any panties. What the hell else had he been taking care of? She was positive she was blushing as brightly as the sunset, but she refused to care. "All the kids are fine?" Yes. That's right. She was much more concerned about her smallest patients right now than the fact that her nipples were trying to break through the T-shirt.

"Clarence sent most of them home. Nelly's still

286

there." She opened her mouth, but he cut her off with a wave of his hand. "Jesse's pulling the night shift again."

She slammed her mug down onto the railing. "I've got to go. What the hell am I doing, standing around looking at you? I've got to get to work." She tried to hurry back into the cabin, but something held her back.

Not something—someone. Rebel had grabbed hold of the arm that wasn't acting as a nipple shield.

"Madeline, relax. She's fine. Everyone's fine. You did the right thing."

"But I should—"

"No, you should stay here, eat dinner and get a little more rest. What was it Clarence said?" He went through the motions of scratching his head like he was really thinking about it, but as far as Madeline was concerned, he was doing a shitty job of humoring her. "Oh, yeah. You're on call. Jesse's got your number if the smallest thing gets out of hand."

She tried to jerk out of his hand, but he was having none of it. "But—but—but—"

"No buts. We called Tim, who brought in this CSI guy from the state troopers. He collected the samples and marked all the evidence and took it to be processed. The trooper said they were gonna get a warrant for the rancher's property too. The law is taking this seriously, Madeline, and that's because of you. You got those test results back in three days. The CSI guy was impressed at how organized everything was. You did your job better than anyone else could have."

"Really?" She was tempted not to believe him. Someone from off the rez had come and taken things seriously? It never happened.

Wait. She'd come from the outside. She'd taken things seriously by just doing her job.

Rebel nodded in agreement, a knowing smile on his face. "Now you need to let Jesse do his. He's Nelly's father, after all."

Well, hell, she couldn't argue with that. And, if she was remembering things correctly, Jesse had done a fine job of keeping the kids clean and calm. She looked down at Rebel's hand, which was loosely circling her wrist. And, damn that man, his thumb was stroking her skin. "I'm not happy about this."

He froze and then pulled his hand back. "Which part? The part where you single-handedly saved several lives? The part where you guessed right about the campy and E. coli thing?" He swallowed. "Or the part about me?"

You. The part about you. But strangely, she couldn't put a finger on exactly which *part* of the part about him bothered her. The fact that he was here? Maybe that was it. Maybe. "Why are you here?" she repeated, taking a step away from him and his long arms and strong hands.

He finished his tea and stood. Automatically, she took another step away. Instinctively, she knew a close Rebel was a dangerous Rebel.

"I want to apologize. To you."

Of course, he was plenty dangerous without touching her. Her heart did that weird lurching thing, but she ignored it. "All right, then. You can apologize."

One corner of his mouth notched up. "I know I can. May I?"

Damn this man, she thought. But that was as far as she got.

288

"I'm sorry, Madeline. I acted like an... Well, a real asshole about that phone call."

The lurching thing got stronger. "Yes," she managed to get out. "You did." She wanted to tell him apology accepted, and since they all agreed she was fine, he could just get the hell off her porch. But she couldn't. He was still standing before her, shifting his hips back and forth as he didn't give her a chance to catch her breath.

"And you were right." He took another small step toward her—but, given the overall tininess of her porch, it was more than enough to back her into the corner. "I, of all people, should know about faking it."

She couldn't get anything out. Which was just as well. If she'd opened her mouth, she might have started squeaking or something equally undignified.

"I know who you really are," he went on, politely ignoring her silence. "I know that wasn't the real you, and I know you were doing that for me. For me."

She was being the bitch, remember? An apology was one thing, but the way he was slowly closing in on her made it clear that he thought a simple apology wasn't enough. And it wasn't. It was time to be the bitch.

"Is that so? When did this blinding revelation hit you? Because it sure didn't have you over here for three days. Three days, Rebel. And I don't want to hear the crap about you not used to being certain places at certain times."

He closed his eyes and nodded in a way that struck her as tired. "You aren't going to like the answer."

Did she like any part of this? "Try me."

"I was in the sweat lodge. Albert told me to get my shit together."

There was a small chance she was still in bed, still dreaming, because in the normal world, dead grandfathers did not tell Traditional Masters of Fine Arts to get their shit together. But if she knew anything, it was that the rez wasn't the normal world. And the hell of it was, she actually did believe him—a little, anyway. "Oh? And did he tell you to apologize?"

"Nope. I had to figure that out myself." The color on his cheeks deepened as he took another step forward. "I'm not too smart. It took me a few days."

"It took you a few days to figure out how to say you're sorry?" She took two quick steps past him. At least she wasn't in the corner anymore, but she wasn't sure if she should make a break for the house—he'd just follow her in—or head off the porch. Which would not be a victory since it was her damn porch.

"No." The quick, solid way he said it pulled her up short. "It took me a few days to figure out how to make it up to you. And then," he said as he reached around to his back pocket. For a split second, Madeline was afraid he'd pull out a ring. Instead, he grabbed a sheaf of papers. "There was that whole medical crisis. I'd been planning on coming up to see you Sunday afternoon, hoping you wouldn't pull a gun on me, but I had this dream that night... " He trailed off as he began smoothing the papers out. "I had to get to the clinic. And the clinic is no place to make a formal apology."

Make it up to her? Without a ring? She shook her head. She didn't want his ring. Rings were just things. She didn't want things. She wanted him. "And?" she said, trying to bitch her way through this, because *this* wasn't what she'd expected. He wasn't groveling, and he wasn't begging, and he wasn't telling her that she was making the biggest mistake of her life. He was being his regular old self.

Not dreaming, she realized. If she were dreaming, they'd be naked in a river.

His smile was cautious. "You don't wear jewelry. So I had to get something better." And he handed her the paper.

This made no sense, none whatsoever. She was looking at a flyer that had a trailer—scratch that, a modular home, the flyer said—on it, with a happy family sitting on a porch. At the top, a small square of paper was stapled to the flyer. "What is this?" Even as the words left her mouth, she realized what the small square was. It was a receipt. For nine thousand dollars.

"A house."

"You bought a house?" All she could do was stare at him.

And he was grinning away at her. "I bought you a house. With a porch."

"You bought me *a house*?"

"Actually, I bought us a home."

Us. Home. That was all she heard. *Us. Home.*

"I've been thinking about it," he went on, again ignoring her carp-mouthed silence. "I've been thinking that a man could get used to indoor plumbing and coffee that makes itself. A man could get used to soft mattresses and warm blankets."

He was going to stay. It wasn't even January, and he was going to stay. That lurching thing was going to knock her to her knees.

291

"And I've been thinking. A porch—that's like being outside, only with one wall. Hell, give a man a comfortable chair and a porch is even better."

"A home?" Excellent. She was squeaking.

"We could still go camping when it's nice." He closed the distance between them with one step and pried her hands loose from the flyer. She hadn't even realized she'd been crushing it against her chest. "Besides, I think your pipes are going to freeze this winter."

"Home?" Oh, this just got better. She was down to one word.

He set the flyer down on the recliner, and then his hands were around her waist. "I made a down payment, but they said we could come back and pick out a different model, if you wanted. It doesn't matter to me, just as long as it's got a porch." He touched his forehead to hers and tilted her head back. "Just as long as it's got you."

He was going to kiss her. He'd worked alongside her to fight the campy, he'd brought her home and cleaned her up, he'd apologized, he'd made a down payment on a modular house and now he was going to kiss her.

She put her hands on his chest and shoved him back, just enough that his lips didn't touch hers. Because she knew that as soon as he kissed her the deal would be sealed. He let her push him back, but his hands stayed firmly anchored around her waist.

"You're going to give up camping?"

His grin got wolfish. "You're doing it again."

She would not let him sidetrack her with all that talk of wants and needs—even if he was right. "I don't care. You're going to give up camping?"

He nodded, waiting patiently.

Her wheels began to spin. Apologies and homes were all very nice, but she was going to make sure they both read the fine print before they signed on the dotted line. "If you buy us a home, you have to get used to being certain places at certain times."

He tilted his head. She couldn't tell if he was amused or irritated. "Understood. You'll have to get used to having a sweat lodge in the back yard."

Like she even knew what a sweat lodge looked like. And who the hell had *yards* around here? "You'll have to get used to Melonie coming out to visit," she fired back.

The grin got more wolfish. *If only he had a longer nose*, she thought. "You'll have to get used to people dropping by looking for a medicine man."

She managed to keep the *oh, yeah?* to herself, but the rest of her thoughts devolved into a juvenile he-said, she-said kind of argument, which wasn't exactly bitchy but still wasn't giving in.

"You'll have to get used to going to Columbus." Rebel Runs Fast in the Mitchell Mansion—she'd bet cold, hard cash that Aunt Matilda would drive *herself* down from Cleveland to see that sight. The thought got her dangerously close to a smile.

He ran a thumb over that almost smile, and her bitch resolve wavered even more. "You'll have to get used to going to New York in the winter."

He was trying to outflank her. Well, it wouldn't work. She had ammo to spare. "You'll have to get used to going to gala charity banquets."

Damn it, nothing was ruffling his feathers. "You'll have to get used to gallery openings," he said, like he'd been waiting for her to say it.

293

That didn't sound pleasant. But if it was only for a week or so… "You'll have to get used to me being on call."

"You'll have to get used to being married."

Outflanked. Completely and totally outflanked by a mystic cowboy who happened to be an Indian. Nothing came out of her mouth. Not a damn thing. He leaned in and kissed her, and in that exquisite moment, she didn't care if she was awake or not. She only knew that she was where she belonged.

"I will never let you go, Mad-e-line," he whispered in her ear as he held her tight. "I couldn't, even if I tried. I love you too much." He leaned back and stared into her eyes. She saw herself, crazy white woman with crazy hair who just wanted to do a little good in this world. But she saw him too. A man who walked in two worlds. A man who wanted to find his place.

She looked down at the flyer, with proof of down payment fluttering in the evening breeze on top. It wasn't a ring, that much was certain. But it was a promise, all the same. Then she looked at him again. All the cocky wolfishness about him was gone as he waited. He wouldn't let her go, she realized. Even if she said no.

"Please," he said. The glimmer of fear in his eyes was just that—a glimmer. But it was enough to tell her that she could still outflank him, still take him down with one word. "Please say yes."

But that wasn't the victory. This wasn't even a battle. This was the rest of her life.

The rest of their lives.

"Yes."

Victory had never been sweeter.

Epilogue

Nobody Bodine stepped to the edge of the shadows. The thin stand of pines was more than enough cover for him to see what he'd come to see. He'd been here on and off for months now, looking at what he'd lost.

It was the same. It was always the same. Rebel Runs Fast, the one man in this world he counted as a friend, sat on the far side of the fire. He was beading tonight, his attention focused on his next project. Some nights he sat and just watched the fire, some nights he worked, other nights he had his brother and his family over to sit around the fire with him. Sometimes, he went riding.

Rebel was never alone.

His wife, the white doctor, was always with him. When he worked, Madeline sat on her padded chair next to him at the fire, reading with this weird little book light attached to what Nobody assumed were medical journals. When Rebel was lost in those trances that came to him, she inched closer to him, watching him with the kind of intent devotion that could only be true love.

No one ever looked at Nobody like that. Not even close. What he got was fear from strangers, and disgust—contempt even—from those who thought they knew him. No one knew him. Only Rebel had ever come close.

Rebel looked up from his beading, his head cocked to one side. Nobody froze. He was silent—hell, he was always silent. Nobody ever heard Nobody, and nobody ever saw Nobody, not unless he wanted them to. But Rebel was not just anybody. He was a medicine man. He saw what the spirit world wanted him to see, heard what the spirit world wanted him to hear.

Before he'd married the white woman, he'd been the only person to ever see and hear Nobody.

To Rebel, Nobody was a part of this world. He'd belonged here in this world, just as the wind and the rocks and the river belonged here. To Rebel, Nobody wasn't just a nobody, who came from a nobody and would always be a nobody. To Rebel, Nobody was a man to be trusted, a man to be believed. Nobody was a man who counted.

Nobody didn't trust the white woman. He trusted no one—except Rebel—but the white woman was especially suspicious. She seemed to be a good woman, from what he could tell from the shadows. She was a doctor, and she had patched him up without question.

But she was still an outsider—a woman, and a white one at that. Her judgment of him was different from others—she had never known his mother, and knew nothing about the hell that had been his childhood. But she still sat in judgment of him and found him wanting. Nobody wasn't good enough to share Rebel with her. That much was clear every time she jammed her hands onto her hips and scowled at him. Which was every time she saw him.

Which was why Nobody stood in the shadows of the pines, watching from his hiding spot.

Rebel was sitting straight up now, looking at him. Well, not quite looking at him. His eyes were searching the trees. He didn't know where, exactly, Nobody was. But he was getting close. Nobody stepped back farther into the shadows.

"When you are ready," Rebel called out to him. "You have a place by the fire."

When he was ready? He would never be ready.

He didn't belong here.

He didn't belong anywhere.

About the Author

Award-winning author Sarah M. Anderson may live east of the Mississippi River, but her heart lies out west on the Great Plains. When she started writing, it wasn't long before her characters found themselves out in South Dakota among the Lakota Sioux. She loves to put people from two different worlds into new situations and see how their backgrounds and cultures take them someplace they never thought they'd go.

With over 1.2 million copies published in over twenty-one countries, Sarah has published over 40 books. Sarah's book *A Man of Privilege* won a RT Book Reviews 2012 Reviewers' Choice Best Book Award. *The Nanny Plan* was a 2016 RITA® winner for Best Contemporary: Short. Additionally, Sarah has given workshops at national and regional conferences, taught craft classes online, spoken at libraries and book clubs, and published articles in the Romance Writers Report. Find out more about Sarah's books at www.sarahmanderson.com. and sign up for the new-release newsletter at http://eepurl.com/nv39b.

Readers can find out more about Sarah's love of cowboys and Indians at:

Her Newsletter: http://eepurl.com/nv39b

Her Website: www.sarahmanderson.com

On Facebook: www.facebook.com/pages/Sarah-M-Anderson-Author

On Twitter: @SarahMAnderson1

On Goodreads: www.goodreads.com/author/show/4982413.Sarah_M_Anderson

By Snail Mail at: Sarah M. Anderson, 200 N 8th ST #193, Quincy IL 62301-9996

Other Books by Sarah M. Anderson

Men of the White Sandy
The Medicine Man
The Rancher
The Shadow
The Medic
The Sheriff
The Wannabe Cowboy

Lawyers in Love
A Man of His Word
A Man of Privilege
A Man of Distinction
Pride and Pregnancy

The Boltons
Straddling the Line
Bringing Home the Bachelor
Expecting a Bolton Baby
Little Secrets: Claiming His Pregnant Bride

Rich, Rugged Ranchers
A Real Cowboy

The Texas Cattleman's Club
What a Rancher Wants
His Lost and Found Family
A Surprise for the Sheikh

Dynasties: The Newports
Claimed by the Cowboy

Rodeo Dreamers
Rodeo Dreams
One Rodeo Season
Crushing on the Cowboy

The First Family of Rodeo
His Best Friend's Sister
His Enemy's Daughter
His for One Night

The Beaumont Heirs
Not the Boss's Baby
Seduced by the Cowboy
A Beaumont Christmas Wedding
His Son, Her Secret
Falling for Her Fake Fiancé
His Illegitimate Heir
Rich Rancher for Christmas
Billionaire's Baby Promise

Billionaires and Babies
The Nanny Plan
His Forever Family
Twins for the Billionaire
Seduction on His Terms

Holiday Novellas
The Christmas Pony

NotMyFirstRodeo.com
Something About a Cowboy
Roping a Rancher

Writing as Maggie Chase
The Jeweled Ladies: The Mistress Series
His Topaz
Their Emerald
Her Ebony
His Sapphire
His Crown Jewel

The Jeweled Ladies: The Rogues Series
His Diamond
Their Amethyst

The Rancher
(Men of the White Sandy #2)

© 2013, 2014 by Sarah M. Anderson

Mary Beth is the kind of woman who wishes she had a five-second delay on her mouth. The swath of verbal destruction she leaves is why she goes west to start over. But any resolve to hold her tongue is lost immediately when she meets Jacob, a Lakota cowboy who says next to nothing—especially about the black leather mask that covers half his face.

Jacob's silence is his armor in a white man's world, but even that isn't enough to protect him—or the mute girl he guards—from forces he can't control. Fascinated by the masked cowboy and drawn to defend the girl, Mary Beth finds herself in the middle of a decades-old power struggle that only she could talk her way out of.

Excerpt from *The Rancher*

Mary Beth followed Robin's gaze, blinking through the streaking evening sun.

Down the center of the street, a cowboy was riding a horse, leading another behind him. As he got closer, Mary Beth could see the cowboy was shirtless. The golden light settled over his dark hat and shimmered off his bare shoulders. His front was still in light shadows, but if the rest of him was as carved as those dark brown shoulders, things were about to get interesting.

"Mmm," Robin hummed and Mary Beth swore the whole restaurant was humming in pleasure with her.

As the lone rider got closer, the shadows eased back a bit, and Mary Beth realized that there was something different about this cowboy.

He had an eye patch.

Whoa, hunk on the hoof, just like in a romance novel. But as she blinked through the angular sunlight, Mary Beth realized that the patch was far larger than the kind a pirate would wear. The swath of dark leather started at his left temple, covered his left eye and continued down over the center of his face, coming to a sharp point over his nose.

Mary Beth shook her head, but the patch remained the same. "He wears a mask?" she whispered to Robin, afraid to break the spell that gripped the café.

"Shhh," Robin hissed.

The masked cowboy rode right up to the café and stopped mere feet from Mary Beth's table before he slid out of the saddle, his leg muscles twitching through his tight jeans the whole way down. He paused for split second, clearly enjoying every female eye trained on his bare torso before he walked up to Mary Beth's table.

"Robin," he said, gently tipping his black felt hat, its brim creased from countless such tips. His one eye, nestled between a strong eyebrow and a stronger cheekbone, swept over the scene before it settled on Mary Beth.

"Jacob," Robin practically sang. She held out the tray with the towel and the water.

Jacob, the masked, shirtless cowboy, gracefully lifted the glass of water from the tray before he set his hat in its place. He took a huge drink, then grabbed the towel, leaned forward and poured the rest of the water over his head.

The water rushed through his slightly overgrown jet-black hair as he stood up, his mask covered with the towel. Rivulets raced down his browned, chiseled chest before he slowly mopped them up, his gaze grabbing Mary Beth's face and refusing to let it go again.

She was sure her mouth was on the table, but she couldn't help it. Every fiber in her body was vibrating as she watched the towel trace passed his pecs, down his lean abs—the muscles moving just beneath the smooth surface of his skin—and follow a faint trail of hair that ended in his jeans. The mask notwithstanding, this man was quite possibly the most ideal specimen of masculinity she'd ever laid eyes on.

A hint of a smile on his face, Jacob handed the towel back to Robin, took the to-go bag, pivoted and walked to the saddlebag of his paint. Mary Beth admiringly noted the huge tear in the seat of his pants, just under his left butt cheek. It was hard to tell what was more promising—his rock-solid chest or that flash of ass. Pausing again for just a second, he tucked the meal in the bag after he whipped out an Anthrax T-shirt that might have been black back in the 80s.

As he began to unbuckle his jeans, Mary Beth heard the entire café suck in a hot breath.

He won't. Mary Beth's brain stuttered in shock. *He wouldn't!*

The top button gave under his nimble fingers, and then the second. Mary Beth couldn't help but stare at the treasure trail of dark fur that crested at an even darker line peaking just over the undone buttons.

Jesus Christ, is he even wearing underwear? She gasped, unable to look away as she squirmed in her chair.

Jacob slipped the tee over his head, tucked it in and buttoned back up. As he took his hat off Robin's tray, the whole café—the sum total of women in Faith Ridge—sighed and leaned back in their chairs. Mary Beth wondered if there were enough cigarettes in town for the collective orgasm that had just happened in broad daylight.